Gossamer

NEW YORK TIMES BESTSELLING AUTHOR
SHANNON MAYER

Gossamer

NEW YORK TIMES BESTSELLING AUTHOR
SHANNON MAYER

Copyright © Shannon Mayer 2024, Gossamer

All rights reserved

HiJinks Ink Publishing

www.shannonmayer.com

All rights reserved. Without limiting the rights under copyright reserved above, no part of this publication may be reproduced, stored in or introduced into a database and retrieval system or transmitted in any form or any means (electronic, mechanical, photocopying or otherwise) without the prior written permission of both the owner of the copyright and the above publishers.

Please do not participate in or encourage the piracy of copyrighted materials in violation of the author's rights. Purchase only authorized editions.

This is a work of fiction. Names, characters, places and incidents are either the product of the author's imagination or are used fictitiously, and any resemblance to actual persons living or dead, business establishments, events or locales is entirely coincidental.

Mayer, Shannon

Gossamer, The Golden Wolf, Book 3

CONTENTS

Important Note	vii
1. BUMPY ROADS FUCKING HURT	1
2. A CROOKED FAMILY TREE	27
3. CRACKPOT DOCTOR	40
4. ALL SORTS OF UNEXPECTED	46
5. MAGIC HAVOC	63
6. VALKYRIE FLIGHT 101 BLOWS ASS	77
7. NORN OF YOUR BUSINESS	92
8. LEAVING IS SUCH SWEET….AH SHIT	115
9. DINNER PARTIES ARE THE WORST	129
10. NOT MY PRINCE CHARMING	143
11. SEE YOU LATER, ALLIGATOR	154
12. NOTHING STINKS LIKE TROLL SHIT	162
13. EAT ME, MOTHERFUCKER	177
14. BINGO CARD OF DEATH	189
15. IS THIS FOR REAL?	201
16. DREAMS AND NIGHTMARES	212
17. CALL ME DADDY	220
18. WHAT THE FUCK, BEBE?	234
19. WATERSLIDE OF DEATH	246
20. NOPE, NOPE, NOPE	258
21. HEL-RACIOUS	269
22. ROTTEN TO THE CORE	285
23. REDEMPTION OF THE DEAD	293
24. WOOD DOESN'T ALWAYS FLOAT	306
25. LOKI'S PLAN	311
26. SPLIT PERSONALITY	315
27. THE END. MAYBE	320
Acknowledgments	329

| Connect With Me | 331 |

CAGED BY FATE

1. Diana	335
2. Diana	353
3. Raven	369

| *Keep Reading* | 383 |

How would you like to have a few extra chapters from Havoc's perspective?

These chapters correspond to specific points in the book you are about to read. Look for an axe image at the start of the chapter as a reminder to refer to the extra chapters if you wish.

Download the chapters by scanning the QR code, or navigating to the link below: www.shannonmayer.com/gethavoc

https://offer.shannonmayer.com/btwr7rowbe

Remember! If you see an axe, that indicates a bonus chapter is available.

The ideal places to read these is just before chapters 6, 12, 18, and 23.

1

BUMPY ROADS FUCKING HURT

The whole thing about facing down your past is that supposedly after you've done it you can move forward, healthier, happier, all that shit. But the truth isn't so clean and tidy. I'd faced my past, killed my mother (in case you've forgotten, yes, she deserved it) but in the process had taken a pretty good wound myself. Short story, I was most certainly bleeding out, all over the back seat of the SUV, on my way to dying.

Said SUV flew down the back roads of Montana, the bumps hitting hard, aggravating the edges of my wound as I bounced in the back seat, one arm around my middle.

"Cin, talk to me," Richard said from the driver's seat. I could see his fingers wrapped tight around the steering wheel, knuckles white. "Let me know you're still alive, Sis."

"You picked the worst, pothole filled road, didn't you?" I moaned as we hit another crevice that felt like we'd just launched through the Grand Canyon. "Just to see me puke? I won't do it."

He laughed, though there was a strained edge to it. "There you are. Okay, we're almost out to the main road. You sure about Alaska? That's where we need to go?"

I swallowed hard, trying to focus on his question, because it was loaded.

My best friend, Bebe, in all her cat glory lay quietly, glowing like a miniature star, the tips of her fur bright with the sun she held within her feline body.

Let's do a quick recap of how I'd found myself here.

I'd had to face my mother down on our old pack lands in Grayling, Montana, in large part because Han, my mate wanted me dead. And while I'd won the fight with her, my brother Kieran had ambushed me immediately after. He'd stuck a spear deep into my side. A spear that carried Norse magic and as such my natural healing abilities as a shifter didn't seem to be doing much in the way of keeping me alive.

Seeing as I carried the sun within me (energy, life force, whatever you want to call it, and also the reason why Han wanted me dead) and my life or death was tied to the end of the world, I'd done the only thing I could.

I'd given over the responsibility of carrying the sun to my small friend. Bebe had taken it willingly, which is how the transfer is made. It's how I'd ended up with it in the first place, offering to carry the burden, unknowingly of course.

By transferring the sun to Bebe…if I died, the world wouldn't crumble around us.

Basically, it was a stop gap for a desperate situation.

Never mind the fact that Havoc, the one man I'd come to depend on as a place of safety, was now hunting me. He himself had told me to run from him.

I had no doubt in my mind that he was a better hunter than his brother Han, and that should have terrified me. But in the state of near death, I didn't feel much but a numb mind and a blazing fire of pain in my body.

I didn't realize I'd closed my eyes. Bebe tapped a paw against one of them.

"Stay with us, girlfriend. Tell us about Alaska. Richard asked if you were sure." Her chartreuse eyes were locked on my face as I blinked down at her.

I laid a hand over Bebe, squeezing her to me. "Yeah, I'm sure, Alaska will be safe."

Was I sure? About as sure as I could be. The last few weeks I'd been running blind, trying to understand what I'd been thrown into—end of the world, legendary monsters, curses and Norse gods. Any one of those things on its own would have been enough to handle. All together...it was too much.

Assuming I survived the wound, I needed to get my footing. To be somewhere I could think through my next steps. Firstly, for me, there was no better footing than home ground. No better place than the one I'd run to the last time my world had been upended.

Secondly, the fact that Grant—my vampire friend — had more books than a university on old mythologies was a serious draw. He was a collector of sorts. He was also the oldest living person I knew and maybe... maybe he could talk to Theodore, the vampire I'd traded Han's journal to in Portland. There was a chance that Theodore could give us more information on just what I was dealing with.

That last fact alone was enough to take me back to my old apartment and hope I was right.

So Alaska it was.

Bebe was incredibly warm under my hand, and she was purring, the rumble of her tiny body soothing my heart at least. I wasn't alone.

I couldn't leave the curse with her, I would never do that to a friend. Which meant I had to survive this wound.

"She's still bleeding a lot," a voice said from behind us. My head was fuzzy, but it sounded like Berek. Berek was with us? "We need to stitch her up. Whatever that spear did, it's affecting her ability to heal."

There was a shuffling of bodies. "Here. I can do it. I've stitched up thousands of things. People. Animals. Mouths. Even a few assholes."

I frowned. My eyes were closed again, but maybe that was for the best. I didn't want to see the concern on anyone's face. I knew how bad it was—a hiss escaped me as I was shifted onto someone's lap.

"Hold still," he grumbled. "Can't believe I'm doing this for a coffee date."

Jor? How was Jor in the car? He was too big, and he didn't have hands so how was he going to stitch me up? With those needle-like snake teeth of his?

I cracked one eye open.

I was laying across the lap of a thickly built man, his torso easily taking up one and a half of the seats. His eyes were locked on my side as he used a needle and thread to stitch the sides of the wound together.

His eyes were shaped like a snake's, right down to the shape of the iris and the lack of lashes. Oh...fuck, this was unexpected.

"Jor? How are you...in here?"

As in Jörmungandr. The Midgard serpent had taken on...human form. I mean, as much as a snake could look like a human I supposed. He smiled down at me, his grin far wider than any human, almost touching the lobe of each of his ears, teeth so fucking sharp they could have been needles indeed. He rolled his shoulders. "The skin suit is a bit tight, but that's life, and I wanted to see how it felt." He didn't stop smiling, only kept on showing row, upon row of teeth. "Also...I thought it would be good practice for our coffee dates this way. Less noticeable than a giant serpent slithering into a Starbucks."

He winked, which only unnerved me more, and went back to stitching me up.

I nodded and forced my eyes away from the mouth that looked so very wrong in so many ways. I drew a breath and let my nose identify everyone in the SUV. Richard. Berek. Jor. Bebe. Claire. Ship. My heart twanged on Ship. The youngest of my three brothers, we'd been thick as thieves growing up. But when our mother, Juniper, had infected the three boys with her darkness, and whatever demon she carried with her... he'd been the last to turn on me.

And now I had him back. Him and Richard.

"Ship?" I called for my other brother. He groaned from the front seat. He'd taken an injury too, though not as bad as mine.

"Present and accounted for."

I drew in another breath and Jor grumbled about me not moving. But I couldn't find the person I thought for sure would be here.

"Where's Dad?" I whispered.

"Mars...stayed behind. He's going to try to get

through to Kieran I think," Richard said. In his voice though, I heard the doubt. Because getting through to Kieran was highly unlikely. I let out a low groan as we hit another hard bump.

A grunt from the far back. "Claire and I are here too."

Berek—was Havoc's second in command—and Claire. His new girlfriend. The woman who'd wanted Havoc for herself when I'd first met them all. I didn't hate her, but we weren't exactly close which was why it surprised me that she'd come along for the ride.

I didn't twist around to look at them, couldn't with the wound in my side. "Not complaining, but why are you here?"

"Because you need our help, and Havoc told us to protect you at all costs," Berek said. "Even from him. Maybe especially from him. He always said that if he'd been the one to try and take out those who carried the sun, that the world would have ended four hundred years ago."

"So sweet," Jor muttered. "I think I might just kill myself for the syrup of it. You might as well be Romeo and Juliet for how fucking sweet it is."

The needle caught a spot that was close to a nerve, and I sucked in a sharp breath.

"Sorry," Jor muttered.

"S'okay." I closed my eyes and focused on breathing shallowly so I didn't make it harder for Jor.

His hands were steady but that didn't negate the fact that we were driving down a dirt road while he stitched me up.

Maybe everything had just been a bad dream, from Shipley walking into my bookstore in Alaska, to me trying to save my sister, then being caught and cursed by Petunia to become a golden retriever, finding my mate only to realize he was a violent psycho Norse prince, meeting Soleil--the girl who carried the sun before me...taking on a second curse that was never meant to come to me.

Shit show was an understatement.

But that would mean the good that had come from all that wouldn't have happened either. Meeting Bebe. Finding strength in myself I never knew was there. Reclaiming two of my brothers and finding my stepfather, Mars.

The moments with Havoc that were burned in my mind along with the feel of his mouth and skin against me. And if I was being real honest with myself, if from all of this I'd only gotten to meet Havoc....it would have been worth it.

Mine. The word whispered through me. Maybe it was my wolf. Maybe it was my imagination, but I felt it all the way to my bones. Havoc and I were...something more.

Jor chuckled, breaking through my thoughts. He lifted both of his arms and flexed, my blood on his fingers. "Look at us trying to save the fucking world as if we were the Avengers facing down an impossible task. Look at us!"

He shifted his legs under me as he tried flexing like fucking Schwarzenegger and pain lanced up my ribcage.

I groaned and Bebe glared up at him. "The impossible task is correct. Us as the Avengers...that's stretching it. Now stop fucking around and finish stitching her up!"

Jor lowered his arms. "You're a bit scary when I'm this size."

"Keep that in mind." Bebe flicked her ears flat to her head. "I have razor blades hidden in these cotton balls."

Jor did a double blink which was freaky as fuck in his snake face. "Point made."

He carefully went back to stitching me up, Bebe watching him from where she was now curled tight to my side.

My mind drifted as waves of pain rolled through me.

Christ on a donkey, this had been a lifetime crammed into a few short months. A shudder went through me, then again, it could have been the hard bounce as we went through a wash out, skidded sideways and barely stayed on the road, and the depth the needle went in with the bounce.

"Sorry," Richard said. "We're almost to the main road."

"You said that five minutes ago," I groaned.

Jor's hands left my side. "All I can do. I mean...if you died then I guess I'd be free to just exist in the world, but what's that to a bunch of coffee dates, am I right?"

No one said a word. The weight of what he was saying was enough to make us all stare at him. He didn't seem to care. Just kept on grinning.

I dragged myself off Jor's lap—not that I didn't trust him, per se, but right then I was feeling more than a little paranoid. Because Jor wasn't wrong. My death benefited some people—monsters, whatever—for sure.

Havoc was coming after me. The one person I had been certain would fight to keep me alive, was now hunting me. By all counts, he was the better hunter of the two brothers. Really, I hadn't needed Berek to say it out loud to know it. Han was...he was not a fighter—he'd let others do his dirty work since I'd met him.

Havoc was more than willing to get into the trenches and fight tooth and nail.

Jor sighed. "I mean, really, the downside--besides losing my coffee date—is that if you die while carrying the sun Ragnarök won't happen. Which ruins my day. No coffee. No razing the world."

The world was saved if the carrier of the sun died now.

Bebe locked eyes with me. Jor didn't realize we'd given her the sun. Not yet. She hopped down to the floor and crouched down, out of sight. Smart, very smart.

Then again...maybe I *should* take the sun back. Take it back and just...let Havoc catch me. If he was really hunting me now, and my death saved the world, wasn't that better?

"What's one life?" I grit the words out as I adjusted myself. "One life compared to the world?"

If I thought things had gotten quiet after Jor's suggestion that he would be free if I died, it was nothing to the dead silence at my suggestion.

"You sure about that?" Richard looked in the rearview mirror. "What if they've been lying all along? What if you dying now does end the world, and send us into Ragnarök, or whatever apocalypse you are tied to?"

Jor hummed thoughtfully. "Your brother makes a point. Things have shifted—I mean, everyone seems to be trying to get their fingers into the pie."

Ship twisted around in his seat, a grimace on his face. "What are you saying?"

Jor rolled his wide shoulders, a ripple that made me think of snake coils adjusting. "Saying that even I don't know what might happen if Cin were to die now.

She" —he pointed at me— "has thrown curve balls that I didn't know existed. Tyr offered her help. He never does that. Petunia and Freya showed up to the battle. And honestly the stink of my father is all over this. So who knows? It's a mystery."

Who knew indeed. How did I find out what was happening? Who could I go to for help?

I frowned.

"What's going on in there?" Bebe reached up from her spot on the floor and tapped my forehead with a paw. "I can just about see the smoke rolling out your ears."

I shifted in my seat and groaned as the stitches pulled, flesh tearing a little. My guts felt like they'd been stirred around and then shoved back inside my middle.

"It won't heal, not that one. You were right about that wolf number three," Jor said and Berek grunted. "You need a god to help you with that, since it was a god's weapon that made the wound."

Jor grinned at me and made a stabbing motion with two fingers towards my middle.

Richard spun the wheel on the SUV and we bounced out of the rough road—the move stole my breath and I just held it until we were up onto pavement. He looked in the rearview. "Wait, did you say we need a *god* to help her heal?"

I shook my head. "I'll just shift. That will speed things up."

Jor grimaced. "Actually, if you shifted now that could tear open the stitches that I *was* able put in place. I'm no god, much as I hate to admit it, my little coffee buddy, but I'm something more than, you know, a human doctor."

Bebe grumbled, "Then we need to find a god? Why not someone who's already helped? Tyr? Freya? Petunia? No, maybe not her. What about Loki?"

"You got a number for any of them?" Richard asked. He was one of the few who could hear Bebe, cursed as she was, her soul trapped inside that of a tabby cat. I wasn't sure if he was being sarcastic or not. Because really, we'd found some weird shit when it came to the Norse pantheon.

Like Freya's Facebook page that led to her Instagram account, that led to her TikTok.

Petunia had cursed me. Freya had thrown us under the bus.

Loki…maybe? I lifted my hand to touch the brand on the side of my neck. Loki's snake brand. He'd not been honest either.

"We can't trust them," I breathed out, a shiver of pain cutting up my middle as I exhaled a little too deep. "They all have a stake in this, either to make Ragnarök happen or to stop it. If we pick wrong…well then, I'm dead. And until we know for sure what the outcome of my death would be, I need to stay alive."

"Even Tyr?" Bebe asked quietly as she climbed back up and onto my chest, her warmth sinking into me again.

I didn't know how to reach him. Sure, he'd helped me, but I'd mostly seen him in my dreams.

"Then we need one of them who wants to stop Ragnarök from happening," Berek said, unaware of Bebe's suggestion.

"That could still mean her death, if her death would stop the end of the world," Jor said. "That's the problem. I just want a coffee date."

I frowned and tried to think past the pain throbbing through my middle. I hated that Jor seemed to be right, and that my body was not healing as it should. Being a shifter, my body should have been healing already and...well, it most certainly was not. My injuries from my mother—cracked jaw and crushed windpipe—were well on their way to being as if they never were. The wound from the weapon...that one was alternately burning hot and icy cold.

The flares of pain getting worse.

I closed my eyes. Tyr had helped me, he'd given me the spear, he'd stood on my side of the fight. But could I trust him any more than the others?

Bebe squirmed where she lay across my middle. I let my eyes drift to half mast, seeing the sun that she carried within her. The reason why Han and now Havoc wanted to kill me.

She'd taken it, willingly, when I'd been on death's door. Because she knew as I did that if I'd died before the night of the Dead Moon was over, while I carried the sun, the world would end.

But now, we were past the night of the Dead Moon. Which changed things. This was a choice I could make, and I could save those I loved.

"I will take it back, Bebe," I whispered.

"No," Richard said. "No, not until we're sure...that you will make it."

I smiled, tasting blood. "But if I die now, Richard, then Ragnarök is undone. The spear was magic, right? Norse weapon and all."

Jor cleared his throat. "Well, what if you're wrong, Sunshine? And then what would happen? I would not get that caramel macchiato I've been dreaming about. So I think you should try to find someone to stitch you up. A minor Norse god would be acceptable, I think. If you still want to die once we're sure your death would save us all, I'm sure we could hand you off to Havoc."

My two brothers let out dual growls, and Bebe let out a low hiss. Jor lifted his hands in mock surrender. "I am not wrong."

He wasn't.

I groaned. "Where, Jor? Where do we find someone to heal me then. No games."

"Extend our coffee dates." He smiled, too many teeth, his mouth gaping.

"An extra fifteen minutes," I said.

"Is that all your life is worth to you?" He pulled back, his smile turning into a frown of epic proportions. "Truly?"

"I am dying, Jor. If I die, no caramel macchiato at all, not one single coffee date." I made myself smile at him, tasting the blood as it coated my mouth. "Deal, or no deal?"

"Blast," he grumbled. "I tipped my hand, didn't I? Fine, an extra fifteen minutes each week."

A shot of pain sliced through me, all the way to the tips of my fingers and toes. "Done. Now talk to me about something, so I don't pass out."

I closed my eyes as Jor gave directions to Richard. Somewhere north. We would cross the border into Canada and then...the words fuzzed

I did not fall asleep, I was in too much pain for that to happen. The best I could do was try not to writhe. Bebe's weight on my chest was warm, and she did not try to move away which was good. Her paws massaged along my collarbone, as if she could soothe away the pain.

"Hang in there, girlfriend," she whispered. "Just don't...don't die, okay?"

Her words and gentle presence helped my heart, but not my body.

Jor cleared his throat. "Something interesting? Hmm. Let's see. You know, I travel via waterways? Well, I can go to any water way, in any part of the world. It's quite the trip. Almost instantaneous."

His voice took on a note of educating us, explaining how he travelled.

"Salt, fresh, any size of water would do. I suppose I've never tried something small as say like a puddle but in theory it would apply. You see when I travel, all the options open up to me like a map, and I just pick one and poof, I'm there!"

Bebe's nose tucked under my chin and whispered to me,"This might be the worst we've had to deal with. But we can make it. We'll figure it out."

"Not wrong. On the worst part. I don't know about the rest," I whispered back. Because it wasn't just the pain in my middle cutting through me. There was something wrong in the region of my heart.

I had my connection to Han, which I had no choice over, but it was...less. And that bit of a disconnect didn't bother me. But I also had a connection to Havoc. That one was more, and the connection was battered, as if it had been thrashed against a rocky shore.

Havoc with his eyes so dark that it was like looking into an abyss. Scarred. Powerful. Deadly.

Mine. My wolf whispered and I shook my head. "Not anymore."

Mine!

I groaned. There would be no arguing with her, not right then.

My golden gave a soft woof and I was surprised to see her separate from my wolf. Inside my head I could see them...the wolf I'd known my whole life, the golden who'd been with me only a short time and a third option... the golden wolf who'd emerged as I'd fought my mother.

Three choices. Three paths.

I held up my hand and Jor stopped talking about how once he'd traveled from Europe all the way to the west coast of the United States using a large wishing well.

"Talk to me about why Havoc is...what happened? Why is he hunting me now?" I stared up at the ceiling of the SUV, noting the splatters of blood. Wondering if the blood was mine. Probably.

I didn't care who answered the question, but I was surprised when it was Claire who spoke.

"We think Sven did it. Berek and I think that it's a spell that Sven used. A spell to make him hunt you."

Somehow, that didn't surprise me and did make me feel a bit better. Havoc wasn't hunting me because he wanted to, but because he was being *forced* to. "But why? Why when Sven was helping Havoc to protect Soleil and the others, he's tried to protect in the past?"

Claire cleared her throat. "I don't know."

"We can only assume that Sven knows something

we don't or has information that we don't and he's acting on that," Berek said. "In all the years I've known him, the woodland king has never changed his stance that he's helping Havoc."

"Could Havoc throw off this spell?" Ship asked.

It was the question I was asking myself.

We all kind of looked to Jor. He was the only one in the SUV that had knowledge of spells, magic, and Norse gods.

Jor shrugged and twisted in his seat. "I might have a theory. I mean, it's more of a coffee date subject though, if I'm being honest."

Jor didn't say anything else. Just looked out the window. As much as I wanted to yell at him and tell him to spill the fucking beans, I just didn't have it in me.

I bit back a moan as I adjusted my position, understanding clear. "Richard. I find myself craving a chai latte. Would you mind going to a drive through, and get us all something hot to drink? Maybe a caramel macchiato for Jor?"

My brother was not stupid, and he and I had worked marks together before. He picked up what I was putting down without breaking a beat. "I could use a shot of caffeine myself. It'll be a long haul to Alaska, and we still have to get across the border."

Shipley spluttered, as did Claire. But Berek was

also quiet, as if he understood we were going to have to convince Jor to tell us what he knew.

We had to get him to help us one way or another.

Bebe bobbed her head. "Smart. I like it. Richie, get me a steamed milk with whipped cream."

Richard grunted. "The irony of a cat asking me for whipped cream on her milk is not lost."

"Get your head out of the gutter," I said.

Bebe tipped her head at me. "How was he in the gutter?"

Jor laughed. "Oh! A pussy asking for whipped cream? Damn, it even took me a second! And I'm usually pretty suave you know. Snake that I am." He gave a throaty chuckle that left me feeling dirty, and he really hadn't said anything all that bad.

Richard cleared his throat, his voice a bit strangled. "Anyway. On to the closest coffee shop that is on the way to…wherever it is we are going aside from north to Alaska."

"A friendly lady who likes to heal others, and she is on the way north, like I said." Jor tapped his fingers against his thick thigh. "I mean, she probably won't be all that happy to see me, of course, so before we get all the way there, I should probably do something about this form. Or probably just leave. That will be best."

A friendly lady. Who had attachments to the Norse pantheon and was a goddess of some sort.

I shivered and Bebe snuggled closer. "You're getting cold, Cin."

"I know." The warmth was leaching out of me, along with my blood. I lifted the blanket they'd wrapped me in to see the wound pulsing with a life of its own. If I'd been more with it, I might have been a little bit afraid.

Terrified. The wound seemed to be eating me alive, reaching out from the point of entry and working its way across my torso.

I wished...I wished that it was Havoc whose lap my head rested on, instead of the bare leather seat. That it was Havoc taking me to a healer.

All I did was close my eyes. Either my brothers and Jor would get me to a healer in time, or they would not.

I almost didn't care.

Almost.

Time slid by, I drifted in and out of consciousness as Jor chattered away about how he was one of the only ones who could travel like he did. Jumping from place to place. I regretted asking him to fill the silence. If I had to listen to him say how 'I am incredibly important and special' in one form or another, I was going to shove him out of the car.

Richard found a coffee shop, and then everyone was ordering, and I just...I didn't even want the tea. I closed my eyes, my hands barely touching Bebe's back.

I knew this feeling too well. We weren't going to

make it to the healer. The cold, the fog, the drifting in and out—I was dying.

Jor was saying something about the theory he had, about how Sven had turned the spell up on Havoc somehow, but the words were all garbled to me.

"Bebe, you'll be safe with them. Stick with Richard," I whispered as my arm slid off her, my body going limp. I knew the approach of death; I'd seen him come for me before and I'd barely dodged his claws the last few times.

When my brothers had shot me full of silver.

When I'd nearly drowned.

When I was beaten to a pulp.

But this time...this time I wasn't sure I'd be able to yank myself out of the depth I'd fallen into.

"Hey. Hey!" Someone was yelling as I slipped down the seat, as I fell into unconsciousness. The smell of coffee and cinnamon filled my nose as my spirit was whisked away.

It was as if the SUV had disappeared and I fell through the earth below, through the tarmac of the road, the world as I knew it gone.

My body tumbled over and over, wind tearing at my face until tears streamed, and then I was jerked to a hard stop just above the ground, so I was looking at the individual frozen blades of grass, then released. I landed in a puff of icy crystals until I lay flat on my belly in an embankment of snow. So cold, I was so fucking cold. Was I truly dead? I pushed to my feet and looked down at my side. My wound was open, the stitches gone, but I wasn't bleeding. The flesh gaped, and I couldn't help but touch it, poking at the bits of my insides I could see. Nope, couldn't feel a thing.

I supposed that was good.

"That's a nasty cut, little bitch."

Her voice...it couldn't be. Gods, no, this could not be happening.

I looked up to see my mother—Juniper—standing across from me in the snow. Her head hung at an off angle. Just like I'd left it.

"You're dead."

Her smile reminded me a little of Jor's with how wide it stretched, almost to her ears. "About as dead as you are about to be."

The snow didn't melt around me. There was no warmth coming off my skin. "You're dead," I repeated, as much for myself as for her.

Juniper shrugged. "I always knew you would kill me. One day. The same way I killed my mother. It is the way of an alpha female. To take the place of the one before her."

"So now you *are* my mother?" I laughed and my wound flexed along the torn edges of my muscles. "Funny to claim it now."

"I gave birth to you. That makes us connected, alpha to alpha." Juniper didn't move toward me at least. She wore the clothes she died in. I was naked as the day I'd been born.

I threw my hands in the air. "You *gave birth to* me. I know Mars was not my father, but you're trying to say what...that you aren't my mother?"

"You were a means to an end. I needed to be pregnant with you, to get what I wanted. You were an unwanted child."

A means to an end?

I frowned and knew that if this had been any other time in my life, I would have been devastated by what she was saying. Not anymore. "What end was that?"

She rolled her eyes. "Power. What else is there?"

I laughed; I couldn't help it. The wound flapped and danced with my mirth as if it were clapping for my efforts. "Wait, you got pregnant with me for power?"

Her eyes rolled, weirdly, in opposite directions. "You are dying. What does it matter now?"

"Because it does," I said. "Because it's obvious that you got no power at all from this deal of yours. You got nothing but me, a daughter you hated."

It was a childish response; I knew it even as the words flew from my lips. As if she would deny hating me now? Not likely.

Her lips curled into a snarl. "I am aware that I was

lied to. Suvenia said that if I were to give birth to the child of a Norse god, I would have more power than any other shifter in the world!"

I had no idea who Suvenia was…but she had obviously lied her face off to Juniper. Which didn't bother me in the least. The knowledge that I was a daughter of a Norse deity was a bit much. Juniper could be lying about that, but I kind of doubted it.

The one Norse god that had tried to truly help stood out in my mind. Dark hair. Short beard. He'd given me the spear to fight with against Juniper.

I struggled to swallow. "Why…why are you here?"

"I was sent to bring you to the other side."

"That's a shit deal for me." I spit the words at her. "Why not someone who actually loves me?"

Her pause was heavy as if she were weighing what she would say next. "They are all still alive."

Nothing could have stilled me more; nothing could have made me fight more than those five words. "Then I am not going with you."

"You don't have a choice."

Only I felt like maybe, just *maybe* I did. Perhaps I had more strength than even I knew. Time to test it out.

I took a step back, then another and another. "I won't go with you. I'm not done with living. Not yet."

She didn't follow me. She just shrugged.

"I will be here, when you are ready to die in truth."

Her head bobbled side to side. "I can't force you to stay here. I can no longer force you to do anything."

"No. You can't."

I had my family. Chosen and blood. And I would not leave them. Not if I had anything to say about it.

2
A CROOKED FAMILY TREE

Maybe I should have been more specific about going back to my family—maybe I shouldn't have thought I'd just wake up and be okay. A lot of maybes rolled around in my head as I was yanked away from Juniper, as whatever death waited for me disappeared.

I told myself it was a good thing that I was no longer staring at her and the terrible angle her head hung at. That it was good I wasn't dying. Or at least I assumed I wasn't dying. Another *maybe*. Really, anywhere away from Juniper who'd been sent to gather my soul or whatever her gig was, was good.

Except I was not back in the SUV when the scene settled.

I was not back with my brothers and Bebe. Where I was...I had no idea. "Fuck, where am I?"

The world spun around me, bits and pieces flashing in front of my eyes as I floated just above it all. Snow. Water. River. A snake that looked like it was made of metal, glowing bits sparking here and there under its scales as it wove its way under the water. Tree branches stretched out wide all around me, some of them covered in rot.

I floated and fell slowly, seeing it all.

A sparkle of gold. Cloth that fell in sheer swaths around me, wrapping me up in a gossamer soft gown.

My feet touched something that was almost solid, giving way under my weight like a carpet of moss, like what Sven had created in the old, abandoned church. I blinked, fully expecting the tree man to pop out and explain his actions. Only he didn't. As far as I could see, I was alone.

I wasn't back with my family. But I also wasn't out of the woods yet. Literally.

"I'm not dead." I did a slow turn, the material moving with me, fluttering against my legs. Above me was an inky black sky, with only a few stars in sight. Nine bright burning stars to be exact. As I turned, I found myself staring up at a tree that was easily a hundred feet across, its limbs reaching impossibly high into that dark sky. Some branches were covered in leaves. Others in fruit. Some were burning. One was covered in thick ice and snow. It took me a moment to recall what I did know about this part of the Norse world.

This was…this was a place that only existed in stories.

The tree of life. A central place from where you could travel to any of the nine realms. A magical place that was impossible to find.

"I'm *pretty* sure I'm not dead," I repeated as I reached out to touch the tree. The bark was worn, as if it had been touched a great deal, smooth like glass under my fingertips. I leaned into it.

"A thin line between life and death for one such as you. You aren't really here either, daughter of destiny, but yet you stand in front of me. Finally."

The voice rippled around me, coming from all directions, and I jerked my hand away from the tree. I kept moving in my slow turn, trying to pinpoint the voice. Female I thought, older, like a grandmother, but not kind. More like a firm grandmother you didn't fuck around and find out with.

"Someone like me? What do you mean by that?" I kept searching for where the voice had come from.

"That part is simple. You are a daughter of destiny. One born to change the world. I've known that since you were in the womb."

I grimaced and took a step back from the tree. "Nope, I don't like that."

"The ones marked for this kind of destiny rarely

do." A laugh flowed out of the strange echoing voice. "But who would you trust to do what must be done? Someone else? I think not. You are the one I've trusted from the beginning. Since I first met you."

I frowned. "What must be done?"

"A quest, all heroes must face a quest. Usually, to save something important. A loved one. A friend. The world."

"I don't want—"

"You would let your little friend hold the sun? She is mighty of heart. But her choices...well, I think we can safely say her choices might not always be the best."

A breeze picked up, tugging on the sheer dress, pulling me closer to the tree. I let it move me.

"I don't want Bebe to be hurt, and I think her choices are solid. Better than anyone else I know."

The voice snorted. "Nah, fooey. You know that big black wolf is hunting you now. And with the spell that Sven has put on him, he would hunt you to the end of all the worlds. The question is," a face slowly began to form in the tree bark, a body stepping out next, then limbs as long and gangly as Sven's, only the bark was knotted, gnarled, darkened with age, "there, that is better."

I didn't step back. I didn't lower my gaze. I just stared at her.

The tree woman's face pinched as she narrowed her eyes—bright yellow—down at me.

"The question is, what happens next?"

An open-ended question if I ever heard one. "Are you expecting an answer? I don't know what happens next. If I knew...well maybe all this shit wouldn't have happened."

She held her hands, palms up and flexed her fingers, the wood of her bones crackling and creaking.

"Daughter of destiny. There is much you must do if you wish to change things as they are. And you can. That is what you must hold to; it is what I have seen for you."

The wind tugged at my hair. Dark brown and gold strands flew around my face. I wasn't entirely sure I knew what she was saying. "You mean, I can change the outcome of Ragnarök. Is that right?"

She bobbled her head left and right, the sound of wood crackling as she moved. "Yes and no. The oracle that might have given you answers is dead. Killed by my son."

"Well fuck," I muttered.

"Indeed. Much fuckery has occurred, as you might say. All of which has brought us here." She spread her hand, fingers bending one at a time. "I am Suvenia, the spirit of this tree, the mother of this place."

Suvenia. The one who'd lied to Juniper? Was it

coincidence that I spoke with my mother, and then her betrayer right after? Somehow, I doubted it.

"You..."

"No. I did not lie to your mother."

I frowned. "But...she didn't have power. Nothing more than a strong alpha shifter would have."

Suvenia laughed. "She had *you*. I saw you in her belly, and I saw the power you would wield. If she had raised you to be her daughter in truth...there would have been no stopping the two of you—you would have united every shifter in the world. But she hated you, believing that she'd been tricked into having you."

My heart and guts twisted and tangled inside my chest as if they were fighting to get out of my mouth. The path that could have been taunted me.

Suvenia sighed. "She brought you to me when you were first born. And when she did not get the power she wanted from me, she bound herself to me. I believe her words were along the lines of 'If I cannot have power, then I will live forever.' I did not think it possible and yet...she did it."

My jaw did drop then. "All her searching for the mate bonds, is that what it was for?"

Suvenia nodded. "Perhaps not initially, but yes. They led her back to me. Believing that I was the one who would outlast every single one of the pantheon, she tied her life to mine." She waved her hand. "But. There are other things you need to understand."

I was still stuck on the fact that my mother had bound herself to the tree of life. And that apparently, I had some serious power in me because I was a daughter of a Norse god.

Could I throw lightning? Call fire to me? Or was it just an all over magic like a witch?

Somehow, I didn't think it was any of those things.

She waved her hand, and a mounded hump of earth rose, just high enough that she could sit on it. "As old as I am, I know much. But not all. Here is what I can share with you. You must find a new way forward. A way to stop Ragnarök once and for all. And you have the power within you to do it."

I laughed. "That's all? You want me to find a way to stop the end of the world, a prophecy that has been around for thousands of years—"

"Tens of thousands if we are being accurate," she said, another shrug crackling like twigs snapping.

I held both hands up. "I am a shifter. A werewolf. And yes, I have carried the sun—"

"And done what no one has done thus far. You have thwarted Han. You faced his general, and beat him. He has a general in each of the worlds that he's chased the sun."

I frowned at her. "His general being my mother?"

"Yes."

Suvenia said all this like it was normal, and the truths she was dropping weren't mind-numbing.

"How long do I have here to ask you questions?"

"As long as you need. Time does not spin out here, as it does in the real world. Your spirit is with me, your body is on the cusp of death. But you are not dead. In that you were right when you defied your mother. You will die when you are ready, and not a moment before."

My eyebrows shot up. "Comforting."

"Isn't it, though?" Her face crackled and I thought she might be trying to smile.

I looked down at the dress wrapped around me, seeing flickers of color in it besides the white—gold and silver, a bit of blue. They seemed to dance across the material, appearing and disappearing at random points.

"It is a reflection of your soul," she said. "It is gossamer silk, strong and yet undeniably beautiful. Some might think you easy to manipulate, but when they try to pull you apart," she plucked at a string and the silk held firm against her tug. "They cannot make you do as they wish."

"Are you saying I'm stubborn, and that's why this has come to me?"

Her laugh caught me off guard. "You are the daughter of a god—a daughter of destiny. *That* is why you were chosen. An unexpected child. The first Norse god born in the last three thousand years—a child that I encouraged to be born. And as such, your life is outside of the prophecies. Your life...and your actions, can be the difference—"

I waved both hands at her. "Stop, stop right there. Tell me who my father is. Please."

The old tree spirit smiled, her face crackling. "I think you have met him; you know in your heart who he is, do you not?"

My father, the one that no one knew, the one that had helped me. She was right, I already knew it. "Tyr, he is my father."

"That is correct. He is your father. He can help you some, but it is difficult because Loki marked you first. That complicates things some. You have become an agent of chaos with that brand of his." She tipped her head at me.

I had never known who my father was, in all my life, and while there had been times I wondered—who wouldn't?—I had made my peace with not knowing years ago. I had Mars. He'd been the father I needed until Juniper took him from us all.

Rage flickered through me. "Did my father, did you know my life would be—"

"That your life would be difficult? Yes and no. Mostly we were trying to protect you from the other gods. They wanted to kill you. And they saw your destiny as something that could save us all. Or end us all. They were right on both counts."

The anger drained from me, like a plug had been uncorked.

Save or destroy the world. It was still going to be on me.

Suvenia groaned and leaned back against the tree. "Do you see my branches? Some are dying. Some are being destroyed. *All* are in danger because of…You are my only hope to survive—Ragnarök may not be as we once thought, but it is as good a word as any for the end of all that we know. The destruction of my tree, of everything that holds our realms apart. Nine realms, all cast into nothingness if you do not find a way to save us."

I stared at her, the wind around us moving the tree side to side. Animals scurried around the branches; I thought I saw a deer bound from one large limb to another.

"Close your eyes, and look again," she said softly. "Let your father's blood speak truth to you."

I did as I was asked, feeling the weight of the moment, my body tight with tension. When I opened my eyes, the tree was no longer a tree.

Spinning orbs hung overhead, barely tied together with thin strands of color, nine plus a pulsing energy in the middle that had been the tree. The threads tying the realms, and all the worlds together, were fraying, but still holding.

For now.

"And what makes you think I can do anything about it?" I wasn't angry any longer, I wasn't even afraid, not in this place of non-existence. "I am a single person. Even if my father is Tyr. It doesn't mean anything; it doesn't make me a hero."

"That is where you are wrong. Even your name, it means destiny. Does it not?"

I nodded reluctantly. Cinniúint was a mouthful, but the tree spirit was correct. It meant destiny. "I always wondered why Juniper gave me the name."

"She didn't. Your father did. Because he understood what waited for you, better than anyone." Her words and voice softened. "He saw what you could do, given the chance. He saw what you could be to all of us. And he believed that you would face the task head on."

My father had named me, and strangely enough, that gave me a warm and glowing sensation right in the middle of my chest, as if Bebe still lay across me.

"Why are you being so…helpful? Everyone else is speaking in riddles, and dancing around what has to be done, who is good, who is bad."

"There is nothing to be gained from keeping this knowledge from you. The path you face is not for the weak of heart or mind. Even telling you all I know, will not be enough for your journey to be clear. What you must do to save me and our worlds…will be a trial like no other hero has faced. Will you...will you fight for me, daughter of destiny? Will you save our worlds and all the souls within them?"

My throat tightened, followed by a strange tingling sensation that rolled through my limbs. Why was I crying? Why was I suddenly dropping to one knee? I bowed my head, dark and golden hair falling forward in a curtain around my face. The tree spirit was no queen, but her power was suddenly everywhere, around me, in me, calling me to a task that would likely end in my death in one form or another—that much I knew in my heart.

She was the mother of all mothers, the one who birthed all the realms, and I could see all the worlds reflected in her eyes. If I didn't fight for her, I wasn't sure who else would.

"Yes," I whispered the one word.

Her hand settled on my head. "Then go. It is time for you to take upon you the quest that will be offered. It will not look like what I have asked, but it will take you on the path you need. Water and ice, darkness and death. Face it all with your head up, Cinniúint. Face it head-on with the heart of gossamer that you hold within you."

The tree around us shivered, and a crack split down the middle, wood groaning and shrieking as if it were being hacked at. Splinters exploded through the air, one piercing me through the top of my right ear. Pain and blood, I clasped at the splinter.

The tree spirit gasped and clutched at her heart. "Hurry...we need you, Cinniúint. We need you."

3

CRACKPOT DOCTOR

"We need you! Cin! Don't give up!"

Someone was yelling and right in my damn ear where I was sure the splinter still stung from the tree. I wanted to slap them away, but my body was heavy with...something that felt like a hundred pounds on my chest.

"Out of my way, cat!"

"I'm her best friend, don't you fucking tell me to get out of the way!"

Bebe, that was Bebe screeching. I was alive then?

A hand pressed hard over the left side of my chest, mashing my boob flat, another hand was pressed against the wound in my side.

"Her heart is beating. She's...she's healing. You haven't lost her. It was a close thing, but if Jor hadn't alerted me..." The voice was not one I knew. Matter of fact, like a doctor would deliver news to a patient's family. Was I in a hospital then?

I wanted to open my eyes and see the person talking, but honestly, my lids were so heavy that they might as well have had anchors on them. I just let them stay closed.

"What do we do now?" Bebe curled up in the small space between my head and my shoulder, her tiny head resting on my throat. I wanted to reach up and clutch her to me, wanted to tell her that I was here, that I was ok. That I could hear her. That I was alive and well.

"We let her sleep," Berek said. "She needs to heal properly."

A grunt. "Agreed. And we get to Alaska as fast as we can." Richard spoke with authority. "That's where she said she needed to go, so that's where we go."

As if the others would just listen to him. Funny enough, there was no argument. Not even from Jor.

That did make me open my eyes, slowly, unsticking them as if they'd been glued shut, the world blurry and fuzzy. I was staring up at a...well I wasn't entirely sure what I was in at first. A building of some sort, but that was kind of stretching it.

Gems and rocks were strung up over head by thin strands of filament and small lights flickered in and amongst them like fireflies, only they weren't little bugs.

They were tiny glowing flowers that flapped their petals as if they *were* bugs. Drugs, they had to have shot me full of drugs to be seeing flying flowers. Which of course would make sense if I were in a hospital, only I was sure I wasn't in a hospital. Not with hanging gems over my head. Not with the smell of burning incense instead of antiseptic flooding my nose.

"Where?" I managed the one-word question, but my throat was dry as if I'd not had anything to drink in days. How long had I been out?

Richard leaned over my face first, and the tension around his mouth and eyes was tighter than I'd ever seen. "Think you could *not* die on us again? Whatever grays I have are all because of you."

I shook my head—or tried to at least—"Not dying. How long?"

"A day and a half," Richard said. "We made it across the border and met our new friend. Jor went ahead of us and got her to follow him. She brought us here after stabilizing you. We're in Northern Alberta."

Another person shoved Richard out of the way and an unfamiliar face leaned over me. Her features were all sharp angles and prominent bones, as if she'd been carved from ice. Her skin was pale, and her hair so light and lacking in color I would have called it white. Her eyes reminded me of the night sky above the tree of life, dark, with a few specks of light in them. By all that you would think she was old, but by the smoothness of her skin she was in her mid-twenties. Of course, the moment she spread her wings above us, I was pretty sure she was not a twenty something hitchhiker that Ship and Richard had randomly picked up, or even some hippie healer they'd stumbled across. She was the healer Jor had wanted to bring me to. I mean...I was guessing anyway from what I was piecing together in my muddled brain.

"You were dead. For like, a good day and a half." Her nose wrinkled up. "You smell like it too."

I stared up into her dark eyes. "I was...talking with someone. It took some time."

She scrunched her face up, pouting her lips and wrinkling her nose and eyebrows all at once. "Right. So anyway. She's alive now. The wound is healed. Try not to engage with enchanted weapons. I can't guarantee I'll be around to help you again."

And with that last bit of stellar advice, she pulled back, and waved a hand over my face as if she were done with me. Bebe butted her head under my chin. "Please don't do that again. This almost dying business is giving me grays too."

I managed to lift a hand and hug her tight to me. "I will do my best, Bebe."

There were so many questions I had, but I forestalled all but one, because I couldn't smell one of our party. "Where did Jor go?"

The pale woman with the wings sniffed. "He ran away. He figured you were dead. So the end of the world was here, but he didn't look at the cat, did he? Didn't notice she was carrying the sun, did he?"

I smiled, though the motion felt strange on my lips. In all the chaos that had been, it looked like Jor *hadn't* noticed I'd handed off the sun to Bebe, just in case I kicked the giant bucket of life. "I guess he didn't."

Bebe sighed. "You want it back?"

I moved as if to sit up, and my two brothers were right there, helping me, their hands at my back and wrapped around my biceps. Their quiet strength was a comfort, like Bebe's unwavering loyalty—something I'd not had a lot of in my life, which made it all that much more precious. "Probably best. But we have a backup plan now. If it looks like I'm about to bail on this world, you take it."

She sniffed. "I don't want it anyway. Can you imagine Havoc trying to fuck me? What a mess that would make of him." She sniffed again. "Not that I'm not amazing, just...well the whole cat versus pussy issue."

I held my hand out to her, and she bopped her nose into the center of my palm. "I'll willingly take the sun from you, Bebe." I felt the rush of the sun's warmth flow through my veins and settle once more in my bones.

"No glitter for you." Bebe looked me over. "Maybe because you've already held the sun?"

A heavy sigh erupted like a small explosion from the other woman, the one with the wings. I turned to her. "I owe you my thanks."

"You do and you don't. I…I healed the wound, but you were on the cusp of death. Technically you were dead, but I was able to hold you to the edge until you decided to come back. It was your decision."

I winced and sat forward. Richard kept a hand on my back. "Decided to come back?"

Her eyes flicked over me. "For some of us in the pantheon, it's a decision to live or die. Likely you would have been able to come back, even without me. Still wounded of course, but you would have survived. It would have taken you longer, is all."

I winced and touched my side where the spear had gone deep. Kieran had done that to me, stabbed me straight through my guts. I mean, who needs enemies when you have family that will literally stab you in the back…er…side.

4

ALL SORTS OF UNEXPECTED

I floated in and out of sleep while my body caught up to the healing that Eir had given me. Eir being the one with the wings and the pale skin and hair. She was a Valkyrie, and one of the only healers around capable of dealing with supernatural type wounds. At least that's what I picked up from the stilted back and forth between her and my brothers.

She was not a goddess, just a minor...something. A healer, and she didn't like Jor, not one bit which of course left her to be suspicious of us. She'd followed him only because he'd begged her not to let me die, and apparently, he never begged anyone.

"Are we seriously going to Alaska?" Bebe whispered the question. "I mean, I wondered if it was just to throw everyone off the scent. You know, seeing as we are dealing with wolves and the whole tracking business."

"I know Alaska, Grant is there, and he might be able to help," I said quietly, thinking of all the old books Grant kept in the backroom of the store. "And it's as good a place as any to figure this out."

"Figure what out?" Richard asked as he sat next to me. "What are you figuring?"

I grimaced and slid my legs to the side of the bed I was laying on. Was I still weak? You bet, but I also knew that every minute counted. And I hadn't told them yet that I was Tyr's daughter.

I mean, how did you just say to someone, hey, I'm the daughter of a god? No, it wasn't going to be that easy. Maybe I didn't need to tell them? Maybe I could just float under the radar while I absorbed the news myself.

"Is there any way we could charter a flight? I'd like to get my feet off the ground and stop leaving scent trails everywhere," I said.

Richard's eyebrows shot up. "You have a mate bond to Han, correct?"

I reluctantly nodded.

My brother pointed a finger at me. "He can find you anywhere."

Berek leaned against the one wall, Claire silent beside him. "I suspect that you have a similar connection now to Havoc—maybe not a mate bond, but perhaps a pack bond? Which of course he was trying to create prior to all this mess."

Of course he had been, and I had suspected it too. Every time he'd fucked me, the bond between us had strengthened.

I knew that. And I'd let it happen. Because a part of me had thought maybe, maybe he was better than... well anyone else I'd let myself get tangled up with. That he wasn't a bad guy after all.

"Yeah, there is something between us." I rubbed at the back of my head.

I won't deny there was an uncomfortable shot of pain that I wanted to attribute to the spear wound but was in fact a little higher in my torso. A little closer to my heart. I didn't want to be the girl who thought she could change the violent red flags that a man presented, I didn't want to be the girl who let her fantasy get in the way of reality. Yet here I was, doing exactly that, feeling like maybe Havoc wasn't all bad. That maybe I could convince him not to kill me.

As if love was strong enough to make him...better.

"Cin?" Ship was the one who broke through my musing. "What's going through your head, you look sad?"

I nodded, focusing on the problem in front of me, and not the Havoc that was rippling through my tattered heart. "Berek, are you and Claire still connected to Havoc? Still part of his pack? I mean I assume so, but I have to ask."

Richard and Ship looked at each other and then to me. "We cut him out already. Soon as we left," Richard said.

I'd almost forgotten that they'd been building ties to Havoc too. As if Havoc and I were both their alphas. I gave them a nod. That was good. Even if it stung something in me, I didn't want to look too closely at.

I could have checked the bonds myself, but I was tired. Exhausted, and I needed all my strength to try and smother those bonds I had to Havoc. To block him as best I could.

Claire nodded. "We are. You think he might track us? To find you?"

That was exactly what I was thinking, or maybe hoping was a better word. "You should go, head east, get a plane, keep flying. See if you can draw him away."

Berek was already shaking his head. "Won't work."

"Why not?"

"Because even though he knows we are with you, it's not us he's tracking. He'd use us for confirmation or if he can't find the bond. That's the only way he'd look to us instead of to you." Berek ran a hand over his hair. "That's what I'd do, and he's a better strategist than me."

"Let me check the bonds; it might take a minute." Also, I didn't know what I'd find.

The others filtered out of the room, leaving me alone.

I forced myself to look inward, to the different bonds that were tied to me. My mother was gone. Richard and Ship's connections to me were solid, a warm presence. Bebe was there, woven through my heart, strong and fierce, such an unexpected bond that I was grateful for daily.

Han...was still my mate, by whatever power Loki had created the connection with...I couldn't help but touch the brand on my neck. The bond was there, and I couldn't break it, no matter how I'd tried. My mother knew how to *steal* mate bonds, but I had no idea if it was possible to actually remove them.

Havoc was another issue altogether. I could see *that* bond clearly, and it was stronger than the last time I'd looked at it. Golden and black, it pulsed with its own heartbeat, woven tightly together, braided over and over.

Calling to me to reach out and touch it. To bring my chosen mate to me, to let him find me. I itched to do just that, to let him find me as stupid as it was, I couldn't deny that I wanted him close. That I felt safer with him through all I'd faced.

I swallowed hard and reached for the bond between us and realized that it was awake.

And he was thinking dirty, dirty thoughts. He was

thinking about us in the church. The last time we'd fucked.

I dropped my head, pressing my lips to the soft underside of her jaw and working my way along her neck. She tasted of sweetness and spice, and I let myself savor her flavor.

She arched her back, silently begging, her muscles quivering. A low, throaty rumble slid out of me as I pressed my body down onto the bed and slid down her body, branding her with nips and sharp sucks on her bare skin, leaving tiny marks.

Mine.

The word echoed between us.

My wolf knew what I didn't want to admit.

She was mine. The bond between us was stronger than anything I'd ever felt which was why I was fighting it. But everything Cin was...was everything I wanted. Everything I thought I'd never have.

Mine.

I could feel her fighting it too. We both knew it was fucking stupid to even try. But neither of us could stay away from each other.

A smile ghosted my lips as I worked my way back up her body. My mouth latched onto one of her nipples, sucking it in deep, rolling the nub and then growling as I drew it out, feeling her shake under me. I knew what my magic did to her.

I fucking loved it.

She gasped as I let go and slid further down her body, biting, marking her skin up as I went.

Possession.

Mate. She was my mate and when this was over...no. No I couldn't do that again, I couldn't risk the pain that came with losing someone you loved...

Mine.

She dug her nails into my shoulders, drawing scores across my back, the push of pleasure and pain had my cock throbbing.

One more time, just this one last time I'd fuck her and I'd get her out of my system.

Just one more time.

Even I knew it was a lie as I settled at the apex of her thighs, unable to stop marking her.

Unable to stop touching her, to make sure she was really here. That she was with me.

I sucked her clit into my mouth, rolling my tongue over it. Sweet and spice.

She was all I could have wanted and nothing I could ever have. Life for me never went that way. There was no happy ending. No hero's welcome.

There was this moment, and that was all.

I gasped as I fell to the floor, his memory of us together so poignantly sweet that I could barely breathe.

Love. He'd said the L word, the fucker.

Run, Goldie. The command was sudden and sharp,

his thought rippled down the line between us, and it was as if he'd reached out and touched me. I couldn't stop the shiver that slid down my spine and pooled in my belly. Damn. There was something wrong with me, for sure. 100% I should not be feeling lusty when I knew that Havoc was on a hunt to kill me. That he would literally cut my head from my body given the chance.

That's what he'd been spelled to do, no matter what he felt.

But that tiny voice that said maybe I could be the one to make him better was stupid, and persistent. *Love*, that little voice whispered. He said it.

I wanted to drop kick that voice to the moon.

There was no room for love. Not when the world was on the cusp of blowing up.

I called the others back inside. "I can sense Havoc. He's a long way off, feels like he might still be in Grayling, and not moving." I sure as shit wasn't going to tell them that I'd gotten a piece of his memories.

"Maybe the spell isn't working?" Bebe offered. "Maybe he won't hunt you?"

Richard shook his head. "We can't bank on the spell not working."

"And we don't know what Han will do now," Berek said. "We don't know if he has a spell on him too, or if he's just a psychotic killer that will hunt you regardless."

Another valid point. I changed the subject.

"Richard, can you sense a bond to Mars?" I scrunched up my face in the bright light. "You said he thought he could reach Kieran." Which meant Mars could very well be in danger.

Richard shook his head. "Nothing. The bond to him is there, but faint. He's worried, but not hurt. Like Havoc, I think he's still near Grayling if I had to guess."

I didn't like that I couldn't reach Mars too. That there was no bond between us, there hadn't been time to reinstate it by the looks of things. I opened my mouth to suggest maybe we try to get him back, maybe send Ship for him.

"We have to keep going," Richard said, his eyes on my face. "We can't go back for him, Cin, you know that and so does Mars."

Ship's face fell, and he lowered his head to his chin.

"Where does that leave us?" Claire asked. "Do we just keep driving?"

"I still think flying would be better," I said. "Get our feet off the ground, quit leaving tracks, and putting a large distance between us and them. That would give us the most time."

Berek nodded. "I agree. The more time and distance we can place between you and Havoc, the better."

Nope, I didn't like how my heart twisted up at that, or how my wolf and my golden both drooped.

We spent the next hour searching for flights. The nearest airport was six hours *south,* and the first flight that could carry more than one person would leave two days from then.

"And that's assuming any of us could get on a flight," Ship said. "None of us have any ID on us."

Eir circled through the room twice, checking on my wound, the tips of her wings brushing all the bits and bobs hanging from the ceiling. "Healing well."

"Thank you." I bent my head toward her. I didn't know if I should bow or what, but she'd saved my life. No matter what she said about me making a choice to come back from the edge of death.

Her eyes roved my face. "You have a bit of his look, you know."

Oh, shit.

I swallowed hard. "My father?"

Her smile was there and gone. "Yes. I fought at his side in several battles. He saved my life twice."

"Really?" I leaned toward her. "Is he—"

"He is just, and fair. And he is an exceptional warrior, though the legends don't speak of him much." Eir touched a finger to one of the globes hanging from the ceiling, spinning it. "There is a storm coming. Even if you were able to get a plane, it would be grounded."

I stared at her. "You have something in mind?"

She shrugged. "It is a last resort. But this place you go to, there is a vampire who rules, isn't there?"

How the hell did she know that?

Before I could even ask, she waved her hand at me. "I've been listening to you all for the last few days. The things you've all said. How you hid from your brothers for so long, how you thought the bonds were gone. A vampire's home ground is often hidden, and all those closest to him would fall under that hiding."

"Fucking Grant!" I whispered.

She arched an eyebrow. "Perhaps best not to fuck him, since you are already bonded to two wolves?"

I shook my head. "Manner of speaking. That's why I was safe for so long there?"

Eir leaned closer and lowered her voice. "It's not a well-known trait of vampires, but it's how they keep their feed supply away from any who might be looking for them. Family members and the like."

Grant…he'd helped hide me. Had he known that he was hiding me? "Do they have to bite you?"

"No, he does not. This is very interesting. He must hold you in high regard." Eir slipped out of the room.

Bebe was at my feet. "I heard all that. Bonus for us, right?"

"Yeah." I nodded. All the more reason to get back to Skagway as fast as we could. Maybe I couldn't hide forever, but I could hide for a little while. Long enough to find some answers.

Richard was flipping through his phone when I

looked over at him. "Eir is right. There is a big storm coming. Everything is going into lockdown."

A waft of cool air flowed in as Eir stepped back into the room and she snapped her fingers, drawing all our eyes to her. "I have secured a flight for you. Very small, and…unusual in its engines…but it will carry you all to the place you need to go. I think it is best you leave soon." She paused and gave me a serious look. "I do not want either Han nor Havoc on my doorstep."

Richard stepped between me and Eir. "Why are you helping us?"

I pushed him aside. "Don't be Dick. She knew…she knew my father."

There. I said it. Out loud even.

Eir dipped her head in my direction. "Her father saved me. I repay him by helping his daughter in a time of need."

"Thank you, Eir." I got to my feet, testing out how wobbly I was. Not too bad. I had no doubt I'd sleep on the plane seeing as the healing fatigue was tugging at me still. But that was a minor price to pay for staying on this side of the dirt.

"I will have them prep the plane." Eir said then turned and left us once more.

Bebe danced along at my side. "Any strippers in Alaska? I mean thinking about it, it would make sense that there would only be girly strippers. Because the guys...I mean the cold and all that shrinkage. What a waste!"

Richard choked on a laugh. "Oh my gods."

No one else heard her of course. I sighed. "I am quite sure we could find at least one male stripper. Maybe we could light a fire for him."

"I could light him on fire," Bebe muttered as she sashayed along with us.

Richard was on my left as we exited the small cottage with all the strange dangling rocks and floating flower petals—and stepped out onto a plateau that overlooked a valley far below. Thunder rumbled in the distance, turning me right around.

Black clouds boiled toward us, flashes of lighting ripping through them far too often for my liking.

"It is time to make haste. The storm will be on us before long." Eir motioned for us to follow her.

We hurried down a path that wove along the edge of the plateau. "Lots of birds here?" Ship asked. "I keep hearing wing beats."

I tipped my head. He was right, I heard them too. The steady thump of wings pumping through the air. Not small wings either, they sounded big with a heavy percussion.

As we rounded a corner, skirting a huge pile of boulders, the wings came into view.

A half a dozen women with wings like Eir's, spread wide and catching the updrafts. No single woman looked alike— they were all different skin tones and hair colors, from light to dark, and everything in between. Two had skin with silvery tones, like they'd been metallicized, one had skin that looked marbleized, white with black lines running across her muscles.

And muscles...damn there were a lot of those. Their muscles rippled as they tread air with ease, adjusting their wings to catch all the currents. Weapons—mostly swords—were strapped to their sides, and there were a few that carried longer weapons on their back, the handles sticking up between their shoulder blades.

The next thing that I noticed, was that each of the women wore a thick strapped harness that was padded through the shoulders. From each of their harnesses was a long cargo strap that was then *attached* to a pile of metal below them.

Eir pointed to a pile of metal strapped together with...no...that could not be what she meant for us to use.

"That's the plane?" The words came out in a high-pitched rush as I pointed to the metal pieces.

I use the term plane in this context: there were wings, and a basic structure with straps and belts, that would make you think 'plane'. But there were no walls. No seats. No engine. No propellor.

I stared at the contraption and then up to the

woman treading air above it. "This is not a good idea; those straps are far from—"

"Hurry up, they don't have all day, and neither do you." Eir put a hand to the middle of my back and gently pushed me forward. "Your father...well, this will not cover what I owe him, but it is a start. Go. Before the storm hits and makes take off impossible." She gave me another shove, this one less gentle, for good measure.

"Are you sure you aren't trying to kill her?" Ship said. He wasn't big on heights. He'd do it because there were others there watching, but he'd be sweating buckets.

"I agree with him," Bebe said. "I don't see like a cat harness, and I'm guessing we are going to be super high up, and going super-fast and I am super fucking sure I don't like this idea."

"Afraid of heights?" Richard asked.

"Afraid of falling from heights!" Bebe snapped back. "This is a terrible, stupid, awful idea!"

I looked at Eir, and thought about the fact that being near Grant would help hide us all. She gave me a subtle nod. I trusted her despite how short a time I'd known her. "You're sure?"

Her smile was tight. "I...this is the way you must take. The path you must fly."

There was something about her voice that made me think of Suvenia, the spirit of the tree of life. That was the deciding factor. Whatever we had to face, this was a part of it.

"We go. Now." I put a little weight into the words, using my alpha strength to get everyone moving.

And that's how we ended up strapped into the bare bones plane, as if we were on some mushroom induced high. It didn't seem real. I mean...who would have believed it if we'd tried to explain to them how we traversed the last distance between northern Alberta and Alaska?

No one, that's the answer in case you weren't sure.

I clutched the straps that were above my head. The five-point harness was a great touch, the straps under my legs nice and snug, but as Bebe was repeatedly pointing out, it meant nothing if we fell. There were no parachutes attached to us, no back up plan.

"Bebe, stop squirming!" Richard yelped as her claws dug into him. She twisted her head around to look back me. She'd decided to go with Richard, pointing out that if she was the backup carrier of the sun, we needed to be separate. In case one of us fell a billion feet to her death, the other had to be willing to take the sun on. Her words, not mine.

I chose not to point out that we'd have to be touching in order to pass the sun back and forth, but she was obviously panicking. And I couldn't blame her, this was going to be...not fun.

All in all, we'd settled on stuffing her down the

front of Richard's shirt just prior to the harness going on. The reality was if one of us went down, we were all going down.

"I can't help it when I'm nervous!" She yowled. "This is…I don't like this!"

Above us one of the Valkyries spoke, as if she were an airline attendant. "Valkyrie flight 101 preparing for take-off. Please keep your hands and feet inside the plane at all times—"

"It's not a plane, it's a fucking joke of an amusement park ride and I hate it!" Bebe snapped.

"Please remain seated for the entirety of the flight, and ensure that your seatbelt remains on at all times—"

"Like we have a choice," Ship muttered. He was to my left, his face nearly as pale as Eir's, though his skin had a bit more of a green tinge to it.

"And do be sure to leave us a review on Google, we appreciate your patronage. Have a good flight!"

Before anyone else could bitch, moan or otherwise complain, the skeleton of a plane lurched straight up, so our feet dangled a solid four feet above the ground.

Straight up and then it wobbled side to side. My belly rolled and I swallowed hard. "Bebe."

"Yeah?"

"You were right, this was a terrible idea."

5

MAGIC HAVOC

Bebe glared at me from her spot inside Richard's shirt as we dangled from the bare bones of the plane. "I told you this was a terrible idea, but would you listen, no—ooooooooo!"

She screeched as we flowed forward and the Valkyries holding us up dove off the cliff edge, dragging us along behind them. I yanked my knees to my chest and even then, the soles of my feet caught the edge of the cliff. My belly lurched firmly up into the back of my throat, and I held my breath as we free fell toward the bottom of the valley.

If it had been a rollercoaster, or maybe even a zipline, I would have enjoyed it. But as it was neither of those, with no safety checks other than our measly harnesses, terror flooded me, and I grit my teeth against the sounds that worked their way up my throat.

Death itself wasn't the issue. It's what would happen to the world, to everyone left behind if I kicked it. We still didn't know the answer to that little question.

Perhaps what scared me more was what if I fell, and I didn't die? What if I fell and because of whatever glitch I had going on, I just…was aware of every broken bone, every injury that was sure to happen if I smashed to the bottom of some valley?

Not good.

We dipped left and right, suddenly weightless as the Valkyries dropped in a straight dive.

Fuck it. I let out a scream, unable to keep it back. To be fair, we were all howling, but the wind whipped our screams away from us as we fell, the treetops coming closer and closer until I could see individual leaves on branches in stark detail. I yanked my knees up again as the very tops of the trees kissed the soles of my boots.

As fast as we'd dropped, we started to level out and the Valkyries were laughing at us. "Fun, right?"

They were giving us thumbs up as we clutched our straps. I had no idea what my face looked like, but by the continued laughter, I realized that they'd done the whole drop and dive on purpose.

For fun.

To see if we could handle it.

"Don't argue with them," I said as I saw Ship's face

turn a distinct shade of swampy green, and his mouth opened. "Great fun, thanks!" I gave them both thumbs up, though that meant letting go of my harness for a moment. I didn't feel bad about grabbing the harness as fast as I had let it go.

My brother shot me a glare. I didn't care. This was our way to avoid Havoc hunting me, to avoid Han hunting me, and a way to get to Alaska quickly without worrying about humans and all their damn rules. The winged ladies were helping us. Eir was helping us.

We were safe, for a little while. That's what I told myself over and over as the wind tore through my hair, as the cold bit at my skin.

The rush of wind around us made talking impossible. From what I could see, Bebe's eyes were closed, and I hoped she was sleeping through this. At least the time would pass quickly for her.

Whatever sleep I might have had, was not going to happen. Which left my mind plenty of time to race along.

What was I supposed to do with the knowledge that the tree goddess had given me? Daughter of Tyr? I couldn't remember what his designation in the Norse pantheon was. I only knew bits and pieces of that mythology. Though I supposed I couldn't call it a myth anymore. Not really. It was a reality that I had found myself in.

This new twist of reality was...unknown to me. But that didn't mean I couldn't figure it out.

I made a list in my head. The first thing I needed to do when we got to my home was to dig out everything I had on the Norse history. Try to see who the major players were, try to see just how I might find a way around the whole needing to die, triggering Ragnarök business. I mean, a legacy left behind is one thing, but being the person responsible for the destruction of all nine realms? That didn't sound like something I wanted to be known for.

There were several books on Norse mythology—reality, whatever—but I wondered if Grant might not have something in storage that gave more information than the usual run of the mill books. Being not only a vampire, but a collector of sorts, he kept special and rare editions at the back of the bookstore. An area that really was just for Grant. I hadn't bothered with it as most of it was written in other languages that I didn't know. Some of them long dead.

"I wonder if Theodore will talk to him?" I muttered the question to myself, knowing that no one else would hear me.

I ducked my head against the wind, wishing that Jor had stayed with us. He at least had a direct knowledge of the challenges I faced.

Unless I could reach out to someone else and get some direction? I closed my eyes and tried to think about what Tyr had looked like. Short beard, dark eyes and dark hair, shaved side of his head. A few beads woven into the longer strands.

I blew out a breath and searched through the bonds that I had to my few people. I carefully sifted through them until I found the slightest, smallest twinge of something.

The thinnest sliver of a bond was there between Tyr and me. Based solely on blood, and that one interaction, if I hadn't been searching for it, I wouldn't have seen it.

I pushed some of my energy into it, and it responded immediately.

With my eyes closed, I was seeing the underwater cave where I'd first met him.

He was sitting on the stump that Ship and I had dragged in so many years before. "Tyr?"

"That is a good trick." He nodded at me. "How did you do it?"

"Shifter bonds," I said. "I wasn't sure it would do anything but..."

He smiled. "But here we are."

I didn't wait for pleasantries. "I don't know what the fuck is happening. Or what I'm doing. Or...or anything! You said you could help me, so help me."

He leaned his elbows on his knees. "Eir has helped you. She pointed out that the vampire's hold on his area will help hide you?"

"Yes, she told me that."

"Good." He smiled and leaned back. And said nothing more.

"You're shitting me. That's it?"

He laughed and stood. "You...you don't have a place in our prophecies, Sunshine. Everything you've done is seemingly impossible. Guiding you is not something I can do. I can offer support, like giving you the spear. Making sure Eir told you what you needed to know about the vampire."

I refused to take that 'sorry that's all I can do' bullshit. "Tell me about Sven. Tell me why the fuck you'd let Juniper tie herself to the tree of life."

He grimaced and paced in front of me. "Sven...I don't know why he wants you dead, I don't know how that benefits him. But it is obvious that he sees something in you that he fears. And he has put all of his power into compelling Havoc."

I frowned. "Han is no longer spelled to kill me?"

"As far as I know, he is free of the spell."

My frown deepened and I fought the urge to pace with him. "Why wouldn't Sven send them both after me?"

"Maybe he thinks that Han will still want to kill you without the spell," Tyr said. "It wouldn't surprise me."

I grimaced. "One spelled, one not. Both hunting me. Maybe."

"Maybe."

Not a lot of help there. "Tell me about Juniper."

"That is more complicated." He sat back down.

"Try me."

"I...I read a very old prophecy. A single line on a page that had been torn out of a book and hidden in another. It led me to your mother. I believed that she would be the answer to stopping Ragnarök."

I snorted. "How's that prediction feeling now?"

He smiled. "I believe that the prophecy was about you. No one else agrees with me, but I...I know I am right."

"Tell me the prophecy."

The bond between me and Havoc twanged, like someone had plucked at a guitar string attached to me. My eyes flew open, the scene with my father gone.

Fuck, what was Havoc up to? Was he trying to find me?

A shiver ran through my body, from the nape of my neck to my tailbone, and I gasped as he tugged on the bond to me, harder, insistent.

Demanding.

Mine.

I wanted to be able to deny him. Oh, how I wanted to deny him. But he was difficult to ignore with my body already singing his damn praises.

And my heart whispering that he'd said that one

word. Even if it was just in his head, he'd said it. Our minds lie far less than our lips.

I swallowed hard as Havoc's demand came at me again. Not once, not twice. Over and over, as he dragged his power over my body the same way he'd slid his hands and mouth over my skin.

It was a good thing Bebe had abandoned me for Richard because I wasn't sure I wasn't going to have an issue here with what Havoc was doing to me.

By issue, I clearly mean having an orgasm mid-flight.

"Fuck me." I lolled my head forward, struggling to breathe through the feel of him against me. What was he doing this for? I didn't understand why he would play with me this way. Was it just to show me he could? It flickered through my mind that it might be as simple as making me hold still while he hunted for me. Because this...thing...that he was doing to me, it was wrecking my ability to do anything but feel.

My heart beat in time with the thrum that was a steady beat between my legs, washing over me in waves, pushing and tugging me toward an orgasm. If I hadn't been strapped into the mock airplane, I would not have been walking. I'd have been flat on my back, waiting for him in real time, writhing under this phantom touch.

That was it. He was using our connection, his ability to make me lose my mind, to hold me still. I groaned, wanting to find a release, knowing that I could do no such thing, strung up as I was.

My legs went tight, muscles spasming, with each trail of his invisible touch.

Worse or maybe better? I *felt* his mouth travelling up my inner thigh, lazy, moving in circles, all the way to my core where he latched his mouth and sucked at me so hard, that I opened my eyes fully expecting to see him there, his mouth on my skin, dark eyes locked on mine. But the space between my legs was empty, no matter what I was feeling.

"Havoc." I groaned his name, the sound whipped away by the wind and the whoosh of wings above us. I should have told him to stop, because this couldn't be. None of it could be between us. And I knew that no matter how far gone he was in the throes of whatever spell had him, that he would stop if I told him to stop.

But I didn't.

Nope, I wasn't that much of a saint and if this was going the way I thought it was going, I was not going to miss out. I gripped the harness, digging my nails into the material, as I tried to get my breathing under control. Not that anyone else was going to notice me—everyone else was hanging on for dear life too.

Havoc's invisible hands gripped at me, invisible and yet there as surely as I clung to the harness, his fingers against my thighs, his mouth against my clit, tongue laying into me with a slow, definitive pressure that had me struggling to breathe.

"You are mine, Goldie. There is nowhere you can run that I can't find you."

Again, I *felt* his mouth against my core, lapping at my center, hot and wet. I jerked under his touch, gasped as he drew his tongue over me, again and again, circling around my core.

Whatever magic it was, I didn't want it to stop.

I might have moaned his name again, probably said something like 'don't stop' but I could barely think past the rippling of sensations. The draw toward a crest of pleasure that I'd never found with anyone else.

Nothing compared to him.

Mine.

And I hated myself more than a little for it. Because right now, he was the bad guy, no matter that there had been moments of light, where I trusted him. No matter what I saw in his head when he looked at me.

He ordered me to run—he knew what he was capable of and at least a portion of him understood that he had been spelled to hunt me. Sven had laid a spell on him, to force him to kill me, and I had no doubt he'd do just that if he caught me.

A tiny voice circled around my heart and tried to point out that he wouldn't have told me to run if he didn't want me to live. I knew that. It didn't change the truth.

If he caught me, I was dead.

He sucked hard on my clit, his magic plucking at every sensitive part of my body and it took all I had to clamp down on the scream that built up inside of me alongside the orgasm.

I couldn't stop the way my body bucked as release rocketed through me, jerking on the straps. Did I make the plane tilt? No fucking idea. My world imploded, the weight of his body on mine, his skin pressed hard to my own.

Impossible? Sure. But I still felt it. Still felt Havoc's tongue doing lazy circles, a growl slipping through him and into me. A demand inside of it. A command of obedience.

Stay. Stay where you are, Goldie.

I didn't know how long it took for me to come down from the aftershocks of the orgasm. I stared into nothing as I tried to get my breathing under control, his alpha command so strong that if I'd been on my feet somewhere I wouldn't have moved. I wouldn't have so much as budged an inch.

But I wasn't on the ground. I was flying through the air with someone else moving me along.

By the time I was able to throw off the compulsion, at least an hour had passed. Sweat had dried down the sides of my face, and the sweat on my back had cooled, leaving me chilly in the high air currents.

Gods above.

I pressed a shaking hand to the side of my face.

What if he pulled that shit when I *was* on foot? I was absolutely screwed.

Sure, I'd die with a smile on my face but…I wasn't ready to die. Not even like that.

The plane seemed to shift to the left, and then our flight was dropping lower. A soft lethargy flowed over me, and I tried to fight it. I really did, because it wasn't just the after effect of an orgasm. It was the command that he'd sent into me. *Stay.*

With a growl I fought my way from the sleep that tugged at me. He'd mouth fucked me into oblivion, using it to make me stay so he could find me, making sure I didn't go too far.

The more the lethargy tugged at me, the more I was sure of it.

"Fucker." I sat up straight and forced myself to take long deep breaths of the crisp air. I would not go to sleep. Even here, where in theory, I could just go to sleep and still be safe.

He wouldn't find me here. But it was the principle. I was a damn alpha female, I did not bow to him, I did not bow to anyone.

An hour slid by, and then another. I didn't know how fast we were going, or how far we'd come, but the ground below us was starting to look familiar. The trees thinner, the terrain harder. Alaska was not for pussies, it chewed them up and spit them the fuck out.

This place was strong and wild, full of beauty and danger that you would find nowhere else in the world. I loved it.

I was home.

On a quick glance upward, the Valkyries didn't seem to be showing any sign of pooping out. Every time I looked up at them, they were flying in the same formation, facing forward, not an ounce of fatigue showing.

Shipley, Berek and Claire were all asleep as far as I could see. Richard was awake, and at this distance I could see his mouth moving as he talked to Bebe.

I sighed and set to lifting my knees to my chest, then lowering them slowly. The burn of my muscles was something to take my mind off the heat that had been between my legs. Even hours later, just thinking about it made me tingle all over and tugged on that bond between us.

"Fucker," I grumbled, yes, for the second time. Havoc was a fucker, and he'd…he'd fucked me in more ways than one. I could feel the connection to him, stronger than the one I had to Han, and it was humming along, as if I wanted it there.

I didn't. Of course I didn't.

Yet, my weak words were just that—as weak as my desire to get rid of him.

Because somewhere in the moments between fighting and fucking, and trying to survive, escaping him and being caught…something had happened between us.

Something more than possession. More than lust.

I ran a hand over my face, wishing for a distraction.

I didn't want to acknowledge that Havoc meant more to me than just a tumble in the sack now…now that he was bound to kill me.

"Fuck my life," I whispered.

A Valkyrie's voice echoed through the air, as if coming over an intercom speaker in an airplane.

"Passengers, please be advised we will need to take evasive maneuvers. Make sure your tray tables and seats are in an upright position, and your seatbelts are tight. We are expecting excessive turbulence."

Well. There was my distraction I was so desperate for.

6

VALKYRIE FLIGHT 101 BLOWS ASS

You know, the flight really hadn't been all that bad up until that little announcement. It had been a bit chilly, had a quick visit with Tyr, and I'd had an amazing orgasm. The straps didn't dig in too hard, but really...I couldn't complain. Okay, there was no inflight service. Well, if you didn't count the lip service that Havoc had provided. And I wasn't complaining about that.

"Did she say what I think she said?" Bebe screeched, loud enough to be heard over the rushing wind and the clank of the plane's bits and pieces as our flight path adjusted. "Extreme turbulence? What the hell does that mean?"

I gripped the straps above my head and yelled up at the Valkyries. "What is it? What are we evading? Is it the storm, did it catch us?" I mean, they had said turbulence. So maybe the storm? One could hope, but I had a bad feeling.

Because I couldn't see anything. I mean, we were so fucking high that anything that took us out up here would fuck us big time. There were no storm clouds any longer, just the chunks of land below, some still white with frost and snow, others gray rock, bits of trees.

A Valkyrie, the one closest to my rigging, looked down at me. "Flying rooster."

Rooster? Had I heard that right? That couldn't be right, it had to be the wrong word. Flying Twister maybe? I turned around as best I could, trying to see another bird, or whatever the hell we were suddenly evading. But still there was nothing.

The winged troop of women suddenly dropped into a dive that spun us to the right, up over a hill, and then down again to the left.

Bebe, Claire and Ship were screaming their heads off. I gritted my teeth as the Valkyries dragged us through the narrow chasm of a canyon, moving side to side as if they were trying to dodge bullets. But I didn't see anyone behind us, and there were no bullets flying.

What in the actual fuck was going on? Color me distrustful, but I couldn't help but wonder if they were doing this just so they could *say* that someone was after them, and that we were killed in the process.

Ooops, our bad, sorry 'bout that.

Of course, right when I was certain that we were being fucked with again, that was when I heard the rumbling roar of something really, *really* big coming up behind us. Or maybe it was above us? I twisted around again. This time I got a glimpse of something that made my eyes bug out.

Scales. Wings. Teeth. Huge. Bright orange eyes locked on us.

"That's not what I think it is, is it?" I yelled.

"That's Rooster. He's a frosty damn bastard," the same Valkyrie yelled. "And we are crossing his territory in order to get you far enough into Alaska."

I blinked and looked back, but Rooster was not visible. For the moment.

"Are you saying his attack...it's not personal?" I yelled my question.

"Exactly." She bobbed her head once.

I didn't ask her more questions, not when she was flying hard to keep us all alive.

I grabbed the strut closest to my head so I could spin myself slightly to the side and get a better look at the beast that was coming hard on our heels.

Finally, he appeared fully, seemingly slithering through the canyon as he flew behind us.

Rooster's body was lean, and he fit through the canyon, but the twists and turns were slowing him down, so I only caught glimpses of the big beast.

Dragon, yes, but his scales were all browns and

greens, not at all what I would have guessed for a northern dragon. Then again, dragons weren't exactly well known anymore, most had been killed off by the humans. Not a surprise there, murderous fearful little shits that they were. The humans, not the dragons.

The dragon's deeply orange eyes were narrowed, and he kept baring his teeth in our direction. But he hadn't blown fire, or anything else for that matter.

"Northern dragon!" Berek yelled. "This is bad!"

Okay, so Rooster *was* a northern dragon, which made it less likely it would be fire coming out of his big ass mouth, and more likely...my thoughts skittered to a stop as the air temperature around us suddenly dropped.

"Hang on!" The Valkyries shouted as a unit and then we dropped rapidly toward the bottom of the canyon, the icy whitish blue walls around us a blur as we raced for the water far below. An ice storm followed us along with a roar from Rooster, shards of pointed chunks of ice flying through the air as if shot from a gun.

The Valkyries ducked and dived, dodging the worst of the particles. That didn't mean none of us got hit, and their ducking and diving jerked us around, the plane groaning as they yanked it in all directions.

A shiv of ice cut across my right forearm, slicing muscle and flesh as easily as a razor blade. Yelps and screams from the others only seemed to urge the dragon on further.

I really was doing my best not to look at what was coming for us. The river below surged and frothed like a giant blender, white caps slamming against rocks and debris.

This was not going to go well if we ended up in there.

Gods' balls, I'd had enough of rivers. I jerked my knees to my chest, but it didn't help, and the moment stretched out. We were in a solid straight stretch of the canyon, and I didn't see any bends coming up. Fuck, that was not going to help us outrun the flying Rooster—

The dragon burst out from behind us, and the world slowed down.

Screams. The Valkyries tucked their wings in tight. I stared up at his open mouth as he lunged forward and grabbed the tail end of the plane, jerking us to a mid-air stop just before we hit the water. Ice frosted on the plane, radiating out of the dragon's mouth and curling toward us. I watched in horror as the ice slid up over the Valkyrie closest to him. Her body froze, her eyes still moving as her wings turned into frozen blocks.

"Cut the straps!" I screamed—we didn't have a choice. There was no escaping the ice. It curled toward each of us, Valkyrie and passenger alike. If any of us were to survive, we had to get free.

At least we were over water. It was something positive. Right? I mean, icy fucking cold water that would kill us in a matter of minutes—shifters or not. But better than being turned into giant ice cubes.

It was the only chance we had.

Berek and Claire dropped first, then Richard with Bebe.

Ship looked at me as I jerked at the straps. His blade cut through his own straps. And as he fell, we both realized the same things.

I had no knife.

"Fuck me up again!" I yelped as I got one of the straps off. A Valkyrie dropped to me, and she shoved a sword through the remaining straps. We locked eyes.

"Go. Find a way. Save us all."

I fell, facing the sky, watching the dragon tear apart the flimsy plane, while my savior was tied to it. She spun and tried to get herself untangled but it was no use. She was yanked into the dragon's mouth, her eyes still on mine. Her last words still on her lips as she disappeared.

Save us all.

The other Valkyries scattered, and I could not blame them. They'd lost two of their own, one to the ice dragon, and the other because she'd saved me instead of herself. My guts roiled like the frothing water below me.

But there was little time to dwell.

I hit the water hard, like hitting a cement sidewalk, the icy cold pulling me down and under, stealing the air in my lungs as I was yanked into a sheer tumble of waves. Rapids. We'd dropped straight into a series of rapids. Bashed left and right, I hit my shoulder, knee and hip on rocks, my hands cut open as I clawed at a boulder trying to get out of the swirl that was dragging at me. I couldn't tell what was up and down with the rolling of the current.

Relax. That was what I needed to do. I blew the air out of my lungs and dropped to the bed of the river. From there I pushed up from the bottom, the urge and need to breathe fighting with the ability to get to the surface.

With a last surge I broke the surface and dragged in a lungful of air, gasping and coughing.

"Richard!" I screamed for my older brother as soon as I could get enough air. Not because I thought he'd save me, but he had Bebe. And Bebe would get absolutely fucked up in this water. I couldn't let her die.

A wave rolled over my head, and I was shoved into another current, spun around and smashed against a log battling the same current. The last time I'd been in a river, fighting for my life, Havoc had saved me.

He'd pulled me out, dragged me from a death that

would have ended the world—not because I meant anything. Just because I was another job to complete. I was a responsibility he hadn't wanted.

When had that changed?

"You aren't like the others who have fallen to the curse. They were all scared. Terrified. As they should be. You...you are the first to fight back in all these years."

He believed in me. And that was enough to give me the strength to push me. I launched myself toward the closest shoreline, fighting the waves as if I were wrestling with Havoc. And yes, it was nearly as futile as if I'd been fighting the much larger man. The river was violent, and cruel, letting me get almost to safety, before I was dragged back under by an unseen current, as if hands had been latched onto my ankles.

Over and over again, I fought for the shoreline. I would not stop fighting.

The cold and exhaustion wrapped themselves around me, sinking into my skin and bones, numbing my mind until there was only one goal. The shoreline.

Keep going. That's all I could do. Keep swimming. Rapids turned into a fast-rolling river, and I finally made a little progress, my knees hitting the shallow riverbed, pebbles and rocks rolling out from under me. I fell forward, clawing at the meager edge, dragging myself up until I was fully out of the water.

I sucked wind, gasping and shivering as the reality of my situation hit hard. There was nothing I could do but keep going. I couldn't stop trying now. The choice was to stop trying and die or keep going and *maybe* live.

I forced myself to sit up and look up and down the edge of the river. But the damn thing had a slight curve, and I couldn't see much more than a few hundred feet back upriver. The others could be anywhere along here. Or they could have passed me and ended up downstream.

I wasn't sure how long I'd fought with the currents. Or if my brothers and friends had fared any better against the pull of the water.

"They're here," I whispered to myself, teeth chattering. I reached for the bond between me and the boys first. They were upstream, alive.

Relief flooded me. Trembling, I got to my feet. The cold would kill me but not if I shifted. Decision made, I went to call my wolf forward, knowing that it was best in this situation.

But she stood there and looked at me. Black wolf. Golden retriever next to her.

No golden wolf.

We are individuals, Cinniúint. *We come together only when needed.* My wolf tipped her head and sneezed in my direction.

The shift between two legs and four was painless. Golden fur rippled around me, and by the size of my paws, I was a golden retriever again. I sighed. Ah well, maybe my wolf knew better. The retriever was better suited to the water, and with a thick undercoat would survive the cold better when it was water I was dealing with.

Feeling a little brighter—that retriever mentality was a serious vibe—I trotted up the side of the river barking. Trying to get someone's attention.

I found Shipley and Claire first. They were huddled together, shivering, lips blue with cold.

Ship saw me and nodded. "Smart. We should shift, warmer that way."

Claire was shaking so hard, I wasn't sure she'd be able to pull it together. Ship shifted first and Claire just sat there, staring at him.

He gave a low woof, a command in it to shift. Even I knew it wasn't enough. She shook her head. "I can't. I need…I need someone stronger to make me."

She was stuck then, it happened sometimes with extreme fear, injury or general trauma.

It takes an alpha to kill an alpha female.

I could try and make her shift. If what Juniper had said was correct, then…there was no reason it wouldn't work, even though I wasn't her alpha. In theory. And if I didn't…she would suffer and we would possibly have to leave her behind.

I whined, not liking that. My golden wanted to protect her.

I gathered my alpha strength, and let it rumble under my skin. I locked eyes with Claire.

She tried to lower her gaze, but I held her there. And gave a sharp bark.

"You need to shift."

Claire's eyes widened and her body shimmered, shifting to her four-legged form in a breath. Her wolf was a deep chocolate with threads of deeper red running across her ribs, like tiger stripes. No doubt she hadn't thought I'd have any say over her as a golden.

But even as she stood there, shaking, I felt something unexpected.

In that one command, because I'd done it to protect her, a deeper connection had been formed. Nothing too permanent, but I could see it and feel her energy through it stronger than before. She was part of my pack...assuming I could count myself, Richard, Bebe and Ship as my pack.

That was not what I wanted. I didn't need more people depending on me, tied to me.

But right then, Claire was terrified, and it was my job to help her through. I sent a gentle push of calm energy toward her, thoughts of safety and warmth.

Her terror ebbed and her breathing eased. She looked at me and gave a soft woof of thanks.

A small part of me hummed with pleasure, because this meant my golden was strong too. A different strength than my wolf, sure, but still strong. There was compassion in my golden that balanced the violence of my wolf.

I could see why they couldn't combine unless the situation was dire. They were too different.

"Alright, let's find the others." I trotted off ahead of them. Assuming—hoping—that they were upriver, at least from what I could sense. Ship fell into a steady pace just ahead of me, his nose twitching.

Claire tucked in close to my hip, the pack bonds keeping her closer than normal.

I breathed in deeply, but more than that I reached for my connection to Richard and Bebe. They were pack. They were family.

I tipped my head, hearing the screech at the same time as I locked onto Bebe's ties to me.

"This is fucking awful! Even with fur, this is the worst! Do you know how long it's going to take me to get warm! Years!"

"At least you're alive, we don't know if the others made it," Richard's voice rumbled back.

We took a corner and there was Berek on the shoreline, already on four-legs. Funny, but I recognized him even though I'd never seen his wolf before. He was a deep gray wolf that would disappear in the shadows of a forest with ease. He turned and looked at me and I felt that same twang as I had with Claire.

His allegiance had switched to me, sometime along the way. I'd begun to sense it before, like at the hospital when he'd been shot and even used it to send him energy when he'd been shot. But it was stronger now and he was more...mine, less Havoc's.

Richard and Bebe, well they weren't in as good a spot as Berek. They were on a rock protruding out of the middle of the river.

Bebe saw me, her eyes widened. "Cin! We tried to grab you! We saw you go tumbling by!"

"I tried," Richard corrected, wincing. "But I broke my leg I think, caught between the rocks, and I lost my balance when I reached for you." The water bashed into the rock they sat on, still in the middle of the river. I eyed the distance. A broken leg was not good, but we'd deal.

We always did.

"Richard, you remember how we used to play keep away? Tossing the ball as far as we could?" I asked.

He grinned, though his lips were tinged blue. "I do."

"Bebe is the ball," I said.

"You will not!" She screamed, but Richard was fast. He scooped her up and launched her toward the shoreline before she could truly protest.

"You bastard!"

"You'll land on your feet," he yelled back.

And he was right. Bebe dropped onto the shore, all four feet landing at once. It didn't stop her from turning around and spitting curses at him.

I bumped my nose into hers. "He can shift now."

"I could have ridden on his back!" she snapped, her wet fur attempting to fluff up in indignation, which just made her look partially fluffed, and wholly pissed.

"But if you were to slide off, it would put us all in danger," Richard said what I was thinking. "Because we'd have to dive into the rapids after you."

Bebe stared at him, then looked at me. "Fine."

I barked at Richard, encouraging him, giving him some of my energy, though I didn't have much it was something. He shifted, right there on the rock. His face contorted with pain, but he pushed through. It wasn't something many shifters liked to do, simply because it hurt severely to shift when you were injured—especially with things like broken limbs. But in our family, we knew that the pain of shifting injured outweighed the risk of being trapped by whoever had done the hurting.

Richard leapt upstream but didn't get far, the water pulling him downstream fast. I waded into the frigid river, and felt Ship take a hold of my tail so I floated another wolf's length out. As Richard fought to get to me, I reached for him.

I managed to get my teeth into his left paw, and he clamped onto the ruff around my neck, and just like that we were dragging him back to the shore. Soaking wet, but we'd all made it out of a death drop that I hadn't been sure any of us would survive.

"We need to get out of here," Berek grumbled. "That dragon will come back once he's done chasing the Valkyries. We'd be easy pickings along the river."

As if hearing him, the beast in question let out a bellow that rocked through the canyon, overpowering even the sound of the river. The air crackled with cold and the threat of an unnatural ice storm. We had to move.

"Then we go," I said.

"Where?" Bebe shook her head, sending out a spray of water.

I looked to the north, feeling home, knowing we were almost there. "We're headed to my place. It's not far."

I just didn't tell her that not far was still going to be farther than she would like.

7
NORN OF YOUR BUSINESS

"'Not far' is a pile of shit!" Bebe grumbled.

My tongue lolled out as I trotted along at a slower pace than I would have liked, but with Richard hobbling on three legs, we couldn't go at full speed. The break was healing, but he needed food to help fuel the process. The big thing was that we were away from the river and the northern dragon that patrolled the water.

"Not far in the scheme of things. We'll be there in a few hours," I said. "Take in the scenery, enjoy the moment and all that shit."

"Are you sure it's safe?" Claire asked, her voice tinged with fear despite the calm I'd sent her. I couldn't blame her, not really. It wasn't every day you ran into a dragon trying to alternately freeze you into an ice cube and tear you to pieces.

Whatever fear I had was no longer registering. I was numb.

Too much had been thrown at me for me to be overly fazed by what had just happened. But maybe Claire and Berek had been more sheltered than me. Even more than Richard or Ship and Bebe.

No, I was not the normal one here.

Hell, I wasn't even just a shifter, I was some sort of minor Norse god? What exactly would that mean for me now? What was the power that I supposedly had? Not killing dragons, that was for sure.

I shied hard away from those thoughts. What I needed was a hot tea, a warm blanket and a soft chair to absorb some of the impact of figuring out just who and what I was and how I could apparently change the trajectory of what destiny had in store for me.

Tea and a warm blanket could fix this. Right, no problem.

"Safer than most places," I said, coming back to the conversation. "Havoc doesn't know that's where I am from. Neither does Han. Eir said…well she said that one of my friends there, Grant, created a natural hiding spot. Which is why I was safe for so many years. I think it will give us some respite to figure out what happens next."

That was the biggest issue at hand.

What next? What steps would I take to keep all this

together? What did I have to do to stop Ragnarök, save the world, and hopefully not die in the process?

I'd stopped Han from killing me, eliminated the threat of my mother—even if Kieran was still out there, and I had no doubt he'd try to kill me again given the chance—but in all that I had gained Havoc as a hunter. The fate of the world was still tied to my life or death if the way I was being hunted meant anything.

I wanted to sigh and curl up in a corner, to see if I woke up from a long nap, maybe this was all some sort of pizza and beer induced dream sequence.

Instead, I did what I often did. I turned my thoughts to what was right in front of me and took in the scenery.

Alaska this time of year was pretty, and about as warm as it was going to get. Tiny purple and pink flowers dotted the landscape around us, trees were bunched up in tight patches where snow still sat at their bases. Yup, snow and flowers, it was a special combination.

The mountains in the distance were completely covered with snow, and glistened bright white, shining in the midday sun, as if encrusted in diamonds. Not that the sun would be setting any time soon. Not here in mid-summer.

I glanced over at Richard. He was jogging and hopping along, his right hind leg dangling for the most part. Here and there he tested it, then jerked it away from the ground with a grimace. He never complained, never said a word about the pain that I knew he was feeling. But I could sense it all the way through our pack bond.

I pushed some of my energy through to him, and he shot a look at me. "I'm fine."

"Fucking indignant nincompoop energy," Bebe said. "That's what I think. She's your sister, let her help you."

I huffed a laugh. Having Bebe so tightly tied within my new pack was interesting. One, because she could sense the energies as well or maybe even better than me. And two, because Richard grunted and bobbed his head, giving in to her. She outranked him, which meant she was above Ship too.

"She's a demanding one," he said. There wasn't an ounce of anger in his words though.

Because even better than her outranking my brothers, Bebe was my second in command. That was the thing about being in a pack, you could feel where strengths and weaknesses put you in the hierarchy. That way no one argued, and it helped to keep fights to a minimum.

Maybe that was why my own mother had never let me into her pack as an adult, because then everyone would have known that I was stronger than her.

Holy freaking shit storm.

The truth hit me like a blow between the eyes. My

whole life, my whole existence...the words blurted out of me.

"Holy shit. Juniper kept me out of the pack because she knew I was stronger than her. Not just to be a bitch, but to hold all her power and to keep everyone else blind to my strength?"

I wasn't entirely sure, but saying it out loud, I felt the truth of it.

"Just figured that out, eh?" Ship trotted alongside me. "That's why she freaked out all those years ago when Mars tried to bring you officially into the pack when you were eighteen. Before that, the only person who would have known was her, being your mother."

"Yeah." I shook my head. "It never would have occurred to me before now. I've never really been a part of a pack as an adult. Not ours at least."

"Never occurred to me either," Richard grumbled. "We thought because you were not Mars' daughter, by blood, that was why. But after her meltdown, even he didn't let you in the pack those last few months he was with us. Maybe he knew that it kept you safer by keeping you out."

Richard wasn't wrong. I'd *never* actually been part of the pack, except as a child—and children were de facto tied to their parents only, so they couldn't be manipulated by other adults. I'd stopped asking after the fight Juniper had put up on my last birthday that

Mars had been with us. Given up on it ever happening and tried to prove myself all that time.

Assumed it was because I wasn't worthy.

Sure, I had bonds to my family, and that was something that I'd worked hard to cut through, but those hadn't been true pack bonds. Likely that's what made it easier to cut the ties.

Those connections had nothing on this interweaving of energy and understanding of one another. Of feeling Claire and Berek, of Bebe's energy and even my brother's. Hell, even that distant connection to Tyr was there.

And I had a feeling it was because I was an alpha, that it was all at the front of my mind.

I shook my head and snapped at a long strand of grass that bobbed ahead of me. "You think Juniper actually made it so I couldn't fully integrate?"

"Would make sense," Berek said. "If she truly learned how to steal mate bonds, it might have come with the knowledge of other types of bonds too. Or maybe…"

I winced. "Or maybe she was looking for ways to cut me out, and stumbled on how to steal mate bonds?" I didn't mention that she'd also tied herself to the tree of life. Not that it had saved her in the end.

"That's what I'd guess," Ship said. "She started looking for stuff not long after you were born, I think. Started bringing in shamans and other pack alphas."

Bebe kneaded her paws into the ruff around my neck. "Doesn't matter, girlfriend. You've got us now. And we've got you. *We've got you.*"

Her words soothed some of the ragged edges of my heart, of the past and the hurts that were there.

"Yeah. That we do. Everything she put us all through, everything that happened…we'll heal those wounds together," Richard said.

My heart, man my heart was bursting and I had to keep my eyes locked on the path I was taking because I would have started bawling.

"I got you too," I managed to say without my voice cracking too much.

We all fell into silence as we drew closer to town.

Skagway hadn't changed much since I'd left, not that I was surprised. It hadn't been that long since Ship had walked into my little bookstore and turned my life upside down. If I'd had a bingo card, I wouldn't have covered a single square on it.

But it felt like with everything that had happened, I'd been gone a lifetime.

I was different after the time that had passed, that was what I was feeling. I had changed in more ways than just carrying the sun.

As if thinking of it triggered its strength, warmth flooded through me. Damn, I should have thought of it sooner and I'd have been able to warm myself up. I wondered if I could pass the warmth on to the others.

"This way." I led the group of wolves around the outskirts of town, avoiding all the main roads, and around through the woods to the backside of the bookstore. "Wait here, I'll get the door open."

I shifted back to two legs, buck naked but that was life as a shifter, and crept up the stairs that led to the apartment above. The door was locked, but the extra key was still under the pot of dead flowers that Taini—my previous roommate—had put out what seemed like a lifetime ago. I hoped she and Copper, her girlfriend, were safe. I hoped they were far from here and sitting on the banks of some river at a café, sipping hot espresso and eating warm croissants.

The door opened with a creak—I never greased the hinges, they were another alarm if someone was sneaking into the apartment—and I peered in. "Denna?"

No answer. Not that I'd fully expected her to make it here ahead of us. The ghoul was a good friend, and I'd sent her away before we'd gone to face my mother in Montana. Sure, it had been a bogus message for Grant, but it was meant to keep them both busy, and out of harm's way.

I didn't want my gentle friend being caught in the middle of this mess—again.

I looked back and motioned for the others to follow me up into the apartment. "Keep the lights off for now, until I get a hold of Grant," I said. I needed to let him know we were here, so we didn't set off any alarms. I needed to ask him if it was true he kept the area protected.

Ship and Berek shifted as they stepped into the apartment. Richard and Claire did not. Richard, I understood, he was dealing with the broken leg. But Claire…she stayed in her wolf form which was odd until her emotions hit me solidly in the guts, embarrassment at the front of the list.

"I'll grab you some clothes and you can use the bathroom first." I headed to my bedroom.

Embarrassment rolled through her at the thought of being naked in front of my brothers and Berek at the same time. I couldn't really decipher why, because generally as shifters, nudity was just kind of a part of the deal. We all shifted from fur to two legs nude.

But if I were a guessing girl, I'd have said it was the newness of her relationship with Berek. Wolves could be possessive…in case you hadn't noticed.

Rubbing at my arms I knew one thing for certain.

I needed to find a way to dull down the connection to them all. As it stood, I could sense each of them acutely. Richard's pain. Claire's embarrassment. Ship's worry. Berek's worry. Bebe's worry and what felt like lust? Who the hell was she lusting after now? I stuck my head out of my bedroom to look at her. She was curled up on the corner of the couch, her eyes closed and just the tip of her tail flicking every other second.

Not that I didn't want a pack...but Berek and Claire weren't really mine. It was a circumstance that had pushed them into my circle, nothing more. And I didn't want to hold people to me that didn't want to be there.

I sighed and went back to digging through my closet. I still had clothes here, I hadn't been able to take everything with me when I'd run the first time.

I yanked on a shirt and jeans quickly, then took a set to the bathroom and motioned for Claire to follow me. She padded silently into the bathroom, and I flicked on the light. "There's no window, you can have the light on, and no one will see you."

She bobbed her head and woofed a soft thanks, butting her nose against my leg in acknowledgment. I stepped out and shut the door behind me. "Berek, Ship, I don't have any clothes that will fit so grab a sheet or something. Toga it up."

Ship grunted and made his way to the second bedroom, and a moment later he came back with a sheet for himself, and one for Berek.

"I'll wait." Richard laid on the threadbare rug in the middle of the living room, lowering his head to his paws, a heavy sigh sliding from him. His leg would heal, but it would take at least a full day. And I had to believe we had a full day before we had to move.

I had to hope that Grant could do what Eir thought he could.

Bebe flicked her tail, as she watched Richard lay

down, wincing as his back leg bumped, her eyes narrowing. "You are being stupid. You should at least let your sister help you with that. Let her float you some more energy."

"I will be fine, Bebe. My sister is also still healing if you hadn't noticed," Rich growled.

She huffed and a flash of annoyance laced with...concern...and a healthy dose of attraction. I stared. She wasn't serious, was she? No, she might have a tiny crush on him, but that was it, she barely knew him. I mean...no, I had other problems that required my attention.

Bebe's love life was so far down my list of concerns right now, it about fell off the page.

"I'm going downstairs, there's always food in the office fridge."

No one responded to me, not even Bebe. Everyone was exhausted, that came through loud and clear.

Besides, I needed a few minutes to myself for several reasons.

I needed to call Grant and find out how big his range of keeping us hidden was.

I needed to see what I could find in the books in the store on what I was hoping would help me understand my situation.

Last but not least, I needed to try and numb the bonds between me and Havoc, and me and Han. Even if Grant could hide me, they would have still sensed my general direction.

Han I was pretty sure I could numb out, I'd done it before with some success.

Havoc, I was not so confident I could quiet those bonds. Even thinking about him made the connection between us spike and throb. I gripped the railing and had to breathe through the onslaught of need.

"Not now," I hissed, the railing crackling under my hand as I squeezed for all I was worth.

Moving through the dark, I was down the rest of the stairs and into the bookstore before anything else came through from Havoc. Breathing in, I could easily pick up the scents of paper and ink, book glue and the faint tang of coffee still lingering from the morning.

Warmth spread through me, and not just because I was inside and out of the cold. This was home, this was a place that I had felt safe for ten years. Ten years of peace. Of safety, and of knowing that I'd found a place that I belonged.

First thing first. I called Grant, fully expecting him to pick up. He might be able to get the journal back to me. Maybe.

The phone went to voicemail, surprising me. "Grant...call me when you get this. I need that book that Theo has." I didn't leave him a number, assuming he'd see the caller ID. I tapped the phone with one finger. I hoped he was okay.

Crazy to be worried about a vampire, but he was my friend.

Next, I had to dull down the connections between me and the wolves I'd picked up, so I could focus on the task at hand. Everyone's emotions all at once were too much.

I started with Berek and Claire. Looking inward, I found the ties binding us together. Soft, rather thin, like gossamer thin strands that I could barely see. I hesitated, memories flooding through me, things I hadn't thought about in years. Because I knew what it was to be cut loose from an alpha.

Juniper stared down at me. The dirt was cool under my bare legs, the smell of the forest not enough to get through the snot and tears running down my face. My arms were wrapped tightly around my body as I waited here.

"You see?" Juniper all but purred the words. "You cannot feel a connection to the others because you are not wanted. That is how pack bonds work, Cinny. You must be wanted for them to hold tight to you. You must want to be attached to us too." She laughed. "And I can tell that is the last thing you want."

A shudder rippled through my naked body, and it took all I had not to shift back to my wolf form. At least as a wolf, I could run away. On two legs...I was trapped. "I..." I didn't know what to say. I was only eighteen, and my mother had yanked me from four legs to two, just using the power of her voice.

The power of her as an alpha trumped my desire to run away.

"Do you deny it? Do you wish to be tied more tightly to me?"

I couldn't look away from her face and for the first time...I was honest. "No. I don't want to be tied to you."

Her smile stretched across her beautiful face, and she spread her arms wide. "Then let the connection between us be dissolved."

A burn ripped through my soul, a flurry of pain cut through me, and it felt as if I were cast out into an ocean storm, drowning as my wolf howled. We'd never be a part of the pack.

We'd been outsiders, only able to sense Juniper truly as the mother-child bond allowed, but still there had been something. Hope that I'd be let in...

I loved my siblings. I loved Mars. I didn't want to lose them. I curled around my body, protected the tiniest of threads that bound me to those I loved.

Juniper kicked dirt at me as she walked away. "That is the only lesson I will ever give you on bonds, little Cinny. Remember this."

I blinked, back in the present moment.

Juniper had cut through the bonds, but I'd clung to a few strands that barely held together, like spider silk, the familial bonds tying me to my siblings.

When I'd left Grayling, I'd dissolved my connections to my brothers and sister, no problem. Because

Juniper had done the lion's share of the work all those years earlier, cutting me from the family. I wasn't sure that my siblings would have even noticed that they'd lost that last thread to me.

"Why now?" I muttered and rubbed my hands over my face. It wasn't difficult to put a damper on the connection between myself, Berek and Claire. I could have cut them loose completely, but they had to want it too.

And *that* is exactly why it was so difficult. Most shifters *wanted* to be in a pack. It was what the wolves they carried with them wanted. Very, very few shifters actually wanted to go it alone.

Shifters like Han and Havoc, lone wolves in every sense of the word, and the ones that had the newest ties to me...they should be very easy to remove.

And yet they'd been the most difficult of all, every time I tried to cut them free.

A hiss of air escaped me and suddenly I struggled to breathe. Han couldn't possibly *want* to remain tied to me. I mean...sure he wanted to kill me, but actually remaining tied to me? Surely, I should be able to cut him loose now.

I looked to the threads between myself and Han.

They were black and green now, muddied like a swamp, and yet the line connecting us seemed to throb with a life of its own. The connection of mates tied together in some shitty sort of destiny. But he'd rejected me. I frowned, eyes closed looking harder at the bond, I reached out and ran a hand over it. It was warm, and thick, sticky almost. Weirdly, it gave off a sense of Loki's energy. Which made sense since he'd created the connection.

I turned my inward vision to the tie between me and Havoc. That was…it called to me, humming with a life of its own the same way Han's did. Only Havoc's tie was a siren's song to wait for him…to let him find me.

The thing they both had in common was the immense girth (get your mind out of the gutter) of the bonds. They were thick as if they'd been developed over years, and not weeks.

Why were they so different than any other bond I'd seen?

My bonds with Claire and Berek, I could see that those could be pulled apart if I wanted to, because they didn't really want to be a part of my pack. They had a pack, they belonged to Havoc, and I'd somehow stolen them away.

But the two wolves who wanted to kill me, those two I couldn't cut loose, and I wasn't going to waste my energy trying to.

I rubbed my hands over my face again. I was trapped by them both, unable to escape them any more than I'd been able to escape Juniper when I was a little girl.

I took the next half an hour layering every bond

that was attached to me, whether it was pack or mate, and muffling it. I buried them deep within me, so there was no more forward connection.

Imagining I wrapped the bonds in concrete, then buried them under six feet of earth, the connection faded to a mere pinprick. It wouldn't give me much warning if one of them showed up, but they also would struggle to find me.

I could almost feel Havoc's rage, like one last gurgle as I shoved his connection away from me.

"Best I can do," I whispered, wiping the sweat from my forehead.

And even with me putting all my effort into blocking the bonds with them, I could still sense Havoc and Han in the distance.

I could only hope that they couldn't sense me. That Grant's vampiric abilities were going to keep us all safe.

"I'm so damn screwed," I whispered as I opened my eyes. With barely a thought I released myself from Claire and Berek. Easy, because they didn't really want to have ties to me. Not with everything that was happening, and they had a pack already. Two down.

I swallowed hard and looked at the bonds between me and my brothers and plucked at the strands. Tried to unbind them from me.

They held. Tears leaked from my eyes. They wanted to stay tied to me and it dissolved a little of the fear that sat in my belly. I wasn't alone. My brothers—blood or not—were choosing to stay with me.

I didn't bother trying to unbind myself from Bebe. That wasn't about to happen. I did however damp her down a little, so I didn't have to feel her lusting after my brother for god's sake.

Shaking a little, having done as much as I could with the bonds, I found myself headed toward the historical section of the store instead of the kitchen like I'd said.

I paused at the front door.

A notice informed me that Bob and George were on vacation and wouldn't be back for another week. That at least gave us a home base for a few more days. And it kept my human friends out of the crossfire, a relief and one less worry on my plate.

Continuing on, I let my fingers trail the spines of the books, reacquainting myself with the feel of the leather and bound cloth, the raised letters of favorites. Calm slid through me, the quiet slipping under my skin and soothing the edges of ragged fear that had been chasing me. The very back corner of the store called to me.

In the semidarkness, the only light came from the security cameras that were scattered around the room. It was enough for me to see by, and in a few short minutes, I had three books on the Norse. Mythology, history, and pantheon.

I took them to my chair, curled up and started reading. The first book was *"Norse Gods and their Roles in Ragnarök"* which was great, until it wasn't. It really, really wasn't. And here I thought things couldn't get worse...how wrong I was. Much of what I was reading was so new to me, and horrifying in its details of how the world would end—especially now that I was living it. That there was no hope, that there was no way to escape Ragnarök.

Han and Havoc...they'd been hunting the sun and moon and once they were caught well, that was the end of things. Jor would raze the world. No one would survive. Fire and destruction to the max.

I skimmed, absorbing the material as fast as I could, not only because I knew my time was limited, but because the words were not exactly warm and fuzzy feeling as they leapt off of the page and pretty much slapped me around. As far as the legends went, there were no happy endings of any sort.

I picked up the second book, *"The Mythology of the Baltic States,"* skimmed it as well, my heart pounding erratically. Not good, none of this was looking good.

I all but tossed that book down and scooped up the third book. *"To Follow the Norse: becoming a Viking."*

The early Vikings and their belief systems were wrapped around the Norse, and the book gave me a glimpse into how the gods wanted to be treated. How they viewed the world, and how they liked to be worshiped.

Like gods. I huffed a laugh at the simplicity of it, "Why the hell write a book about the fact that gods are dicks, and when you don't treat them as such, they ruin your life?"

I said the words out loud and groaned, folding forward so my forehead touched my knees. This was the shits. The absolute shits. There was very little about Tyr, Havoc, Han…certainly nothing about a daughter of destiny named Cin.

My one real hope was that Grant would be able to get me that fucking journal.

"Hey." Bebe butted her head against my hanging arms to get my attention. "What did you learn? Something good?"

I groaned again. "Unless I'm missing something important, I learned that we are well and truly fucked, Bebe."

She let out a hiss. "Seriously?"

I took a breath and tried to put everything I'd learned into a few simple sentences.

"Ragnarök is inevitable, there is nothing in any of these books about stopping it. There is no clue about how we can stop the world and all the realms coming to an end—only how to speed up the end." I ran a hand over my face. "The Norse gods themselves aren't strong enough to stop what's supposed to happen. It's why Havoc and Han are the way they are, it's like everyone is bound up in a big web, with some giant puppet master pulling the strings."

I stayed where I was, folded at the waist, the stretch and burn of my muscles giving me something to focus on.

"Well, we just need to find the puppet master then. Right?" Bebe leapt up so she sat on my back, her miniscule weight pushing me a little deeper into the stretch.

I blinked.

Find the puppet master.

That was..."That's fucking brilliant, Bebe."

"Of course it is. I'm a cat and a woman, two of the most brilliant creatures on this spinning rock. I don't know why you're surprised." She curled up on my back, but I sat up and dislodged her. I reached for the book on the Norse gods and flipped through it until I found what I was looking for. Running my finger down the page, the words seemed to glow in the semi-dark.

"Bebe, the webs of fate are bound and made and *spun* by the Norns. They are the three weavers of fate, seeing the future, cutting lives short, and all that sort of shit. They are associated with strings. Like *puppet masters*. But more than that..." I tapped the book. Could it be that easy after all? I doubted it, but the idea of going to them felt...right. "They would know if there's a way to stop this. If they can see the future and the paths offered, then they would know what I need to do!" I was certain that was my answer. The Norns. I had to talk to the Norns.

"Assuming they aren't the ones making it all happen." Bebe snorted.

I ignored her for the moment as I searched through the books again. Because knowing that I had to find the Norns, and then actually finding them, were two very different things.

A scuffle of a footstep snapped my attention to my left. Shipley stood there, still wrapped in a sheet, but he had a plate of food in his hand.

"You need to eat. It isn't much, but Berek found the deep freeze and your stash of meat. Claire whipped it up with what they could find leftover in the pantry down here. It's pretty good for scrounging."

He grabbed a chair and sat down next to me. I took the plate and breathed in the smell. I'd been so wrapped up in my reading that I hadn't even smelled the food cooking. Food I'd promised to bring them all.

A pasta dish loaded with cream, marinara, baby tomatoes and shrimp, parmesan sprinkled over the top. I took a bite and let out a soft sigh. "This is good. Thank you."

"I know, I had two plates already." Ship laughed.

"Did Richard eat?" I asked.

"Yes, we found some steak in the freezer, dethawed it enough that he could chow it down while me and

Berek set his leg. He'll be better by morning, I think. The run on it didn't help."

I nodded. That much protein and fat would help Rich heal fast. I should have told them to do just that, but the pull to the books had been too strong. The need to know how to get myself and my family out of this mess was more important than anything—even an injury like a broken leg could wait.

I shoveled the pasta and freezer burned shrimp into my mouth, talking around the mouthfuls. "I think I know where I need to go. I just..." I swallowed a whole cherry tomato and choked on it. Ship slapped me on the back.

"What do you 'need to just'?"

I cleared my throat and wiped at my watering eyes. The hunger had been held at bay by all the emotions, the fear, the injuries, but now I was ravenous. "Can you get me another plate?"

Ship looked at the empty plate then back to me. "You'll tell me what you found?"

I nodded.

But the truth was...I wasn't sure that anyone else could come with me. Not where I was going.

And man, were they going to be pissed when I told them I had to leave them behind.

LEAVING IS SUCH SWEET....AH SHIT

By the next morning—and two more steaks later—Richard's leg healed. We found clothes for everyone, though it took me sneaking out and stealing pants and shirts off people's clothes lines, trying not to get noticed because some of the locals would know me.

I'd run the bookstore for ten years after all.

As it was, Richard was wearing a flannel shirt and jeans, Berek had a blue polo and jeans and Ship...well he'd gotten the raw end of the deal with baby blue sweatpants and a tie-died shirt with 'Hippie forever' scrawled across the front.

I sat curled up in my chair, reading by a single light. We kept lights to a minimum, not wanting to alert anyone that we were here. Because Grant still hadn't called me back.

And Gods only knew who Havoc might have helping him. Or Han. Or Kieran.

"Are you sure? You think you need to find these Norns, you don't think there might be an easier way?" Berek asked the question...again as he paced between the stacks. It wasn't even the second or the third time. More like the third time this morning. Since I'd told them what I had to do, they'd all taken time to argue with me about the fact that I was going to have to leave on my own.

"Berek," Bebe growled, "if you ask her that one more time, I'm going to claw your tongue out myself."

Richard snorted. "Gods, you're a vicious thing, aren't you?"

Bebe snorted right back at him from where she lay draped over my shoulder and the back of the chair. "Someone has to shut him up. He cannot keep asking the same question, over and over. It's stupid and irritating, and he's just doing it because he wants a different answer." Of course, only me and Richard could hear Bebe, so we didn't pass on the message. It was best that way. Because keeping all these werewolves in tight quarters was getting...uncomfortable to say the least.

Berek and Claire were no longer pack. Which set them inevitably against us. No fights had broken out, but more than once the talks had gotten heated. Just like when we'd all been back at the church together.

I'd spent every minute I had researching everything I could on the Norns and where to find them, and I'd employed the others to help me go through all the books we could find throughout the bookstore. Because the idea of the Norns was good and all, but it wasn't like there was a set of directions on how to find them. No GPS, no Google maps.

By all counts, sometimes the Norns showed up on their own, as fate was wont to do. Other times they had to be found, while you fought your way through the worst monsters and realms to get to them. Now call me a glutton for punishment if you will, but the longer we looked, the more I was certain that second option was going to be my path.

Monsters and terror.

Why not?

"Fuck my life," I whispered as I shut the book I'd been searching through.

"Something worse?" Richard didn't even look up from the book he was reading through.

"No, just frustrated. There are no set answers. Nothing I can say *this*, I'll do this."

Claire whimpered from where she dozed in the corner of the room. She'd been incredibly quiet since we'd arrived, barely speaking, flinching anytime someone moved too fast. Except for Berek, we all gave her space. Whatever she was reliving, whatever she was going through, she didn't want to share.

It was late in the day, and it wasn't long before the

others had slid away to their beds, leaving just me and Bebe downstairs.

"What next, girlfriend? I know you have a plan going on inside that head of yours. You wouldn't be you if you didn't have an idea." Bebe stretched and yawned, flashing her tiny canines.

"Yeah..." I muttered. "Or at least someone to ask for help if he'd answer his damn phone." I'd tried calling Grant several times, with no answer. That made me nervous—Grant had never not picked up the phone. Especially when I called from the store seeing as he owned it.

Bebe stretched and yawned. "Try again. Blow his phone up like a psycho ex-girlfriend who can't believe he'd move on."

I laughed and picked up the cordless phone, dialing Grant's number from memory.

A soft breath on the other side as he answered on the third ring. "Cinniúint." Grant's voice was a relief, though I thought I heard something...odd in his voice. "What are you doing here?"

"Man, have you not seen all my messages?" I about strangled the phone.

"I just arrived back in town, not five minutes ago."

I frowned. "You never leave town."

"This was important. Rather fortunate that you are here, I needed to speak to you. Why are you looking for me, Cinniúint?"

I dove into what I was looking for, holding back on the journal to start. That was going to be the tough item. Theodore had been freaking obsessed with it. "I need to get some resources. Information. Maybe weapons. And a map that doesn't exist. Think you can manage all that?"

"Weapons?" Grant laughed and then sobered. "Shit, you aren't kidding. What weapons do you need? Why do you need weapons as a shifter? And you have an inbuilt sense of direction, what do you need a map for?"

I grimaced and shook my head even though he couldn't see me. "I...can't tell you everything, Grant. I don't want you to get caught up in this shit that I'm neck deep in, I don't want my friends getting hurt if I can help it." I banged my head lightly on the wall, wishing I had more answers than questions myself. "And clothes for three guys, about the size of your second in command." Ship especially would appreciate the change of clothes. Richard had been teasing him mercilessly about his hippie shirt.

Grant let out a low sigh. "I can do that. I'll bring the clothes over. The store is closed for the weekend. Bob and his man are gone on some cruise."

"I know." I mean, I didn't know it was a cruise, but I knew they were away. "You okay, Grant?"

"The kitchen is fully stocked in the store," Grant

said, ignoring my question. "I'll meet you there in ten minutes."

He hung up and I stared at the phone. "How the hell you going to do that and not get crisped?" The summer sun set for all of thirty seconds this time of year, and while Grant was not a newbie vampire, even he couldn't stand out in the sun fully exposed.

I turned around and headed up the stairs to my apartment.

Berek was sitting on the couch, leaning back, dozing.

Claire emerged from the bathroom, her head low. The last two days she had been...weird. Not that I had a great friendship with her or anything, but this was strange even for what I knew of her.

"What's going on?" I asked her quietly. "Are you okay?"

This low headed behavior didn't seem like her, and I couldn't quite put my fingers on why it bothered me so much. She shook her head, "Just overwhelmed is all. This has been more than I expected."

I didn't buy it, not with the fact that she'd run with Havoc and his pack for years. But I let her keep her secrets, such as they were.

"I have a visitor coming. Someone who can help. Maybe."

Berek's eyes flew open, and Ship stepped out of my bedroom, followed closely by Richard.

"Who?" Richard asked.

"Grant. He's...a local vampire." I wasn't going to lie to them, seeing as they'd be able to smell him the second he stepped into the building.

Ship shook his head. "Is that a good idea?"

"It's all I've got, and him being here helps to hide us. It's a good thing." Whatever fatigue everyone had been feeling seemed to disappear. Which meant one thing.

Everyone here would need to eat to keep going past their fatigue points.

"I'll get some food going downstairs." I turned back around. "He won't be long."

"Can we make requests? Like pancakes and bacon, with maple syrup and whipped cream?" Ship asked, a distinct sparkle to his eyes.

I raised an eyebrow at him. "You get what you get—"

"And you don't get upset," Richard finished for me. He lifted his head, "I'll come help you prep."

As much as the help would be welcome, I wasn't sure how Grant would react to having a whole bunch of werewolves literally on his doorstep. Sure, I'd asked for clothing, but still, this was a lot.

"You stay here, Rich. I'll call everyone when the food is ready, and I've prepped Grant."

He grunted and pushed off the doorframe. "No. You are the one who needs to be watched. To be protected. You are our alpha, Cin." He lifted his chin. "I failed you more than once, little sis, I won't fail you again."

Gods above and below my throat tightened. Not in any world, in any dream, had I ever thought I'd gain one of my brothers back, never mind two of them. It still made me want to sit down and bawl my eyes out.

"He has a point," Bebe said, patting his leg. "You're a draw for trouble, Cin, I can't believe it's been quiet these last two days. I keep expecting a boogeyman to jump out of the closet and grab you."

Her words seemed to still Richard. "Don't say that, Bebe. Words have power."

I snorted, and tried to pretend I didn't feel a chill wrap itself around me but couldn't disagree with her. I'd been expecting something too.

"Look. I'll get food going. Bebe, you come with me. The rest of you stay here. The front of the store has bars across all the entrances for nighttime, so nothing is coming through. Nothing is going to grab me from the closet."

"Havoc is strong enough," Claire said softly.

I looked at her again. She wouldn't meet my gaze, and she'd pulled away from Berek, tucking her hands up into her armpits.

"I'm sure he is, but he isn't here and with Grant hiding us, he shouldn't be able to find us," I said.

Any sensation of the bond between us was buried

deep. Whatever I'd done this time was enough to keep things turned down so much so that I couldn't even sense him in the distance. Him or Han.

Good. That was good.

I did not feel bad losing the connection to Havoc. I didn't. And I just needed to keep telling myself that there wasn't a pit in my stomach. Unless...what if he'd closed it down on his side of things? That would have actually helped to erase the connection completely.

But I didn't think he'd get rid of the bond until I was dead. Just a hunch on my part with the thickness of the connection between us.

"He could find you anywhere if he wanted to," Claire whispered. "If he was still bonded to you. There's nothing you could do to stop him."

Her words caused a ripple through the room. Worry spiked in the three I was still tied to. Berek went to Claire.

"Don't say that, Claire. She's safe here."

I turned and headed toward the stairs, unable to keep my face straight, because her words had struck something in me. A question that shouldn't have scared me.

Had Havoc somehow shut the bond down between us?

I reached blindly for the stair railing, at the same time that I reached for the connection between me and

Havoc, digging it out of the layers I'd buried it under, almost frantic in my sudden need to see if he'd...

I gasped at what I found.

Or more accurately, what I didn't find. Nothing, there was no more bond between us.

I stumbled and barely caught myself on my knees.

Bebe danced around in front of me. "What's wrong?"

"What happened?" Richard yelled.

"I just tripped on the stairs!" I yelled back. I wanted to say I was irritated, because now I couldn't trace how close or far Havoc was, the way I could with Han. But that wasn't the case at all.

The connection to Havoc had been a lifeline...and with the connection to him gone...I didn't want to feel *loss*. This was good. Better than good, it meant that he couldn't find me easily. Just like Claire had said.

I made my way to the small kitchen below, stunned by what I'd discovered. Digging through the fridge blindly, I pulled out a stack of steaks that weighed at least ten pounds. I slid them onto the counter and started pulling spices out, seasoning the meat as I struggled to understand just what had happened.

How the fuck had Havoc done it? Or had someone done it for him? No, the truth was that he didn't want the bond to me, and that was what had done it. Even Han hadn't fully released me, it's why we were still bound. I was his fail safe.

But Havoc had let me go.

Sure, it was a good thing, seeing as he was under some sort of spell, and a small part of me thought maybe he'd let me go because he cared. But then again maybe he just didn't like feeling me inside his head... my emotions swirled hot and uncertain.

Maybe he was seeing my memories from my side, like I'd seen his.

"Are you going to talk to me, or am I going to have to claw the words out of your mouth? What happened up there on the stairs?" Bebe sat on the counter, her chartreuse eyes watching my every move. I sighed and pressed my hands onto the edge of the counter.

"The bond between me and Havoc...it's...it's gone. He's taken it from me. Yes, I tried to bury it, but I couldn't shut it down completely. But he did. Which meant that he didn't want it. He didn't want...me."

Bebe tipped her head. "You can't find him now, and he can't find you?"

"Correct." The cap on the spices was loose and the entire container of Cajun BBQ fell onto the pile of steaks.

"That's good, Cin," Bebe pitched her voice to a gentle tone. "You know it."

I swallowed hard, the lump in the center making it difficult. "Yeah, I know."

She walked across the counter to butt her head under my chin. "I know it hurts, girlfriend. Especially when we want those bad boys to prove us right. Or wrong depending on the case."

I sucked in a sharp breath and huffed out a laugh. "Yeah."

It was all I could say around the way my body was reacting to the loss of connection to Havoc.

Her ears flattened out to the side of her head and she drooped a little. "What about your brothers? Did they...let you go too?"

I shook my head, and a smile wobbled across my lips. "They are with me, to whatever end we come to. And of course, you too, Bebe. You're my second in command." I gave her a smile and she bounced up onto her back feet, and reached up with her front paws as if she were praising the gods.

"Damn straight! Bad bitches rule! But we don't need them, the others, do we? Claire has been acting weird anyway." Bebe sat back down, wrapping her tail around her front feet.

"I don't know if we need them, and yes, I noticed that too about Claire. But I cut them both loose. You should be able to sense Richard and Ship, but not the other two." I flipped the first round of steaks onto the frying pan, searing them, then shoving them into the oven to finish, yanked another pan out and repeated the process.

"Oh, dang! I can!" Bebe's eyes went wide and then she closed them. "How do I...turn it off?"

I gave her a quick rundown of how I quieted the bonds. Was it correct? No idea, but it worked for me.

I moved on autopilot. There were frozen gnocchi that I dumped into a pot of boiling water, then dug out four boxes of mac and cheese, whipped those into another pot and while a salad would have been good for anyone else, we needed calories for shifting and healing.

Basically, we were carb loading for whatever was coming.

I left the salad out of the mix, and instead dug around until I found the bag of protein powder. I grabbed the blender and started throwing in raw eggs, bananas, cocoa powder, peanut butter, cottage cheese and far too many scoops of protein powder.

"That's a lot," Bebe kept on saying. "And you made it fast."

"It's what we need. Especially Richard, because even though he's healed, he has a lot of calories to make up for." I grimaced at the steaks. They were overdone, I should have started them last, but…whatever. I needed the protein too. It was easy to forget I'd almost died a few days ago.

I opened my mouth to call up to them, but movement in the back room tugged at my ears. "That had better be Grant."

A figure moved in the shadows and the vampire stepped out. A bag of clothes in one hand, and a small journal in the other. A journal that I'd given to Theodore, the vampire in Portland, for his help. I was more than a little surprised to see it in Grant's hand.

He flipped it onto the table. "We need to talk, Cin, you are in far bigger trouble than you realize."

I couldn't help it, I laughed. "Oh, I realize, Grant. I realize far too well."

He shook his head. "No…no I don't think you do."

9

DINNER PARTIES ARE THE WORST

The guys took the clothes that Grant had brought, and Ship at least changed out his hippie clothes for something a little more manly.

Richard sized Grant up and even held out his hand. "You're a friend to my sister?"

Grant raised both eyebrows. "You're one of the brothers who tried to kill her?"

I grimaced.

Richard nodded. "I am, but I'm on her side now. It pisses you off that I tried to hurt her?"

Grant flashed his fangs. Richard smiled. "Good. Because she needs as many people protecting her as possible."

I held a hand up between the two men and faced Grant.

"You think I don't know I'm in trouble?" I asked him. "Everyone eat. This is going to be a long night."

They all dug in, and even Berek and Claire didn't hesitate. Despite my stomach growling fiercely, I waited for the others to get food on their plates.

Grant looked over our small group. "Do you know you're a Norse god?"

Everyone froze. Yeah, I hadn't mentioned it to them yet. It's not something you just bring up.

I pointed a finger at Grant. "Boom, I did know that."

He blinked several times, his eyes big behind his glasses. He looked like a scrawny teenage geek, from his messy hair and oversized glasses to the canvas shoes and punk rock t-shirt he wore. "Since..."

"Yeah, since when?" Bebe yelled.

"Oh, it's a recent thing, the discovering of that particular tidbit. So far, it's done nothing for me, so I haven't mentioned it." I slumped against the counter and crossed my arms.

Richard and Ship had stopped eating. "You know who your father is?"

"Tyr," I said. "The guy who showed up at the fight with Juniper."

Ship let out a low whistle. "We could be a reality show."

He really was not wrong.

I turned back to Grant.

"I've been reading everything I can find relating to Norse mythology. I think I've gotten a lead, but the lead needs a map, or some direction. Or something to help me get to where I need to go."

Grant tapped the small journal on the table. "This is why I was gone. Theodore called me and said that... he said that if I cared for you at all, I would come to see him."

I stared at the journal in his hand. "That's a copy, isn't it?"

"He wouldn't give up the original, but he allowed me to make a copy, yes. That is what took me so long." He let out a heavy sigh. "That and Denna finding me and giving me a message. What does look to the east mean? Why did you send her east too?"

"Because I didn't want her in danger. I...gave her a made-up message to get her clear of all this." I grimaced. If I made it through this alive, Denna was going to be pissed.

The vampire tapped the new journal. "This is...it's illuminating."

"Must have been hard to read," Bebe muttered. "Being a vampire and all."

Richard glanced at her. "Think that illuminating words will fry him?"

She gave him a feline grin. "I'm glad someone got my joke."

Ignoring them, I flipped open the journal. Sticky

notes had been attached to every page with the tiniest writing I'd ever seen on them. "This is good though, isn't it? That he translated it."

"Depends on how you look at it." Grant adjusted his glasses with both hands and stared up at me. "You are in deep shit, Cin. Your birth was not supposed to happen. The Norse pantheon was done and moving rapidly toward Ragnarök. The fact that you were born fucked everything up."

"Yeah, I kind of got that much." I felt the eyes of the others in the room swing toward me. I waved a hand at them, trying to diffuse the energy that Grant's words sparked. "I haven't had time to fill you all in on what I learned when I was mostly dead."

"But not all dead." Bebe sucked up a few noodles and squinted one eye at me. "Not all dead which is an important distinction."

I nodded at her. "Right. So apparently my father is Tyr, as I said. Juniper is my mother, despite how I wish that wasn't true."

"Please tell me you didn't kill your mother. Juniper that is," Grant said. "There is a whole section in here, late in the journal," he tapped the book, "about what would happen if you killed her. It leaves very few paths for you to take if that happens."

I just stared at the book, because I wasn't quite ready to admit that I had killed her. "And what would happen if that was the case?"

Grant just stared at me, his face paling. "Please, *please,* tell me you didn't."

"Well, she did, and that bitch deserved it!" Bebe snapped. "She was trying to kill Cin, was she supposed to just back down, let her head get lopped off and fully let the start of Ragnarök happen?"

Grant looked at Bebe, obviously he could hear her, as he stumbled back. "You have very little time. That's what it means. It's a ripple effect. In reality, Juniper's death doesn't mean anything…except that it's the first step for you down a path that is…not good. You being here? Second step on that path."

He tapped a line on the book, and I saw a few things I didn't like.

Scrolled across a two-page spread were three pathways, and apparently, I was on the middle one. He flipped the pages. The paths wove across several pages, and I stared at the one I'd set my feet on.

Little images were woven into the path along the way. I flipped the page back and touched the start of it, where a body lay across it. A body that looked like Juniper.

"This is exact, except for the fact that the copy is not marked in blood," Grant said.

I traced it with my finger.

"That looks like Jor," Bebe whispered as I stopped on another image. "Is he coming here? And is that an alligator? Maybe he can turn into an alligator."

I traced the pencil drawn path as it wove through the next few pages. I found the Norns, apparently, and at the end of the path...there was clearly the death of three wolves. The world went to shit after their deaths and since one of the wolves looked like me...I could see where this was going.

"There is a divergence here." Grant took the book back and showed me. "Here, right when you get to the Norns. Something will happen and it will dictate the rest. That's the only chance you have."

At least I was right about that. I had to find the Norns.

I stared at where his finger touched the image of three women. He wasn't wrong. All three pathways touched the same spot, then three possibilities spun out from there.

No problem, right?

I flipped through the book, looking for something else. Anything that would give me...something. Maybe the prophecy that Tyr had mentioned.

"This is just a journal, what's in here doesn't necessarily mean anything." Yup, grasping at straws. Denial. That's a good thing when shit goes sideways.

"The other two paths." Richard leaned over my shoulder. "How do they look?"

I traced them both to their endings.

My picture was there each time, my wolf dead, wolves dead around me.

There was no ending where I made it.

"Fuck." Richard dropped a hand onto my shoulder. "We won't let that happen, Cin. We won't."

His words, and the belief that it would be okay was…it was everything in that moment. But when I looked up into his eyes, I saw that he knew the truth too.

There was no way out for me.

In the other two endings, I saved the world. But no matter what happened I was going to die.

"Looks like you're going to get the sun again, Bebe," I said.

"No, don't even say that!" She grabbed at me, her claws digging in.

Let's be real, my life hadn't exactly been an easy ride up to now, so why did Grant look at me like he expected me to freak out about a few words in an old book?

I hadn't freaked out when I'd almost died.

Hadn't freaked out when I'd had to kill my mother.

Hadn't freaked out when I realized my fated mate was trying to kill me.

Nope, I'd held my shit together.

My stomach rolled, as the truth hit me like an anvil from a roof, nausea pitching a fit in my lower regions. I. would. Hold. My. Shit. Together.

It didn't matter that I had more to lose now than ever before.

It didn't matter that I was slated to die. I would do what I had to do.

"It ain't happening," Bebe said. "You aren't dying, Cin. We've found a way around all this so far, we'll find a way around this too."

"Bebe is right," Richard said. "This is not the end."

Grant snatched the book from me and turned to a page near the end. "This one path means no rebirth of the worlds—your death does that. As it stands, that's what happens after the traditional Ragnarök happens. The worlds respawn, the tree of life is still there, and it rebirths the realms. You...killing your mother was the start of the darkest of the three paths. One where the tree of life dissolves into nothing. One where there is nothing left."

Shit...my mother had tied herself to the tree of life, and I'd killed her. If I thought my stomach was rolling before, it was nothing to what it was doing now. Was I the one who killed the tree of life?

Fuck. Me.

Berek cleared his throat. "Would that mean none of the old prophecies would hold? That Havoc and Han would no longer take part in the death of the sun?"

"Exactly!" Grant snapped the book shut. "Which means we don't know what happens next! There is nothing to guide you, nothing to help all this end in a way that the world survives even on a minuscule level. These three paths in this journal are the closest thing we have as a guide. And they aren't exactly sunshine and unicorn shit!"

Grant's voice was rising both in pitch and decibel as he spoke.

I grabbed a plate and threw a steak onto it, slammed a bunch of gnocchi next to it and started in on the food. I didn't have words at this point. Food was always a good answer when the world got dark.

"There is no other way but your death," Grant whispered, but his words dropped into the room like a small bomb. "And I...I don't want you to die either, Cin. But how do we stop this?"

Without an answer, I nodded as I stuffed food into me. It should have tasted decent, should have filled the pit in my belly. But the food was like ash in my mouth, and I struggled to swallow it all down.

Someone put a glass of water in my hand. "Something stronger," I whispered.

It was replaced with a tall glass of amber liquid. I didn't hesitate, I just tipped the entire glass back and let the whiskey burn its way down my throat, let the fire numb some of the horror.

I had—impossibly—made things worse by killing Juniper. I could see the tree of life dying in front of me, the rot, the branches that were skeletal. And the tree spirit had asked me to save it? I was the one who'd caused it. Even if I didn't realize it at the time...

"You think that drinking is a good idea right now?"

Claire asked, the condescension in her voice thick. Ah, there she was. The bitch who didn't like me. "Shouldn't you stay sober for an important conversation such as this rather than getting skunked?"

I slammed my empty drink on the counter, hard enough to crack the base of the glass. "I need a minute."

The world blurred as I struggled to get out of the bookstore. The front door was locked down tight, blinds shut so that no light came in, which left me stumbling up the stairs, through the apartment and then on to the backyard.

A hand dropped on my wrist at the bottom of the stairs. The smell of aged books and blood tugged at me. I turned to Grant. "What?"

"Don't go far. There is someone looking for you. While I was gone...do you know that I can hide those I care about?" His voice was pitched low, and I could barely make the words out.

"I know."

"Then understand that while I was gone, that protection was not here. If someone was looking for you, they could find you."

"Ok." That was the best I could give him. I pulled from his hold and turned away.

I didn't run. I let the whiskey burn hot and bright through me as I forced myself to move toward the forest that ringed the town.

Bebe trotted alongside me, seemingly appearing from nowhere. "I'm not leaving you."

"I know. Strippers and ice cream, here we come," I muttered. Because it seemed like as good a time as any for our end of the world plan.

She let out a heavy sigh. "I wish it were that simple."

"I do too."

"You know where you're going?"

"Yes. I just need to...shut the panic down. I need a way to calm things so I can think." I put a hand to a thin pine tree and pushed away from it. I just needed a few minutes, a place to center myself.

There was an answer. I just had to find it.

The pond was exactly what I needed. Because the world was going too fast, the pace that everyone was demanding I run was too fast. The complications of a single action too heavy.

"Oh, you aren't seriously going to get in there, are you?" Bebe yelped. "Girl, you're crazy!"

I was already stripping though. I knew that the pond would still be glacier, it was fed from the river that ran down the mountains behind the town.

Calling it a pond might make you think that it wasn't very big, but that would be inaccurate. The pond was easily twenty feet across, and a hundred feet long, and gods only knew how deep. I'd never tried to go deep in it. The surface was cold enough for my purposes.

The mud squelched under my feet as I took my shoes off, and then before I could take it back, I dove in, the sluice of ice-cold water shutting down any thought but the need for air and warmth.

Basic survival instincts clamored at me, demanding that I come up for a breath, that I didn't stay under the water, or I'd die. Simple. Live or die.

Death would mean that all the worlds were done for. The tree of life. All the realms.

Life meant that there was a chance. I just had to find it.

I hadn't had to use this technique in a long time to calm myself, not since I first came to Alaska when the night terrors and trauma chased me from any semblance of normalcy.

Funny that water calmed me, when so many times it tried to kill me.

I swam toward the middle of the pond before I broke the surface, gasping for air, not liking how close to a howl the gasp sounded.

My skin hurt with the intensity of the cold, feeling almost like I was in a fire, rather than the cold.

Bebe paced the edge of the pond. "Seriously?"

"It's great." I hissed the words out between my teeth, barely able to think.

"Okay, so you want to discuss the situation?" Bebe said.

I nodded. "I...the tree of life is dying. I've been asked to save it. But I was the one who somehow started its death by killing Juniper. Because my mother tied herself to the tree."

Bebe's tail lashed. "What is the tree of life?"

Right, I hadn't told anyone about all that, I mean... I'd barely let myself think about what had happened when I'd almost died. Never mind telling them how I'd seen the tree dying, and the tree spirit there asking me to save her.

Probably that was part of the issue now. I'd suppressed all the shit I'd gone through in the last week, and it was eating me up.

"Haven't you been listening when we are reading through the books?" I asked, no ire in my voice.

"No. I've been sleeping."

"Norse Mythology..." I paused, treading water. Though, I suppose it wasn't exactly a myth now. Now it was real.

And I was living it.

"The tree of life is the center of all the nine realms." I bit the words out as I swam around in a circle, as if the movement would help. "The spirit of the tree—Suvenia—asked me to save her. To save all the realms. But if what Grant is saying and the book is saying is true, it's my fault that it's dying in the first place. That Juniper's death set this into motion."

She watched me for a moment.

"That's some heavy shit," Bebe said. "You think we can do it? Save the tree?"

We. There it was again. I blew out a shaking breath. "I think we have to. I have to."

"There is no 'I' in team, bitch. You and me, to the end of whatever."

A shuddering breath slid through me, and some of the fear and anxiety slipped away as I swam for the edge of the pond. I ducked my head under one last time, blowing the last of the air from my lungs, just before I surfaced again.

It would be okay. I'd find a way through this, just like I found a way through everything that the world and my supposed fate had thrown at me.

I came up from under the water to Bebe screeching. "Han! Han is here! Run! Swim! Just get away!"

I looked up to see Han leaning against a tree, watching me, no weapon in sight. No axe dangling from his hand.

That didn't exactly make me feel better as he stared at me, a slow smile crossing his cruelly beautiful mouth.

"Hello, Princess."

10

NOT MY PRINCE CHARMING

Han laughed at me, his features as handsome as ever, even if he was an evil fuck. "You are a pain in my ass, you know that? You are still my mate, despite everything."

I pushed off the bottom of the pond, floating further out into the middle. What the hell was I going to do now? I reached for the connection to my brothers...but then paused. They were tough, but Han was part god. He would kill them. I was sure of it. So, I played along. For now. "I've been told that before. Not exactly news to me."

He ran a hand over his head. "I really would have liked Ragnarök to happen. At least the way I wanted it to, you know, with me ruling after? But it seems you really put your foot into it. You fucked everything up, just by *existing*. Mind you, killing your mother didn't help—did you know she was tied to the tree of life? Unbelievable, really, I guess you really are one of us. A bunch of murdering, vicious killers."

"How do you know that she's tied to the tree of life?"

"You don't seem surprised." He tipped his head. "Interesting. Well, I have it on good authority that the pantheon is freaking out. They think you set this all up. To take them down."

"I didn't," I said unable to muster up more than the two words.

"No, I don't think you did either. Too naïve."

My bones ached with the cold of the pond, and I was pretty sure I felt a slither of a long muscular snake rolling across my ankles.

There were no snakes that swam in this lake, at least not of the size I was feeling.

Which only left one possibility. "Jor."

Han's eyebrows climbed. "You think he's here?"

Next to me, a pair of eyes attached to a big scaly head surfaced, blinking up at me. I pointed at him in case Han missed the movement. "Yes."

Han sighed. "Well, it doesn't matter. The whole prophecy is messed up. There is no point in me killing you right now. It does nothing but soothe my ego. If you die, I don't even know if Ragnarök will happen."

"Impossible." Jor shot his head upward, fangs

descending. "Your ego is impossible to soothe. It's too big."

I laughed, teeth chattering, I couldn't help it. Because I had an image of someone trying to stroke a giant, screeching bundle of an ego that kept twisting away from being touched. I was losing it. Or more likely the cold was getting to me.

"So why are you here?" My teeth slammed together, and it took everything I had to keep speaking normally. "Are you spelled now too?"

Han tucked his hands into his pants pockets, toasty and warm on the edge of the pond. "That fucking mate bond. Even without a desire to kill you...I am drawn to you. I think Havoc will do it anyway—kill you, that is. He was always the better hunter than me. I'm certain Sven spelled him, you know. Made it so he can't help but want to kill you. That he thinks of nothing but your blood and eventual death. The way I once thought of it." Han smiled. I struggled not to react. But maybe he saw something in my face because his smile widened. Though what he saw beyond the pale tinge of my skin, I'm not sure. "And you are more than any of us realized. You carry the sun, and you are one of us. I don't know if that's even allowed."

One of us. One of the Norse pantheon. "It's complicated."

"Prophecies and bullshit usually are." He didn't quit smiling.

"Why are you here, if not to kill her?" Bebe snapped. I noticed she'd moved around so she was as far from him as she could be, across the pond.

"Good question. I think I found myself curious. The urge to kill you, to kill any of the suns, is gone. Which tells me I might have been under a compulsion; the same way Havoc is now. Or if the change in how the end of the world is going to happen shifted things, that's possible too. The compulsion came on me, around the time that Sven started working with me, nearly five hundred years ago." He shrugged. "Games and shadows, magic and blood. Ours is a pantheon of violence, Cin. Welcome to the family."

He turned as if to leave. I looked at Jor who did a full body ripple, as if he understood my silent question. I knew so little about this world, and I wasn't sure how much good it would be reading old books based on a mythology that may or may not be accurate.

The question was, how desperate was I for help? How much was I willing to gamble to survive?

Han was ten feet away now and continuing away from me.

"Will you help me? Or at least, help me for a minute?" For a minute? Moon goddess, I was struggling here.

I blurted the two questions out, and Han stilled in his tracks. He looked over his shoulder. "You would be stupid to trust me. I am not a nice man, Cin. Even without the compulsion on me, there is a point where your death would benefit me. It was always meant to happen."

"I didn't say anything about trust." I had to get out of the water. The cold was too much, I'd been in too long. I started toward the shore, my limbs sluggish even though my mind felt calm. If I didn't get out soon, I would die of the cold—even a shifter had limits. "I need help to understand what's been laid at my feet. Why would Sven spell you? Why would he spell Havoc? Why didn't Sven spell you both if he wants me dead? What does he have to gain from Ragnarök happening at a certain time? Where can I find the Norns?"

Jor rumbled beside me. "I'm disappointed. If Ragnarök is no longer the end days as we understand them, where does that leave me?"

"Maybe you get to be a hero," I said as my feet found footing in the soft mud.

Jor reeled back in the pond like I'd slapped him, ripples flowing out around his massive thick body. "A hero? Why would I want that? Heroes rarely get happily ever after's, Cin. You know that, right? They usually die."

I didn't answer Jor, just kept moving until I was out of the pond. Shivering, vulnerable, and yet I could *feel* the difference in Han. A sense of calm radiated off him. Calm, dangerous, and unbothered by the fact that I was meant to die at his hands at one point, that I'd bested him.

Han looked me over, his eyes dispassionate despite my state of undress and the fact that I was cold as ice which made my nipples all but point straight at him. "What exactly do you need help with?"

"You could start by handing her those clothes," Bebe snapped as she raced around to get between us. "Don't you be looking at her boobs. They aren't yours."

Han laughed, low and deep, a sound that would have done something to me when I'd first been 'rescued' by him. But now, nothing, not even a glimmer of lust. "Actually, if we want to play that game, you are my mate still. The bond is still there. You've numbed it quite well, though, I'll say that. It took me a few days to track you down."

I shrugged, feeling nothing but the cold. "I don't believe in mate bonds."

"No? You did when I first dragged you from that shelter." He took a step closer, my clothes held out to me, heat radiating off him.

A few weeks before, his very proximity would have had me panting, begging on my knees. Now? Not so much. Not even a flicker of desire rippled through me. Because he was the monster that wanted the world to end in fire and destruction.

Or at least, he had been.

I snatched my clothes from him, and yanked on my

shirt and pants, ignoring everything else. "I think mate bonds can be changed, shifted, destroyed, even. I've seen it."

"Ah, your dear mother." He tssked. "She was a peach, wasn't she?"

I grimaced. As if anything else could have reminded me how very wrong he was for me, that was it—he'd been banging Juniper for gods knew how long. That would do the trick. The fact that at any point, spelled or not, he'd found her attractive...it was too much for me. "Besides, I don't do my mother's sloppy seconds."

"Oh, snap!" Bebe laughed and shadow boxed along beside me.

"I can't believe you are trusting him at all!" Jor grumbled from the pond. "This is seriously messed up! I don't want to lose my coffee dates. You can't die yet, Cin!"

I looked at Jor and then back to Han. "Loki made me your mate, to try and save you. Why didn't he just remove the compulsion from you?"

"I doubt anyone knows about it. I barely understood it until it was off me." Han shrugged. "And he bound us so you would save me, yes, but no doubt it was for his own machinations."

I silently agreed with him and found myself touching the brand on my neck. Loki's symbol was etched into my skin, reminding me just how I'd gotten into this mess in the first place.

The thing was, Han was not someone I would ever trust, not in any situation. Because he was a fucking monster. He'd killed women for funzies. My thoughts stuttered over the memory.

Didn't he? What if that had been Sven back then too? Fuck. "Did you kill the vet?" The question blurted out of me. There had been a very kind vet. She'd stitched me up after a fight where I'd been on the losing end of a very sharp piece of glass. Han had taken her home, made her every fantasy come true, and the next morning...well...she'd been dead.

Han grunted. "I don't know. Maybe?"

"Maybe?" Bebe took a swat at his legs. "What the hell kind of answer is maybe? How do you not know if you've killed someone or not? What is wrong with you?"

He bent down to Bebe's level. "I am a monster, little pussy. You'd best remember that. And monsters don't give a fuck who they kill, who they eat, or what they destroy, as long as their main needs are met." His hand shot out faster than I could even see it, to grab her tail, lifting her in the air a few inches. "Be glad I find you amusing."

She screeched and launched herself at his face, but I caught her, holding her to my chest as she all but vibrated with fury.

"You son of a bitch! Don't you ever touch my tail!"

Bebe trembled, but at least she wasn't clawing at me to get to him.

Han laughed, unmoved by her violence toward him.

I stood there, barefoot, staring him down. A twinge ran along my back, the strumming of a bond that I did still have.

Richard. He was calling to me. I took a step. Han moved like liquid and blocked my path.

"You want answers?"

I stared up at him, so close that in another time, another place I would have leaned into him. But he was not my mate. Not for real, it was all manufactured. Even my wolf knew it. The rolling growl rumbled up through my chest, vibrating the air between us. "Yes. I need answers."

"You are on the right path, even if it looks like the hardest one. Find the Norns." He closed the last breath of distance between us, staring me down as if that would intimidate me. Maybe if it had just been my golden, maybe it would have worked. But my golden in me, she was not cowering anymore. I bared my teeth.

"How?"

He smiled and leaned so that his mouth brushed against my ear. "You want more? What will you give me?"

His breath was hot, and I couldn't help the shiver. It

wasn't desire, but sheer temperature change, I was fucking cold, and his breath was hot as a fire.

"Don't give him anything," Bebe hissed, still crushed against my chest. And that close to him? Well, she took advantage.

She swatted the side of his face, slicing him open. He stumbled back, a snarl on his lips. He lifted his fingers and touched the claw marks, blood coating them.

"Oh, you will pay for that."

"Run, Bebe." I tossed her over my shoulder and squared off against Han. "You deserve more than that, for what you've put us through."

Jor curled through the water, right to the shoreline. "Oh, this is so good. I wish I had popcorn! And I can feel the twist to the story coming! Gods!"

Han shot him a look. "What do you mean by that, snake?"

"Serpent." Jor flicked his tail. "I'm a *serpent*. And what I meant by that is simple. The third player is about to show up."

Panic ripped through me. Panic that was not my own.

Richard's panic was hot, and wild and a single word came through the bond between us.

Havoc.

I looked at Han. "You sure you don't want to kill me?"

"You, not at the moment. Your fucking cat, I'd grind to dust," he snarled.

Bebe squeaked, as if she were afraid, but I doubted she was afraid at all.

No, the sound of heavy padded feet closing in on us was the issue. I turned to my left to see Havoc stalking toward us, his icy blue eyes locked on me. His dark fur bristled across his spine, his tail stiff as he stared me down.

There was nothing of the man I knew in those eyes.

"Right." I whispered. "Well don't suppose you want to keep your brother busy while I run?"

Han laughed. "You're kidding me? You want me to play protector?"

A girl could hope.

And right then, hope was all I had left.

11

SEE YOU LATER, ALLIGATOR

"I am not going to protect you," Han repeated. "But maybe...I suppose it will continue to screw things up for Sven if I slow my brother down? Only fair since he had me spelled for so many years."

The mark on my neck lit up, like I'd licked a wall socket. I shook and stumbled backward, toward the pond, muscles convulsing and shaking.

Havoc's eyes never left me. A low grumble trickled past his lips and the sound...fuck me the sound still did terrible things to me, as if he'd put his mouth to my core and just...fucking vibrated.

I whimpered; I couldn't help it. Han's head whipped to the side to look at me. "What is wrong with you?"

Havoc shifted right there, to two legs, naked,

muscles all on display. His smile was wicked, tugging at the scar along his face. His dark eyes—yes, dark when he was on two legs—were as fathomless as any future I might have tried to see for myself. "Because she can't help but want it."

Han's eyebrows shot up. "You really did fuck him?"

"Saved the world," I said.

"And the other times?" Jor asked. "I know there were other times you bedded him, did that save the world then too?"

"Not helping," I muttered as the heels of my feet hit the edge of the pond.

"How did you find me so quick?" I asked Havoc.

Because the bond between us was gone. I slumped, understanding rocking through me. "Claire? You used her, didn't you."

He smiled, a bare flash of his teeth. "She still wants me. I used that."

Han whistled. "Jor, you're right, we should have gotten popcorn."

"You'd just let her die?" Jor gasped. "That's not right."

"You are no hero, Jor," Han drawled. "Nor am I. And neither is Havoc, though I think he wanted to be for so many years. Now he's a monster again. Just. Like. Us."

Havoc was completely naked as he stalked toward me. I couldn't move. I needed to get away, but I was pinned between two wolves who had reason to kill me and a giant serpent.

"Jor," I whispered. "Can you get me to the Norns?"

I mean, if anyone might be able to get me closer to them it was the Midgard serpent, a creature who moved between realms and places.

"Well...that's a hero move," he grumbled. "I don't know. I'm not sure I should. I already broke rules when I helped you back when you were fighting your old pack."

"This is not the time to suddenly go back to your gray morals, Jor!" I snapped.

He grunted. "Can't help it. And you can't...*make*... me."

Make him? Did he mean that he'd do it if I threatened him? It was worth a try.

"Bebe." I called her and she leapt toward me. Havoc took a few steps, his hand held out to the side as his double-sided axe just...appeared out of thin air, like he'd pulled it from an invisible pocket. He grasped the handle and took an experimental swing.

Han sighed. "Brother. We don't have the same task now. Her birth alone fucked everything up—but we didn't know that. So whatever Sven has put on you, it won't do what you think if you kill her."

"Thanks?" I muttered and took another step back so that the water rose above my calves, and I was bumping against Jor's snout. I had an idea. A terrible, horrendously bad idea, but honestly it was all I had.

One bad idea against two men that wanted me dead. "Bebe, work with me."

"You got it, babe!" She butted her head under my chin.

I reached down and touched Jor's head, and he lifted himself up. I slid around and straddled him, as if I were getting on a horse. "Take me where I want to go, or you get the cat claws." I held Bebe over his head.

She hissed and extended her claws so that they touched Jor's neck. His eyes lit up. "Oh, that's good, threaten me with the razors in the cotton balls! I like this, yes, wait, sorry, of course, I am *terrified of cats*, I'll have to do as you want." He ruined it by snickering. I pulled Bebe back to my chest.

Havoc hadn't moved.

His muscles trembled as if he were...fighting with himself.

Han laughed. "I do believe he might be fighting the compulsion. Interesting. I never bothered. Perhaps that's why Sven put all his energy into him, and none into me."

Jor slid backward deep into the lake. "I'll be honest, I don't know if this will work. It could kill you both. I've never taken anyone with me through the water tunnels before."

"What?" I screeched as Jor's magic locked around

us, holding us tightly to his body as he sunk down, swirling and diving.

The last thing I saw was Havoc sprint toward the water, and Han intercepting him.

They went down, roaring and snarling and then the water was over my head, and everything was muffled, water filling my ears. I clutched Bebe and she clutched me, and it was all I could do to hang onto her and my breath and hope that we made it.

Dark, cold water slipped over us. I counted the seconds to keep myself from panicking. At forty-five the temperature changed, warming until it felt like tepid bath water. Things bumped against me, hard, scaled things, bits and pieces of logs.

At a minute, Jor burst upward, and I gasped for air. Bebe spluttered. "What the actual fuck, where are we? Oh, shit, this is not good!"

I blinked, water streaming down my face. We were still sitting on Jor's back, but all around us were alligators and crocodiles. Okay, I was assuming both. Maybe it was only one, I was no biologist. There were a lot of snapping jaws around us, that was the important thing to note. I tucked my legs up on Jor's back.

"Please don't dump us in the water," I said.

"Nah, that would defeat me bringing you here. Welcome to the Everglades! There's a nice little troll encampment over there." He swam along, and the gators hissed at him, but otherwise didn't bother the big serpent. Smart gators. Crocs. Whatever.

"That's where you need to go if you want to find the Norns. Trolls have all sorts of maps, and they are sneaky buggers, so watch whatever jewels you have."

I kept my legs tucked up and only once we were clear of most of the crocodilians, did Jor's words register. "I'm sorry, did you say *troll camp*?"

"Yup, they protect the entrance to the Norn's in a roundabout way. You need to go through them. Should be a good fight. Very entertaining."

Jor dropped us off on a sand bank. Bebe and I leapt off his back and he rolled around to face us. "You know, you really are great fun. I like that about you. You make life interesting."

"Thanks for the help, Jor." I gave him a jaunty salute. "You're a good friend, and I think you might be turning into a hero, despite your protests."

The horror on his face made me laugh. "I am… not…a…hero." He spluttered and then softened, leaning in close. "But maybe I am a good friend. That's acceptable I think."

He spun and flipped himself back into the water, gone before I could ask him for any other suggestions.

The truth of the matter was I'd never dealt with trolls. Like dragons and other creatures, I knew they existed but we all kind of kept to our own areas as supernaturals. Which meant there wasn't a lot of intersection between the different species, and not a lot of good knowledge on how to deal with one another.

"What do you know about trolls?" Bebe shook, casting out droplets of water. Acting for all the world like we'd not just come all the way across the country, landed in a swamp, and had literally zero tools, weapons, or help.

No problem, we were bad bitches, we had this.

I dug around in my memory banks for what little I knew. None of it was great. Most of it bad. "Trolls like the swamp lands, as deep into the marshy areas as they can get, typically, as far from humans as possible." I looked around the sandbar that Jor had dropped us on.

"So...we probably need a boat?" Bebe looked at me, hope in her eyes. I grimaced.

What I didn't want to tell Bebe was that trolls had a taste for fresh flesh, of any kind. As long as the creature was still alive, they'd eat it. While it thrashed and screamed, preferably.

"I don't think a boat will get us through this."

Jor had indicated to head to the west, so that was the direction I started out, Bebe trotting alongside me. The sandbar turned out to be an island, one side leading further inland and covered in thick mangroves. Yellow eyes peered at us from the water between the roots as the light began to fade, the crocs and gators just waiting on their next meal to get too close to the water's edge. Going on in the dark was stupid, and would get us killed or worse, trapped by trolls.

Either way, we'd get eaten.

"We need to stop for the night." I pointed at a pair of mangrove trees that had wound around one another, creating a bit of a bowl in the middle, about fifteen feet up. "That will work."

A few minutes later we were up in the tree nest, and I curled so I could stare out at the ocean. Bebe settled herself on my hip. "Cin?"

"Hmm."

"What are we going to do about the trolls?"

I shook my head. "No idea. I'm hoping that a good night sleep in a mangrove tree, while crocodiles dream of tearing me to shreds, will give me inspiration."

She sighed and a low purr rumbled through her. "Well…a good night's sleep can never be bad, right?"

Sure.

Except that it was anything but a good night's sleep.

12

NOTHING STINKS LIKE TROLL SHIT

There was nothing like sleeping in a mangrove tree for a good rest with the twisted branches jabbing me in every other rib. Between that uncomfortable bed, and the things I saw in my dreams, well...there wasn't a lot of down time for my brain.

The memory was not mine. And yet I knew it, because I'd been there. Only again I was seeing it through Havoc's eyes. I was seeing *me* through his eyes.

"Do you consent to this?" My voice was rough, I knew it, but seeing her so...hurt. I could barely contain the rage in me. Even this, mostly healed, I didn't want to add to her pain.

"I...yes. I consent." She paused, her eyes latching onto mine. *"Do you consent to this?"*

My hands were on the edge of the bed, which sagged a

little under my weight. Had anyone ever asked if I consented to anything? To this life, to this task?

All I could do was stare at her, drink her in. Damn her for making me want her more. Not for her body, but for the heart that beat under her breast. What would it mean to have someone care about me like this?

"*Havoc?*"

A growl rumbled out of me, and she gasped, arching, her body reaching for me as if it had a mind of its own. This woman...she would be the death of me. I could feel it in my bones.

"*Yes. I consent.*"

I slid my body up along hers, the fabric of my shirt brushing against her bare skin, teasing her gently. I held myself up on my forearms, our faces close together but not touching, not kissing.

Gods, her lips fucking begged to be kissed, to be crushed under my mouth, to have me demand and beg her to open to me at the same time. But that's not what this was.

This was a necessity, and she was doing it because she had to save the world. I didn't want this to be a necessity. I wanted it to be...more.

"*On your back,*" *she said, hooking one of her legs through mine and rolling me to the side.*

I let out a grunt of surprise as she straddled me, positioning my cock so that it was right there at her entrance. The tension of holding herself there, of my hands on the swell of her hips, the sensation of her warmth beckoning me.

My cock ached, straining toward her as her body had strained toward me.

How long had it been since I'd...at least fifty years. Maybe more.

She held herself there, hesitating. She could have just slid onto me, and I didn't pull her closer. I waited, sweating and barely holding myself together.

Someone took that moment to knock on the door, gods damned moron.

"Fuck off," I snarled, and it turned into a low growl.

Moaning, her whole body quivering, she pushed down on the tip of my cock, her wet pussy parting for me. It took everything I had to not come right then. She placed her hands on my chest to balance herself, her breasts hanging dangerously close to my mouth.

Perfect, she was fucking perfect.

My cock flexed and I growled again, then swept my hands up over her thighs to grab her ass. I could easily palm each cheek, squeezing them, digging into the soft flesh. I ran my fingers up and down the line of her ass, exploring every curve.

Fucking hell, I dragged her closer to me, as if I could truly join us just by sheer unyielding force.

She grabbed the edges of my shirt and ripped it open, her hands finding their way across my chest, tracing scars.

I could barely breathe with the sensations, with the

overwhelming need to keep her with me. To keep her at my side. Not because she held the sun, not because I needed to protect her.

Only to keep her here, with me.
Where she belonged.

Pain slashed through me, as I realized what Havoc's memories were showing me. This couldn't be happening.

To find out he'd cared for me from the beginning, only to have him hunting me now.

It was like I was being cut apart from the inside out and I couldn't stop it, there was no wound I could see yet the pain was there. How do you heal something unseen?

You don't.

I screamed and thrashed in my dreams, calling to him, trying to get him to stay. But when I jerked awake, Bebe was sound asleep on my hip, her nose pressed between her front paws as if I hadn't moved an inch.

I drew a shuddering breath and wiped the sweat from my brow, my heart aching.

"Havoc," I whispered his name and pressed my fingers to the corners of my eyes to stop the tears that threatened. I couldn't let this change my trajectory, I had to keep going.

Survival. I was good at it, and I had to keep being good at it and that meant not thinking about the fact that Havoc...had been struggling with the same kind of emotions I had been.

The light above us had shifted, and by the fading of the stars, it was probably four in the morning. Maybe a little later. I sighed and did my best to put thoughts of Havoc aside.

I had to figure out how to get us in and out of a troll camp.

Could we sneak in? Did they have a good sense of smell, or sight or hearing? Were they militant and prepped for war with scouts and guards or were they lazy and comfortable in their placement in the world being at the top of the food chain?

I tried to remember what little I'd read about trolls. Not a lot was known about them, and likely what Jor had told me was more than most books could reveal. Obviously, they liked to torture their victims, so that put them in a serial killer category—but were they the smart serial killers, or just mean as fuck and a little bit stupid?

Smart would be harder to get by. Stupid might be the only thing that would give us an edge.

I dropped my hand across Bebe's back, and she let out a tiny squeak in her sleep, her eyes staying closed.

The best thing might be to try and sneak through. Bebe was small enough they'd never see her. And I could shift to my golden form, it was smaller than my wolf and more suited to the water if I fell in. If I rolled in mud, I'd blend in better, and it would hide my scent at the same time.

Decision made, I closed my eyes to try and get another hour or so of sleep.

I took a deep breath and got a whiff of...what in all that was holy was that foul stench? A gag caught me so off guard I struggled to breathe at all for fear I'd throw up. The wind brought me another wave of whatever it was, a scent of rot and shit, and something sickeningly sweet that lingered at the back of my throat, sitting there like it was meant to stick forever.

The bog of eternal stench came to mind.

I clenched my teeth together and breathed shallowly. It was the best I could do without throwing up. Even in her sleep, Bebe's nose wrinkled, and her ears pinned to her head, a low hiss escaping her.

Heavy footsteps crashed through the swamp below us—footsteps that were definitely not human from the boom of them. I grabbed Bebe, and rolled so that we were curled in a tighter ball. She didn't struggle, but her nose wrinkled up again as her eyes opened, and she gagged like she had a hair ball working its way up her throat. I tucked her in tighter to my chest.

"Shh."

She bobbed her head in understanding as her body shook with dry heaves.

Those footsteps were huge...and they were coming closer, bringing the acrid, rotting scent with them.

The gravel in the voice of the first made his words a struggle to understand and I had to focus hard. "Boss said find a couple more. We got more back home. Big dinner tonight."

"Yah. More is more," a second, lighter voice said. "And more is good. More. More. More!" The last word echoed up through the trees and a bunch of birds took flight.

"Grab some scaley-dillys, then. We take a handful each, that's enough."

"I'm tired of scaley-dillys. Canna we get some... bally snakzies?"

They sounded like...kids? Giant, thumping kids tromping through the swamp. I dared to look through the cracks of our tree nest to catch a glimpse of them.

The trolls looked about fourteen feet tall, their skin a deep green, streaked with brown lines like the stripes of a tiger. As they walked, they faded into the swamp around us, the camouflage so good it was spooky. They literally disappeared as they walked, then reappeared a few feet closer, even as I stared right at them. Muscles were fucking *layered* on the trolls, and there wasn't an ounce of fat on them that I could see. And I could see a lot since they each only wore one piece of clothing.

Daisy dukes. Short shorts that rode up their thick thighs and thicker asses. More like a loin cloth than shorts, but the cloth had been painted or stained the same color as their skin so that they added to the camouflage.

"Oh! Scaley-dilly!" The one on the left had the higher pitched voice, and as he shot forward, I was able to see more of his body. He stood with a crocodile (or maybe it was an alligator, I didn't know) in his hand, the 8-foot-long beast thrashing its tail and trying desperately to snap at its captor.

"Bindy hindy!" The second troll said, as it wrapped the croc's snout with a thick piece of rope, then ran the rope over the body a few times to pin the legs tight to the body. With that, he threw the croc over his shoulder and let it dangle, tail first. Like it wasn't normally a top predator in the swamp.

The fact that the troll seemed unconcerned with how close the croc's mouth was to his own head was a testament to just how dangerous they—the trolls—were. Dangerous and maybe I was hoping—stupid.

The two beasts hunted around below us until they had four more crocs trussed up and tossed over their shoulders.

"More!"

"Nah, that's enough scaley-dillys. Big brown wolf meat is going to be a treat!"

My guts clenched and I couldn't help but squeeze Bebe a little tighter. She might have squeaked, I don't know.

But I knew that the only big brown wolf that still

had a tie to me was Richard. I looked at Bebe and mouthed his name.

Her mouth opened and closed as she shook her head. I nodded. It had to be him.

Havoc had cut off his bond to me, more effectively than I ever had been able to. Han could find me but had no reason to—he'd said it himself, there was no spell on him. He'd sought me out...well, he hadn't said why.

That left my brothers and only one of them was a brown wolf. Richard. I'd barely gotten him back in my life. I reached carefully for the bond to him and felt nothing but relief.

He was far, far away.

Whoever the trolls had, it wasn't my brother. But who the hell *did* the trolls have then?

"And the man too!" The first troll said, high pitch giddy. "Man and wolf! Yummy like scaley-dillys for pancakers! Morning dinner is going to be the bests!"

If I hadn't had the bond to my brothers, I would have said they'd come for me. But as it was, I knew they were safe back in Alaska.

It took everything I had to stay where we were, to not leap down and follow the trolls as soon as they were out of sight.

Bebe broke the silence first, but she kept her voice low. "They can't...they'll eat him!"

I shook my head and let her go. "No, it isn't

Richard, Bebe. Use the connection to him, he's safe. A bit pissed, but far away safe."

She closed her eyes and then slowly her body relaxed. "But then, who do they have? Is someone else looking for the Norns? What if it's someone who knows what's going on? Could it be your other brother?"

My heart ticked a little faster. That wouldn't be great. Not that I was going to try and save Kieran if he was with the trolls—I wasn't that nice anymore. He'd made his choice.

Bebe's eyes were filled with worry, and I couldn't say anything that would alleviate it. We were operating on very little information.

"It's a doorway, or a cave…or something that will lead us toward the Norns. That's what we need to hang onto. If we can help whoever is trapped by the trolls—and it isn't someone against us, then we'll do it. But not at the cost of our own selves. There's too much at stake."

"Agreed," she said. "Let's go then."

We slid down the tree and I shifted just before I hit the ground, my golden retriever coming forward happily. I should have realized…

Before I could stop myself, I rolled in the thick mud, my tail wagging like it had a fucking life of its own. Over and over, I dunked myself before I got control and stood up, tongue hanging out, thick coat heavy with moisture and muck.

Bebe stared at me, horror in her eyes, "That's disgusting. Dogs are gross."

I shrugged, tongue still lolling. "Is my fur all covered?"

"You looked like you were playing! This is not a time for playing!" she whisper yelled.

"I know, I couldn't...I couldn't stop myself." The retriever I shifted into was sometimes harder to control than my wolf. Which was wild when you thought about it. My wolf was super obedient. The retriever literally had a mind of her own.

"Yeah." She looked me over. "You're not glowing, you are covered in mud, and you'll blend in with the swamp. Now let's go before we lose our troll guides."

With that we took off, bounding across the mangrove roots, following the distant sound of the clomping trolls. The good thing about following in their wake...all the 'scaley-dillys' were scattered, swimming for cover.

There were no predators bigger or scarier than the trolls in this swamp and all the reptiles knew it.

Overhead the sky continued to shift toward daylight. Toward the breakfast the trolls wanted to take part in.

As fast as we ran, the trolls stayed always just ahead of us. They covered distance easily with their long legs, unbothered by anything, because nothing would challenge them. We followed mostly based on the sound of the crashing as we could barely pick them out as they moved.

We'd been running for twenty minutes before things changed.

A gong, like someone hitting a dinner bell, echoed through the swamp, the tone reverberating in my bones.

Ahead of us, the trolls yelped and began running if the increased rumble of their feet hitting the muck was any indication.

"Faster!" I said, leaping and dodging, caring less about my footing than I should have. I tumbled into the water, landed on top of a submerged croc-a-gator and felt it scoot away from me. Maybe it thought I was a troll.

I launched myself away from the pool of water, yelped as I stuck my foot through a tangle of roots and wrenched myself free, twisting my leg in order to do it. Ignoring the pain, I fought to keep the speed up.

Bebe was a streak of gray beside me, bounding and dancing across the water as if she were Jesus himself... only she was using the backs of the crocs to cross the water.

That one had balls of steel. Lady balls of course.

I wasn't small enough to follow her lead, which meant that she got to the troll camp ahead of me.

Sliding to a stop at the edge of the camp, I rolled into the mud, re-coating myself with muck, covering my scent and my highly visible golden coat.

I lay in the mud and crept forward, the troll camp in full view. I don't know what I was expecting, but what I was seeing was…weird.

Boats of all sizes and shapes sat deep in the mud, some on their sides, some on the hull, others on the bow or stern. They created covers that could have been called huts, I suppose, though there wasn't a great deal of protection from the elements.

From each boat were strung vines and boards and more mud. On top of each of the boats were small mangrove trees. The odd style of cover created a canopy that from above, you'd never know as anything but more mangroves.

I lifted my nose and forced myself to breathe in the scents.

The overwhelming stench of troll was still there, stronger now, but I'd become more numb to it and I didn't gag. Under that stench was the faint whiff of a wolf.

Faint. So faint as if whoever it was, was covered in mud too. Made sense with the muck across the camp.

Bebe lay beside me, as flat to the ground as she could get, a glob of mud on the top of her head. "You see them?"

I shook my head and crept forward. I had to get closer.

The gong sounded again, and a troop of trolls hurried out from under their boat houses, their bodies blending and disappearing into their surroundings between steps.

I struggled to hold still. Part of me wanted to run—the golden part.

Steady, we had to stay steady.

With the overwhelming scent of troll shit, it was hard to tell when the trolls were close.

Which meant they could be right on top of us, and I'd never know it until they were plucking us out of the mud like the scaley-dilly's they'd snagged earlier.

The stress made me pant, my tongue touched the ground—mistake number one.

I heaved, sucking my tongue back in my mouth which didn't help in the least, deep throating the foulness of the troll camp. It was like my body took over and no matter how my mind screamed, I couldn't stop the thrashing as I fought to get the taste out of my mouth.

Terrible, this was beyond terrible. I was going to be found out.

I was going to get us all killed, because the golden in me couldn't hold still all because she didn't like the foul taste of troll shit and mud.

I spun sideways, flipping and flopping like a fish out of water.

Unseeing, I slammed into something hard as steel and a set of hands settled on me. The hands held me still as I gagged and finally heaved the worst of the taste from my mouth, my mouth frothing and foaming, dripping bubbles from my lips.

I looked up at the person holding me. Blue eyes stared down, his cruel mouth curving in a mocking smile.

"Well, Princess, funny to meet you here."

13

EAT ME, MOTHERFUCKER

I didn't know if I should thrash harder or run away or what the fuck to do...because the voice cutting through the cacophony of smells and sounds. Was...Han's.

I settled for jerking away. I yanked myself from his hands and lost a tuft of hair. Staring up at his face, he was covered in dirt, mud and blood—I wasn't sure I would have recognized him if he hadn't spoken. No, that's not true. His eyes and mouth gave him away.

He was in a cage that was about twelve by twelve, and made of thick steel of all sizes and shapes. "I'm rather indisposed as you can see. Want to help us out?"

Us?

The snarl of a wolf from the far side of the cage snapped my attention to the problem bigger than Han.

Havoc tensed, staring me down, his muscles

bunched as if he were about to spring across and tear my throat out. His dark fur was covered in so much mud that instead of black he was brown...a brown wolf.

Bebe spluttered beside me. "What the fuck is this troll shit...? How are you two even here? Did you bring him to help him kill Cin? And why would we help you out? That's insane! We'd be better off to leave you here."

All the questions, and all the worries she had were mine too.

I just stared at Han, not even bothering to add to what she said. Because she was wrong. I couldn't leave Havoc.

Not after...not after I'd seen his memories.

Han sighed as if we had all the time in the world, leaning on the bars. "Look, I can...I can take you to the doorway of the Norns. If you get me out of here, I can show you where you need to go. That way you don't need a troll map. That's fair, isn't it?"

"We can find it on our own. Jor said that the trolls have maps," Bebe snapped. "Come on, Cin, let's leave them to get eaten and get us a map."

Havoc hadn't moved and I found myself just watching him. He was holding it together. Better than he had before anyway.

What the hell was I thinking?

"Odin's big ass, you like him too? What the fuck is wrong with you both?" Han crouched so we were eye to eye. "You know he wants to kill you, the way I did? Right?"

I huffed. "You wouldn't understand."

Han's eyebrows shot up. "I wouldn't?"

The roaring hiss of a trio of crocs reached my ears and we all turned as the trolls began to eat their appetizers of scaley-dillys.

Flesh and bone cracked, blood spewed, teeth snapped, the croc-a-gators hissed and tried to escape but there was nothing they could do to stop what was happening.

Han swallowed hard enough for it to be audible, but his eyes were locked on the gory scene. "I'm not 100% sure we will come back from death anymore, Cin. The rules have changed, for all I know Havoc and I could be torn apart and that will be it. We'll be dead."

Was he telling the truth or was he just saying it to make us help them? Could I live with Havoc dying? With Han dead, that would free me from the mate bond and whatever machinations he might have up his sleeve at a later date.

But leaving him here would mean leaving Havoc too. And there was no way I could do that.

Yes, I realized that rescuing the wolf who wanted me dead was a fool's errand.

But maybe, just maybe I was seeing his memories because I needed to know what he felt. Maybe it would be enough for him to fight off Sven's spell.

I looked at Bebe and gave a soft whine. She stared back and sighed. "Okay, we'll get them out. But how, wolf boy? Is there a key?"

He gave a quick nod. "Yes. It's a star shaped key." He tapped the other side of the cage, and I moved to see the lock. A five-pointed star, so the key would be round with points sticking out of it? The thing was, the key would be huge, looked to be about a foot across, and no doubt it was steel too. There was no way I could carry it as a golden, or even in my wolf form.

I'd have to shift to two legs, which would make me incredibly visible, buck naked, with lightly tanned skin.

"Where?" Bebe asked. "Where do we find it?"

"Fucked if I know." Han shrugged.

Another gong sounded, deeper in tone than the first and we all looked once more to the horde of trolls. The last bit of croc-a-gator was flipped into the air and disappeared down the gullet of the biggest of the trolls. He easily stood close to twenty feet tall and was doubly as thick as the youngster trolls we'd encountered earlier.

The camouflage on him was not as strong. He licked his lips and looked our way, pointing with a thick stumpy finger that dripped with blood. "Bring on the wolf and the man! We feasty deasty yeasty today!"

Han swore under his breath. "Well, it was nice knowing you, Princess."

Three trolls ran toward the cage, and I slunk backward, down in the mud as I watched them scoop up the cage and carry it toward the feasting place. Han clung to the edge, farthest from the door, Havoc next to him, scrambling along the bottom of the cage.

"What are we going to do?" Bebe whispered. "We aren't strong enough!"

No, we weren't. But I knew someone who was.

I shifted back to two legs, hoping what I was about to do would work. If not…I would have no choice but to leave Havoc and Han to their fates.

But I would try. Because Havoc was more than just a quick fuck, he was more than a guy that had tried to keep me alive. I think if I were a betting person, he'd been falling in love with me before Sven put the spell on him.

Lying in the mud naked, I pressed Loki's symbol on my neck, and pushed some of my alpha energy into it. There was no way he'd come if he knew I just needed help. But he was a lech so… "Loki. I need your ass here right now. I'm naked and covered in nothing but slippery, wet—"

The air around us crackled and I rolled to see Loki standing over me, grinning. "I knew you'd come around to see me as a viable…wait, you look like shit."

"I need your help." I pushed to my hands and knees and from there to my feet.

The trolls were rattling the cage as they fought with the key.

Loki's eyes were wide, and his eyebrows climbed. "Why not ask your father?"

"I doubt he has the power you have." Not that I believed that, but the look of satisfaction on Loki's face said it all.

I had him. Ego won over reality yet again.

He smiled and preened, rolling his shoulders back ever so subtly. "Well, that's true. But *why* should I help you?"

"I'm trying to save the world, and you want that still? You want me to save your grandsons? Keep the tree of life from falling to toothpicks?" I asked, doing my best not to panic. We were short on time, and he wanted to have a fucking therapy session.

He grunted. "Damn it. Yes. What exactly do you need?"

I chose to ignore how easy it was to convince him.

My mind had already leapt forward three steps. The boys would get dropped out of the cage at some point, and that meant we'd be running.

"Clothes and boots for me. Supplies for a journey to the Norns. And a distraction. Keep the trolls busy while we head for the entrance to the Norns." I never took my eyes from his, no matter how much I wanted to look at what was happening behind me. The trolls were roaring with frustration.

The sound of metal on metal was there, but no satisfying click of the key working.

Loki laughed. "That's a tidy little list. Here." He rolled his wrist and tossed me a leather backpack that was surprisingly light. "Everything you want is in there, clothes included. You sure you want Havoc free?"

"Sven spelled him to hunt me," I said. "Can you lift that spell?"

A screech of metal spun me around. The trolls had gotten tired of trying their own damn key and were tearing the steel bars apart.

"Hurry up!" Han bellowed.

"I can't touch the Woodland King's spells. That's a big no-no. Besides, once you cross into the realm of the Norns, the spell will be subdued. So why should I do it when it will fade in about four or five miles?" Loki grunted.

His words...the spell would fade on the other side of the doorway...I had the backpack on and was running toward the trolls before I thought better of what I was doing. Crazy, this was crazy. But if Havoc followed me into the realm of the Norns, he would be the Havoc I knew.

The Havoc that I thought might love me...that was worth fighting for and even dying for.

"Listen up you dirty mother fuckers!" I skidded to a stop, the mud making the skid something amazing, leaving long marks behind me.

"Yeah, you wanna fight, you think you're so tough! I'm a tough bitch, I've carried the sun, you losers!" Bebe bounced beside me, puffed right up, as big as a six-pound cat covered in mud could puff.

Han clung to the inside of the cage, Havoc was at his feet, and they were both fighting not to slide out and into the mouth of the big troll, the one who'd demanded they were next on the menu.

All the trolls turned to look at us. My skin prickled with the urge to shift and make a run for it, but I held my ground. "Han, what direction?"

"Fuck, woman, you're going to get us all killed! North!" Han roared.

Havoc howled as a troll threw a net toward us, and then the net...it just fucking disappeared.

Loki appeared at my side. "Really. You are a great deal of trouble. I think that's why I chose you."

This was our chance.

"Run!" I yelled at Bebe as I dropped and shifted to four legs. The backpack clung to me as I bolted forward, a golden once more.

Huge hands swept toward me, the feeling of rushing air the only warning I got. I rolled and ducked and dived. Havoc and Han were out of the cage and then the four of us were bolting north.

"Loki said he'd help!" Bebe screeched as a troll foot

landed next to her, barely seen with their fucking camouflage.

Loki had said that there was everything I needed… in the backpack. "He put something in the bag, something to help distract the trolls!"

Han was at my side in a flash, as he all but lifted me off my feet, digging through the bag as we ran.

I blinked as he turned with a long tube in his hands. "What the hell is that?" Bebe yelped.

"Fireworks." Han lit the fuse and held it over his head.

The pop, pop, pop of the roman candle was a soft noise compared to the crashing of bushes and tearing free of mangrove trees.

And then there was nothing but the silence of our feet and the harshness of our breathing. The splash of water, and then the call of birds as we fled deeper into the swamp.

"Stop, stop," Han said and we all slid to a standstill, struggling to hear anything over the rush of blood in our ears.

Havoc stood on the far side of Han, panting. It was only then I saw the bloody wound in his side. He was injured, and badly.

Han turned and shook his head. "They aren't following us. They are chasing where the fireworks went down."

"It was that easy?" Bebe heaved. "Seriously?"

"They aren't bright," Han huffed. "But they will pick up our scent once they give up on the shiny stars that fell." He tossed the used roman candle away.

As he spoke, Havoc shifted to two legs, his hands clutching at his belly.

I stared at him, the man who'd shared my bed more than once, the man who I'd begun to trust. And even knowing that he wanted to kill me, I wanted to lean into him, to breathe him in and tell myself he would be okay.

That we'd find a way through this. We. Us. Together.

Because his memories told me the truth of how he felt.

"This way," Han grumbled. "Don't shift to two legs like this idiot. You'll be better on four legs through this mess."

Havoc snapped his fingers and pants appeared on his body, along with a wrap of white linen around his middle that pulled tight until he grimaced. I took a step, and his eyes shot to me, darkening until I was sure he was going to lunge at me. But he held himself still.

I held my ground and bared my teeth, despite the urge to cower at his feet. Han held up his hand between us. "I don't know why you aren't trying to kill her, but—"

"Injury." Havoc turned away so I was no longer in

his line of sight. "It's enough pain to keep my mind elsewhere. As you said, brother, perhaps we are not above dying now."

I wanted to tell him what I'd seen. I wanted to tell him I didn't hold what he was trying to do against him. The fact that he was able to fight the urge at all was a testament to his desire to *not* hurt me.

"Hop up, Bebe." I motioned to my back, and she gave a sigh and leapt to sit on the backpack.

"Havoc, you at the front," Han said. "You know where the entrance is as well as me."

Havoc shot his brother a look. "Trying to keep me away from your *mate*?" His words were laced with a veritable green venom.

Han laughed. "I think not, brother, bad enough I had to fuck her mother. I don't do mother-daughter duos."

I grimaced at the image. "Just go. I'll take the back."

They both looked at me and I shrugged. "I'm the alpha, now *move.*" I shoved energy into the last word with as much 'oomph' as I could, and it seemed to work.

That or they were just humoring me.

I let them get ahead of me; Havoc was moving slow, holding his side. Han walked with his hands tucked in his pockets like he was out for a nature walk in some highbrow botanical gardens, and not slopping through the Florida Everglades.

"Was this on your bingo card?" Bebe asked. "I mean...in all the possibilities, in all the shit we've seen, was this....ever on your radar?"

I snorted and shook my head. "Even with the journal...How could it be? Last month I was just trying not to be stuck as a golden retriever."

She sighed heavily. "That's fair. I just keep wondering what's going to come next, you know? Sea monsters? Dark demons? Death and fire?"

Han and Havoc stopped and looked back at us. I turned my head to look at Bebe too. "Why do you keep doing that? Why would you even put that out there? Gods only know who might be listening."

A deep rumble shook the ground and seeing as we were all turned around except for Bebe, three of us saw the trees move.

Apparently, we hadn't thrown off the trolls just yet.

14
BINGO CARD OF DEATH

"You happy now?" I yelled as we raced through the swamp, a herd of ravenous trolls thundering along behind us. There were enough of them that they repeatedly sent waves of water sloshing forward with their giant legs and the momentum they had going on.

"Not really. Being right in this particular situation isn't a great feeling!" Bebe clung to my backpack for dear life, crouched low. Which was smart.

Even as a buoyant retriever, I had gone under the waves twice already. Havoc and Han were ahead, moving easily, dodging the worst of the onslaught from behind, even with Havoc's injury. To be fair, the trolls were throwing trees that went over my head and landed closer to the brothers.

"I didn't want this on my bingo card!" Bebe

shrieked as we hit a firm patch of ground, only to have a croc-a-gator snap at us from our left.

I didn't have more breath to spare an answer.

"Hurry, get to the doorway!" Han barked.

Han. The guy who'd been trying to kill me all along was now telling me to hurry up so I'd survive, and it was freaking me out.

But he was pointing at safety, or at least what I hoped was safety. Just ahead of us was a massive mangrove tree, bigger than any other tree I'd seen in the swamp so far. The middle of the tree had been split open, a narrow 'doorway' that yawned with darkness and flickered with lightning.

Lightning, inside the tree? It screamed magic.

"This is going to hurt," I muttered.

"Not worse than being eaten alive," Bebe yelped back.

Havoc disappeared through the tree first, a crack of thunder ripping through the air, and a howl followed it. I picked up speed, took a step and pain lanced through me, my right hind leg caught on something, jerking me to a stop.

Before I could catch my breath, I was yanked underwater and rolled. A scaley-dilly had caught me, not a log. Right at the finish line. Son of a bitch, I hoped no one had been betting on me making it.

My body was thrashed as the beast rolled, spinning me so fast I would have no idea what was up or down, even if it had let me go. I scrabbled and tried to fight, kicking with my free leg at the croc's face, trying to hit an eyeball.

Lungs burning, the need to grab a breath of air clawing at me. What if I shifted? Would I be able to use my hands to claw at its eyes? Frantic, the idea was all I had. I shifted to two legs and pain erupted up my shin bone as the croc bit down deeper. My human legs were thicker than my golden…I screamed underwater, unable to stop myself from letting out the precious air.

I was going to die.

In a swamp, drowned by a croc while trolls trampled my friend.

Bebe. I had to get the sun to her.

I was going to miss her so damn much. I hoped she got away. That was my last thought as I prepared to drink in the swamp. I couldn't hold my breath any longer.

The croc let me go, and the release was so sudden that I didn't move at first.

Hands grabbed at me, yanking me upward and then I was in someone's arms, my head hanging, throwing up swamp water to the side.

"More, more, more! I'm hungry ungry grungry!" The bellow of the troll's leader was so close, I could smell his breath, and it was no better than the smell of their camp, shitty and full of rot.

How many bits of flesh were trapped in his teeth? How long had they been there?

"Not the time!" Havoc snarled as he tightened his hold on me.

Had I asked the questions out loud?

Wait. Havoc had me in his arms? Why not just let me die?

The trolls threw something big, the whistle of it in the air like a missile aimed straight for us, crashing at our feet as we fell through the tree's doorway.

We were thrown through, falling down, down into icy cold water. We hit it together and I jerked out of Havoc's arms, realizing just how fucking close to death I was. My feet found the bottom of what felt like a river, and I pushed off to the surface with my good leg. The leg the croc-a-gator had bitten throbbed, and I was sure it was broken, but the pain was distant.

I gasped as I broke the surface.

"DON'T DO THAT TO ME!" Bebe screeched. "You...you...how could you do that? I had to go through the doorway on my own and get one of these idiots to run back for you, and Han wouldn't, but Havoc would, and I didn't know if he was going to kill you!"

I spun slowly in the water to face the shoreline. "Thanks, Bebe. You're the best. As always."

She huffed and glared at me, bedraggled, looking very much like a drowned rat, but the mud was gone at least. I doubted I looked much better. The river water washed away the worst of the swamp.

Gritting my teeth, I swam to the shoreline.

"Cin."

Havoc's voice turned me around. His eyes were no longer filled with hate, with death… "You're hurt."

"Yup, par for the course. Thanks for the rescue back there. You going to try and kill me?"

He ran his hands over his head. "Loki was right. The spell is dampened here. I can fight it off."

"Why is that? Not that we're complaining, but explain it to me like I'm a child?" Bebe asked.

"You are a child compared to us." Han sat on the edge of the clear flowing river. "Spells cast in a specific realm, stay in that specific realm. Sven would have to cast the spell here too, for it to be effective. I doubt he thought any of us would step out of Midgard. Pardon me, Earth."

Havoc stayed in the deeper water. His injury bled and the water turned pink around him. To be fair, the water was pink around me too.

"How far are the Norns?" I asked.

Both brothers huffed like I'd asked a hilarious question, which did not leave me with a great deal of confidence.

"Hard to say." Havoc took a step toward me and when I didn't retreat, he kept moving, slowly, carefully.

"The Norns could be three days from this place, or three hundred."

The tree does not have three hundred days. You must hurry, the spirit of the tree of life whispered through me, urgency pushing me.

"We need it to be closer."

"You need to heal," Havoc said.

"Pot meet kettle." I pointed at his side. "How long before *you're* healed?"

His eyebrows shot up. "Twelve hours. Faster if there is food in that pack Loki sent."

I slid out of the straps and threw it out onto the shoreline. Han scooped it and started to rifle through it. "Lots of stuff. Clothes, food, medical supplies."

Havoc was so close now, I could have reached out and touched him, but I wasn't going to be stupid—I couldn't afford to be stupid. His memories meant something, but we were in the thick of this still. "So, if we make it out of here and go back to earth, that spell of Sven's will kick back in?"

"Yes. Sven would have to die for this spell to be removed, as I doubt he will lift it on his own." Damn, just a few words and I was shivering as if he'd touched me.

I had it bad.

I was going to be stupid.

I held a hand to him, and he wrapped his fingers

around mine, warmth suffusing my skin where he was touching me.

He took another step and grimaced as a fresh burst of pink water swirled around his middle. He bent to pick me up and I shook my head as I moved away from him. "You can't lift me out. And I can't walk out on my own. That croc-a-gator did a number on my leg."

"Fuck," Han snapped. "I'll pick you up, but it's the last time."

As if *he'd* picked me up before. I wasn't quite sure what he was referring to, but I let go of Havoc as Han flipped off his coat and strode out into the river.

As he reached me, a flare of annoyance crossed his features, and he scooped me up. Carefully. Was he actually worried about causing me pain? Why?

The mate bond between us flared as his bare arm touched the back of my legs. Well shit, that explained things then, didn't it? Only for me, the bond was an irritant.

For him it was making him...gentle.

Even with Han being as cautious as he was being, I couldn't help the hiss of pain that ripped through my clenched teeth. My leg dangled and the bones ground and bit against one another in a most unpleasant way.

Havoc snarled. "Be careful with her."

Han closed his eyes. "Sorry."

I blinked and stared at him, then looked at Bebe. "Did I hear...right?"

"Yeah, that's fucking weird," Bebe said.

"It's the mate bond," Han growled. "With Sven's spell fully gone...the mate bond is...ramping up. It's why I sought you out in Alaska. To see if what I was feeling was real."

I might have agreed with him, only I wasn't feeling shit on my end toward him. I kept my mouth shut as he walked us out and carefully, damn near gently, lowered me onto where he'd dropped his coat.

Havoc followed us out of the river, and I took a moment to look away from him because it was too much. In large part because there was nothing tying us together anymore. He'd sliced it clean through.

I could have been offended, even hurt by that fact except that I was pretty sure I knew why he'd done it.

To keep me safe, one last effort to keep me alive.

And even with that...his memories had come to me.

"Here, put something on." Bebe dragged the backpack to me. "You look cold. Or at least your nipples do."

I sighed and dug around in the bag, pulling out a sports bra, underwear, jeans and a plain black shirt. Nothing fancy, but it would do. I got the bra and shirt on no problem, everything else would have to wait.

Han grumbled under his breath. "I hate this shit. I'm starting a fire."

Again, I wasn't sure what shit he was referring to.

The fact that we were here, maybe? That he'd agreed to help? Or that he could feel the mate bond and it was making him nice?

Option number three was my guess.

Havoc groaned as he lowered himself beside me. He didn't say anything, just sat there at my side. I finally allowed myself to look around the space we were in, to distract myself from the throbbing in my leg, and the urge to reach for Havoc.

We had bigger problems than what lay between us. I knew that. He knew that.

Didn't mean I didn't want to crawl on top of him and let him hold me.

Bebe sat next to me, grooming herself dry, silent except for low level muttering.

The river was clear as a crystal, visibility easy all the way to the bottom. It gurgled and rolled over a few rocks here and there, but really it was a gentle current. The weird thing was it spilled out of a hole in the wall about ten feet up, as if the water were coming from the swamp. But the water wasn't dark or murky, it was beautifully clear, without a single drop of troll shit in it. When I took a deep breath, I realized that none of us smelled.

"Like a giant filtration system," I muttered.

"Something like that," Havoc said.

I kept up my perusal of the place. We were on a shoreline that was grass all the way to the edge of the river, short cropped like someone had mowed it. All around us were walls of rock that rose well over our heads into a cavern that I couldn't see the top of, further out it looked like a forest grew inside a massive cave system. There was light, but I couldn't tell where the source of it was.

"Are we safe here?"

"For the moment," Han said. I twisted around. He'd gotten a fire going and was headed toward me.

His eyes drifted over me and...they fucking softened. I pointed a finger at him. "Not a chance. Pull your mate bond away if you have to, but you're the one who said it and I agree. We don't do mother-daughter duos."

His smile was sudden and sharp, his eyes flaring with anger. "Fuck you too."

"Not if my life depended on it."

He leaned in. "But what if saving the world depended on it? That's why you fucked my brother, isn't it?"

Havoc grunted. "Maybe it's just because I'm better in bed."

My eyes popped wide, and Han shot a look at Havoc. "I doubt that. She'd have to fuck us both and give us a rating."

"I'm not—"

Havoc laughed. "I'm not doing *that* again."

How the hell could he laugh? It was like...like they

were really acting like brothers again, arguing and comparing their dick sizes as they fought over a girl.

"That's messed up. Boys are messed up," Bebe said.

I agreed with her, but there was nothing I could do about spending time with the both of them. "You going to carry me to the fire, or make me crawl?"

"You don't want the mate bond, you can crawl." Han stood and walked away.

Ahhh, there he was. Nice guy number one.

"Don't be a dick, Han," Bebe said. "We saved your fucking bacon, you pick her up right now or I'll claw your tiny dick off myself."

Han whipped around. "My tiny dick? You mean the one you ogled and talked about riding until you screamed?"

Bebe shrugged. "I've seen bigger since."

Havoc choked on a laugh.

Han stared at her. "You must have been a real ball buster."

She arched her back and did a long downward dog stretch. "You have no idea."

Han stared at her. "You sure you aren't a Norse deity stuck in a cat's body?"

Bebe sighed. "I wish. You think I would allow all this shit to happen to me and my girl if I were a Norse anything?"

I didn't like that the two brothers answered together.

"Yes."

She huffed. "Well, I'm not. I fucked around with Loki. Petunia turned me into this. What do you want, a fucking medal for telling me that I'm nothing?"

Bebe turned and trotted toward the fire, still cursing and snapping at the two of them. Han bent and picked me up.

"I think your friend has been lying to you."

I shook my head. "I don't. I think you've just been lied to so much, that you don't know how to tell the truth even when it wants to claw your balls and dick off."

His arms tensed but then he relaxed and shrugged. "Well, when she tells you who she really is, whoever that might be, don't complain to me. Because I told you so."

15

IS THIS FOR REAL?

"Why the fuck would I complain to you?" I asked as Han set me down by the fire. The warmth soaked into me, and I groaned...nope, that was my leg jostled as he lowered me.

Han grimaced. "Fuck. I'm sorr—"

"Don't you dare," I snapped.

"I'm sorry," Han said. Damn it, he dared.

I poked him in the chest. "I don't feel anything for you, do you understand? I buried that mate bond so fucking deep that I *can't* feel anything for you. You left me to my brothers. You killed Soliel. You fucked my mother! And if Havoc can cut me off, why can't you?"

Han looked from me to Havoc. "Because what you had wasn't a mate bond. You chose each other. There was no fate, or magic involved, there was no meant to be…if anything the two of you should have been fucking repelled by one another seeing as you are *my* mate."

Bebe situated herself on the far side of the fire and had already curled up and by all accounts had gone to sleep, which left me alone with this revelation.

The worst part was that I wasn't fully in disagreement. I'd chosen Havoc. And apparently, he'd chosen me if his memories were true. I'd just assumed that because it felt…more real than what I had with Han, that it was a second mate bond.

That it was meant to be in its own way.

"We didn't have a choice," Havoc said as he pulled stacks of Tupperware out of the backpack. Magic bags were something I'd heard of, but damn to see one in action was nice and absolutely I was avoiding thinking too deep about the actual conversation happening in front of me.

There had been no choice for him, for Havoc. He'd had to fuck me, or the world would have ended. I didn't have a choice. Not that first time. Sure, we'd consented, but it wasn't because we'd actually wanted to fuck.

But if we were being honest, even then I'd wanted him. And he'd very much wanted me. His memory of that night was crystal fucking clear.

I couldn't help it. "Well, that's a pile of shit."

Both men froze and looked at me. The weight of

their stares didn't bother me. I looked at Han first, then to Havoc. "You can act like you didn't want me, if that helps you sleep at night. But the truth is a bit different from that, and you and I both know it. Besides, you were trying to bind me to you, to make the mate bond swap."

Han burst out laughing. "Is that what he told you? That old wives' tale...you believed it? I thought you were smarter than that, Princess. He just wanted a piece of ass, and he got it. Didn't he?"

He wanted to play rough? I smiled at him sweetly. "If you'd been fucked the way he fucked me the first time, you'd take any reason to go back for seconds and thirds."

Han's smile fell from his face and his eyes got dangerously dark. "Don't test me. Not now. You are mine."

Both my wolf and my golden snorted. I agreed. Havoc was ours.

"Test." I smiled and then winced as my leg twitched. "Test. Test. Test. You don't seem to get it, Han. There is *nothing* for us. Mate bond rejected, thank you very much. Maybe Loki could take it off, seeing as he's the one who put it on."

"Then why did you save me?" he asked. "At the troll camp, why not leave me behind?"

"I figured you knew the way to the doorway."

He huffed. "Please. You could have found it. They

would have been busy eating my screaming face, and you wouldn't have had to run."

I glared at him. "Maybe I'm just nicer than you!"

Havoc snapped his fingers between us. "Much as this is super fucking amusing, I'm tired. We need to eat and sleep if we're going to heal." He threw me a Tupperware container and then threw one to Han as well. "Here. Eat and stop bitching at each other. You're like an old married couple."

I huffed and cracked the lid. The smell of roast duck, sweet potatoes and thick cream sauce rolled up to me, flooding my senses. My mouth instantly filled with saliva. "Bebe, come eat."

She didn't answer. The brothers were digging into their food.

I scooped a bite with my fingers and sucked the juices off. I couldn't help the moan as I tipped my head back, I hadn't had food this good in…well ever. I licked my fingers, then took another scoop. "Bebe…you've got to try this."

With a single-minded goal, I demolished what was in the container, stopping only to breathe and whisper my thanks to whoever had cooked up the feast. Magic Tupperware for the fucking win.

I saved a chunk of duck for Bebe. "Seriously, come eat."

"Fine," she hissed, "but I'm not happy. They are

making me out to be a bad guy, and I'm not a bad anything!"

My friend stalked over to me, her hair all standing on end like she was facing down an enemy. I glanced at Havoc who was staring at me, his container unfinished. "What?"

He swallowed and shook his head. I looked to Han. He had a similar expression on his face, almost…pain? "Are you two okay?"

"They were watching you eat, licking your fingers." Bebe took the chunk of duck from me. "It *was* pretty hot. All the little breathy moans, like you were in a porno except you were the only one who didn't know."

Havoc grunted and dug back into his food. "Just eat."

I grinned, and then laughed. "Seriously, you two are way too overstimulated by things that are just every day. I like good food. I make happy noises when I eat."

Neither of them answered me, which was fine, I was exhausted. I closed the lid on the food and the container…got heavy. I cracked the lid and peeked in. There was another round of duck and sweet potatoes and cream sauce, and I could have cried.

"Thanks to whoever made this, you are a goddess," I whispered.

An answering warmth wrapped around me.

Bebe let out a little burp and sighed. "That was amazing. I'm going to curl up by the fire."

Han stood and tossed the container at Havoc. "I'm going for a walk."

Which left Havoc and I alone for the first time in… what felt like forever.

He glanced over at me. "I don't want to hurt you, Goldie."

"I know." I wrapped my arms around my bent knees. "I don't want to die."

One minute I was sitting on the rocks, the next he was lifting me carefully into his lap. I don't know how he did it without bumping my leg, but he managed. He buried his face against my neck and collarbone.

"I should have listened to you, about your mother." His lips moved against my skin, but it wasn't lusty. I slipped my arms around his neck and held on to him, understanding the need to just be with him.

To touch him. My wolf and goldie fucking sighed and pressed me even closer to him.

"She's made a mess of this," I said. I quickly filled him in on how she'd bound herself to the tree of life. That I suspected that was why it was dying now—because I'd killed my mother. "Basically, this is all my fault."

"There was no way you could have known." His arm was wrapped around me, and he gently squeezed my hip with his hand. "None of us did. It was like a prophecy behind the prophecies that we all knew."

He lifted his head, his dark eyes taking me in. He

carefully raised his hand and touched my face. "I dreamed of you. Of us."

Damn it if I didn't smile. "I did too. But I saw things from your eyes."

The curl of his lips told me that perhaps he'd gotten the same. "Did you like what you saw?"

I tried not to squirm. My bare ass was right on top of his cock, and he was rapidly getting hard. But this was more than lust. And maybe it always had been, from the first moment we met. When he'd saved me from my brothers.

"Yes, I liked it. Because I saw a wolf falling in love with his chosen mate."

His chest rose and fell rapidly, a low rumble rolling through him and into me. "Is that so?"

"I suspect you saw the same thing." I lowered my voice. If I was going to die, then I wanted to say the things that were the hardest. "I...was so afraid, Havoc. To let my heart get tangled again with someone who couldn't be with me. So afraid that I wouldn't be enough...for you."

His jaw ticked and he cupped the back of my head, bringing my face to his. "I was afraid I wouldn't be able to protect you. That if you died, it was best that I didn't tangle my heart up with yours."

I let my fingers trace the side of his neck. "Were we both wrong?"

His eyes closed and he pressed his lips to my collarbone. "Yes, we were both stupid to think we could fight this. I want you at my side, Goldie. For however long that is."

I closed my eyes, and a shudder went through me. Tension I hadn't known was there released and I let myself sink into his arms, into him. "I'll take that deal. No matter what we face."

Another low rumble rippled from him, and it touched off a riot of sensation in my core. His hand slipped between us, seeking my wet warmth. He groaned as he dipped two fingers into me, then slid them up over my clit.

I couldn't move, not with my leg and being forced to stay still was a delicious torture as he slowly circled my sensitive nub. Lazy, as if he had all the time in the world, giving harder and lighter pressure, catching it between two fingers and tugging gently, squeezing it while I gasped and tried to make zero noise.

I wasn't sure I could hold on much longer. I knew what came next—Havoc would slide his cock deep into me and I'd fucking explode. But we had a situation.

"Havoc?"

"Hmm." He was kissing his way around my neck, under my jaw, tasting me as if he hadn't already eaten and was hungry for something more, while he played with my clit.

I tried to get my head thinking straight.

"He'd feel it if we fucked, wouldn't he?" I didn't want to think about Han right then.

Havoc groaned and pulled me tighter to him, his hand slipping away from me. "Fuck. Yes."

"Not that I want you to stop, but..."

But.

Gods damn Han was a but now. Butting in on my reunion with Havoc.

"But he won't know if you come." It was my turn to slide my hand between us. To dip below the waistband of his loose pants and wrap my fingers around his cock. He grunted and closed his eyes.

"Eyes on me," I whispered.

His dark eyes flew open. "Evil."

"Tell me to stop then."

His grin tugged up on one side of his face. "Never. Fuck me."

I slid my hand up and down, relishing in the fact that I could do to him, what he could do to me.

I chose him.

And just like that, whatever connection had been destroyed was back. I gasped seeing and feeling the moment from both sides. Feeling my hand on his cock, and seeing me through his eyes as the pleasure spiked and he came all over my hand. My body clenched and an unexpected orgasm ripped through me, matching his, as if me touching his cock had somehow transferred to my own body.

A low groan slid through him, and I sat there shaking, my broken leg pissed as hell that I'd moved at all.

A bellow ripped out of the forest. "What the fuck, man?"

So much for not having Han know we'd been fooling around while he was gone.

I wanted to ask Havoc what the hell had just happened. Why had we seen each other like that. But a soft fatigue settled over me and I sighed.

Havoc struggled to stay upright. "Something's wrong."

I swallowed hard as he slumped, pulling me down with him. I couldn't keep my eyes open either.

"Food," I whispered in realization as I laid my head on his chest. It had to be the food. "Laced." But why?

The question was, would it kill us, or just put us to sleep? My eyes drifted closed and I wasn't sure I cared.

I held Havoc a little tighter and he kept his arm tight around me too, as if he could indeed keep me by his side with sheer will.

I forced my eyes open, one last time. A figure walked up the river toward us. Cloaked in shadows, whoever it was moved with an easy grace born of being a fighter and I made myself stare them down. I let a growl escape before I couldn't hold my head up any longer.

"Such a fighter." A male's voice echoed around us.

"But you can sleep, I will watch over you. You and my sons."

16

DREAMS AND NIGHTMARES

As soon as I lost the fight to the drug, herb, or spell that had been in our most delicious food, the dream came on hard and fast. Dream, but maybe a nightmare. I wasn't sure.

I stood between the two brothers, Havoc on my right, Han on my left. Bebe clung to my shoulders, her belly pressed against the back of my neck, her tail wrapped all the way around.

"Is this...is this real? Are you really with me, or is it just my dream?" I whispered.

We stood on the edge of a grand palace with tall spires that spiked impossibly high into a brilliant blue and white sky. Not white with clouds, white as in streaks of white rippled through the blue, almost like it was an ocean, and not a sky at all.

"Yes," Havoc said. "This is real. Our spirits are here. The question is why are we here?"

"Where is here?" I asked.

"How about why did you go fucking my mate when I was a hundred feet away?" Han snarled.

"What?" Bebe yelped. "I was sleeping by the fire, and you fucked Havoc?"

"We didn't!" I threw my hands in the air.

Han gave me a dirty look. "Oh, you're telling me that was a spontaneous orgasm?"

Bebe sniffed. "If that was a thing, I'd know about it."

"We didn't fuck. And this is Asgard. Home of Odin and the Norse pantheon," Havoc said, tugging me to his side and away from Han. "Someone wants us to see something that is happening here. That would be my guess. Let's leave the rest for now."

As soon as he finished speaking, we moved. No, that wasn't quite right. We didn't move, the world whipped around us like we were strapped to a roller-coaster we couldn't get off.

Up and down, we were yanked forward, over a rainbow bridge that spanned a huge empty space, and then we were slammed to a stop in front of what looked like a business meeting.

The long table was made of a brilliant white stone, and there were chairs all around the edges of it. The people in the chairs were dressed in business attire: suits for the men, business dresses for the women, although they were all different colors.

But despite the high-end clothing, I was not fooled. I mean...the men had beards decked out with beads and bones, half of them wore helmets of some variation, and every person at the table held a weapon.

The women were fierce, their faces painted as if they were going to war.

The man at the head of the table had only one eye, and two ravens sat on the table in front of him, pecking at the bagels and donuts that were spread out. "This is a mess." He slammed the flat of his hand on the table, shaking the entire thing. No one flinched.

"Odin, you aren't telling us anything we don't know," Freya said. She wore her white and blue business suit well; it looked good on her curvy frame.

"Well apparently, I need to say it again! We have no way to know what will happen next! All the prophecies, out the window! All because Tyr couldn't keep it in his pants!"

"I think I've managed to help the situation." Every eye turned to Loki who strolled into the room. "They are on their way to Europe right now. They think that the entrance to the Norns is deep in the old homeland. Which will keep them busy while you figure out said mess."

A sigh rippled through the crowd of what could only be...relief?

"We can't let Tyr's daughter get to the Norns," Freya said. "We've done what we can to slow her down, that was well done, Loki."

He smiled and bowed at the waist. "I mean, why would you want her to get to the Norns? They only have the answers to what is going on, they could help her heal the tree of life. Suvenia is dying, you all know this."

Odin growled, "You are oversimplifying things. You know what could happen if she gets to the Norns. Do you really want that? She and those two boys of Fenrir's...they are twisting fate itself!"

I stared, my heart and mind racing. Want what? What were we wanting? Or not wanting? Why wouldn't they just spit it the fuck out? Was it not what the journal had in it? Maybe I wouldn't die?

"I don't want Ragnarök, I've changed my stance on that, as you know," Loki said. "But that isn't what—"

"It is," Odin snapped. "Stop twisting words, you slimy little shit. You want my throne, that is nothing new. You think I don't know that?"

Loki grinned. "I'll take my leave then, my king. Good luck with...all the things coming."

And just like that, he disappeared.

A man in a suit with a deep green shirt stood up,

and at first, I didn't recognize him. He looked so different than the last time I'd seen him. "Cin is a chance for us...a better chance than we've ever had to live without the fear of Ragnarök hanging over us—"

"No." Odin seemed to like cutting people off. "She was never seen in the Norns' prophecies, she was never meant to be born, which makes her a danger to us all," he spread his hand wide. "Until she swallowed the sun, her abilities were dulled. But taking on that power opened her up. The further into our world she goes, the more she will gain her own abilities—we are seeing that already. Fate is moving with her. She is changing everyone's destiny! She could end up killing us all. It is better that she dies now. The Woodland King was right about that."

And then, like things couldn't get worse...Sven stepped out from a doorway. He bowed deeply to the table, his bark skin crackling, pieces of it falling to the floor.

"Her death...it will ensure the end of Ragnarök. It will ensure the safety of all of the realms, and it will heal my mother."

Lies! He lies! Suvenia's voice whispered through me. I didn't doubt her. Sven was a lying sack of wood chips.

Sven spread his hands. "I have set the brothers to hunting her together, to save us all. I thought Havoc could do it on his own, but his bond to her is too strong. He is fighting me far too much. Han was always more eager to kill. Together, they will be able to catch her and end her."

His lies spewed out of him like leaking sap. Because that is not what the tree spirit at the tree of life had said and I knew in my gut that she'd been speaking the truth.

Although the brothers in question *were* with me, I suppressed a shiver of fear that I was standing in the middle of a giant fucking trap.

Lies and half-truths swirled around me, but I would figure this out. There was no other choice.

What I didn't understand was *why* Sven wanted me dead. Something had changed from when I'd first met him. Either it was the fact that I carried the sun, or it was the fact that I was now related to the Norse pantheon. It was possible that he hadn't realized my connection at first.

That felt like the truth. I hadn't been a player, not even on his board when he'd first met me. I bet I'd really fucked up whatever plans he'd had.

"What does he gain, if I die?" I said quietly.

Sven tipped his head, as if he'd heard me. Slowly, he turned to face me, and the sorrow I'd seen in his eyes when he'd sent me running was no longer there.

"I do believe...she is here, watching us. Learning of our plans like the spy she is. She is not one of us."

Havoc and Han grabbed me at the same time, their fingers digging in hard to my upper arms, and they yanked the three of us away from the scene. We ran, side by side, as the realm seemed to come apart behind us. Chunks of earth flew, as if bombs had been set off at our feet, spears and arrows shot toward us, a boom of thunder shook the air.

There was a tug on the center of my body, right at my belly button, and then I was alone, hurtling through what could only be a dream state by the way I floated, and I finally jerked awake.

I gasped as I sat up, the gurgle of the river and the echo of footsteps were what I locked on. We weren't alone. My leg was three-quarters healed, but I barely gave the pain a thought as I shot to my feet and yanked on my remaining clothes.

Havoc was sound asleep at my feet, and Han... where was Han? Still in the forest? Bebe was curled by the fire, passed out.

"What the hell kind of fucked up is that?" I whispered the question, not sure if I was hearing the footsteps, or not. Maybe it was Han?

"That, Young one, is the power of a liar. A liar with magic is perhaps the most dangerous creature that our world has ever seen."

I spun, stumbled, and found myself staring up into the face of a man who carried both Han and Havoc's features. The jaw line of Han, the eyes of Havoc, a body that leaned more toward Havoc with the breadth of his shoulders.

All that was fine and dandy, but it was the axe he held at his side that had my attention. It was black and rusted and looked like it had pitting from all the blood it had seen.

"You're here to kill me, aren't you?"

17

CALL ME DADDY

The man who could only be Havoc and Han's father tipped his head toward me. "I am not here to kill you, young pup."

Pup. I hadn't been called that in...what felt like forever. "Then you're here to help us?"

He tipped his head to the side. "Yes."

"Then why knock them out?"

"My sons do not always behave when I am around, and I wanted to speak to you without interruption." His dark eyes never left my face. He made me think of the lone wolves who'd pass through our forests from time to time. Always on the outskirts, and always with a touch of madness in them, because wolves are meant to find their pack, to be with others like them. It's what keeps us whole.

"Fenrir," I said, more statement than question.

"Just Fen will do." He rolled his shoulders and motioned for me to sit. "You have a journey ahead of you, and not much time to do it in."

"So, you want me to sit down and waste time?"

"I have suspended time. When you step from this meeting it will be as if no more than a blink of an eye will have passed." He motioned again for me to sit.

I lowered myself to sit, only I didn't reach the ground. A big chair made of logs that could have come straight out of the ocean waited for me. A driftwood chair.

"How are you going to help?" I repeated my earlier question with a slight variation.

"I am the son of Loki, brother to Jörmungandr and Hel herself...help perhaps is too strong of a word." He dropped back into a chair that matched my own as a table materialized in front of us.

A tall stone pitcher and two thick pewter mugs sat in the middle of it. "Drink. We will discuss what we can discuss and see if it...helps."

The wolf in me was curious about this one, about why he smelled like wolf but also like a monster. Why would he help us? The golden in me was unsure, but not afraid and that was enough for me to trust him—for now.

I poured myself a drink and then poured him one too. "Cheers."

Fen tipped his mug in my direction.

We drank and the crisp, clear drink soothed my throat, but made me feel a little lightheaded. "What is this?"

"A drink of the gods. If you weren't truly Tyr's daughter, you'd have burned to a crisp from the inside out."

I stared at him over the rim. "Fuck you."

His smile was sudden and sharp, all hardness and wolfy angles. "Ah, if only my son wasn't your mate."

I wrinkled up my nose. "I'd still pass. I don't do father-son duos."

He laughed and poured himself more of the drink.

"We will talk, and we will see where the conversation goes. That's best."

"Let me take a guess. You came to watch the train wreck, spectate and then leave before we actually need your help?" I said.

Fen winked, as if he was letting me in on a secret. Gods save me. "Do you know that I am the father of *all* shifters? The first, I created because I was alone. She was...unbelievably strong. An alpha female to match my energy."

I choked on my drink. "Please tell me it wasn't my mother."

He shook his head. "No, it was not your mother." He frowned and squinted. "I suppose it would make you the great, great, great, great granddaughter of my first alpha female. That line remained stronger than any other females that came along. They were stronger, had more grit and fire, and generally changed the world around them whether they liked it or not. Being created by a god will often have that effect. That is your line, that is Juniper's line. Though at times, the power can make one a bit mad."

I clutched the mug in my hands. "Yeah, Juniper was that. You didn't think to put a check on all this power you stuffed into their stupid bodies?"

"No, I am a son of chaos himself, pup, I put things into motion and then I enjoy the ride."

"I don't like this ride," I said.

"I don't doubt that."

I wanted to reach across the table and strangle him, to tell him to just spit out what it was that he came here to tell me. Not even tell his sons, just me. But I held my tongue and waited, because if we had all the time in the world then I could wait. I could see this through to get the information I needed.

Which meant I listened to him talk about the drama amongst the other deities. Odin's hatred of his ravens. How stupid Thor was, despite his fighting prowess. How pissed Freya was that her cult had disbanded. About how Loki had switched from encouraging Ragnarök to happen, to trying to stop it, and why that might be.

"He fell in love," I said. "Maybe for the first time, in

truth. But I think that's why. Or at least that's the rumor I heard."

Fen's eyes widened. "No! You think so? Oh, that's interesting...I will have to find out who it is. Hmm. I wonder if it's a human?"

I'd put the other pieces together, and suddenly this little meeting made more sense. He was just like his brother. Lonely and wanting to talk—wanting a friend. "You get along with your brother, Jor?"

A sigh slid from him. "It's complicated."

"Most family relationships are. I don't get on with all my siblings. I mean, it's better now with two of my brothers. The other one, well, I keep waiting for Kieran to show up and try to kill me." I could not believe this was the discussion, but it made more sense now that I put them in the same category as his brother. They both wanted to talk to someone. They wanted entertainment and gossip.

"Kieran is hunting you still. He is working with Sven. As a backup." Fen took a sip of his drink. "Be warned that even if you survive what is coming, he will still try to kill you. The darkness Juniper set in him has taken on a life of its own."

"Awesome." I took a drink and let it soothe a few more ragged edges. If nothing else, I could tell my leg was healing as we spoke, despite Fen having halted time. Slowed it, whatever.

I sighed. "Look, I think that we've spent enough time gossiping. Why are you really here?"

He set his mug down. "Sven knows where you three are. He will re-bind the spell to Havoc in this realm. And he's about to do the same to Han, as I think you witnessed in the meeting I sent you to. They will both hunt you now."

The mug clattered from my hands. "What? Loki sent them in the wrong direction. Sven can't know—"

"That's what the meeting was about, the one you saw. Sven asked permission to expand the spell, seeing as you slipped through to the pathways between the realms. It doesn't matter where you are." He leaned forward and took my hands in his, and only then did I feel how cold my fingers had gotten against the warmth of his palms. "You will be hunted, pup. And all of us need you to survive; my father has made that clear. We need you to make it to the Norns. They will guide you."

"And when I get there?"

He smiled. "Be yourself. Tell them the truth. Don't hold back."

I was shaking, I couldn't help it. "As soon as we snap out of this?"

"You will have five minutes before the spell kicks in again. Maybe less, maybe more."

"And why does it feel like our time in this stasis is now limited?"

Fen didn't let go of me. "A minute."

A minute was all I had before both Havoc and Han would be hunting me. I spoke quickly as I pulled my hands from Fen's and began to strip, tucking my clothes into the backpack and sliding the straps over my shoulders.

"The Norns are where the answer lies?"

"Yes."

Solid. "And I can save Suvenia, and the realms?"

"You can. I don't know how, but it's on you, pup. You can do this. You are strong enough, and more than that...you have the heart to do what must be done. The answer lies in the meeting you saw. Think on it."

The answer? "You can't just tell me?"

"Where's the fun in that?" He grinned.

"You have your brother's shit eating grin," I snapped and he laughed.

My heart and mind were scrambled, and any other questions I had. How many times had I been thrown into a river? So many times. It had to mean something, all of it had been pushing me to this one more time. "The river, that's my path?"

"It will get you close to the Norns but leave it when you come to the raven wing rock. From there you will be on foot to the home of the Norns."

I blew out a quick breath. "Tell Jor that I will try for a coffee date in a week. If I make it."

Fen's eyebrows shot up. "You...are going for coffee with my brother?"

"He saved my life." I shrugged. "More than once, so I owe him a few coffee dates."

Fen's jaw dropped. "Fuck off with you. I should have asked for coffee dates too."

A laugh burst out of me, but it got tangled up with a choking sob because I knew how deadly the two men were that would be hunting me in a matter of minutes. "Is there any way you can slow them down? Without hurting them." Damn it, I was going soft.

But I didn't want Havoc hurt. Han...well he was Han. He could live with a few bruises.

"I will try. They are better fighters than me, and... Sven stripped them of their immortality—they can die, and I don't want them to die. I'll put a time stall on their acceptance of the spell if I can," He tipped his head toward me and the world started to wobble, speed picking up when I hadn't even felt like it slowed. I focused on where Bebe was still sound asleep, curled up in a tight little cinnamon roll. She was going to be fucking pissed...at least initially. But we had one hope.

I blinked and Fen was gone.

I stumbled over to her, and scooped Bebe up. She grumbled as I held her tight to my chest. Havoc rolled to his feet, from his crouch he stared up at me. "How are you naked? You just had—"

"Sven has spelled you and Han to both hunt me...it

will cross all realms now." I couldn't help it, I stood there and stared at him, willing Fen to be wrong.

Havoc snarled and stood. "Fuck. Go. Just go. I'll... I'll try to stop him."

"What's going on?" Bebe grumbled, "I was dreaming I was human again."

I stepped toward Havoc, maybe it was stupid, but I wanted to believe in something that was impossible. "I trust..."

He grabbed me by the face, and pressed his forehead to mine, fingers gentle across my cheeks. "Kill me, if you can, Goldie. I...will never be good for you and Sven, he will always use me to hunt you. And I...I can't...live with this world if you aren't in it."

I gasped and stared up into his dark eyes. His lips hovered against mine, breathing, drinking each other in and maybe I thought that time had slowed. I wanted to drag him to me, to kiss him as if I could take a piece of him with me. I'd chosen him for me. It was not fate.

It was the destiny I'd created for myself.

My cheeks were wet with tears as I clung to him, trying to hold him to me as if it would be enough to counter the spell. "Havoc. I'm not losing you. Not now."

"I know, Goldie. I know."

Our faces still pressed close, the moment stretching.

Han's howl cut through us, and Havoc shoved me away. "Go. Don't look back."

I didn't know how Havoc was holding the spell at bay, but I took him at his word and stumbled back from him.

"That was hot, what's going on?" Bebe finally looked up at me. "Why are you crying?"

"Hang on, we're going swimming."

"What?" Her screech hit a new peak as I turned and sprinted for the river, my leg aching but holding, then dove into the water, holding her tight to my chest. I didn't shift into my golden form right away. The water was cool, but not cold and I held us down as long as I could, hoping to be far enough down the river that Havoc and Han wouldn't be able to see me.

Bebe clung to me, her claws digging in, then getting frantic the longer we held on below the water's surface. The current and my legs propelling us along as fast as I could.

No matter there came a point where I had no choice. I had to surface. We both had to get a breath. I pushed off the bottom of the river, my body doing a circle as we both sucked air. Behind us there was nothing, I couldn't see our makeshift camp.

I couldn't see Havoc or Han, couldn't hear a wolf's howl. Maybe Havoc had been able to slow things down. Maybe Fen was holding them at bay like he'd said.

"You going to explain to me just what the hell we are doing in a river...again?" Bebe clung to me, which was fine. I let my body shift to four legs and as a golden retriever started swimming. Between the current and my dog paddling efforts, we'd make good time.

"Watch for a raven wing rock, we need to get out there. That's the path to the Norns."

"Okay. What the fuck happened?" she might have shouted that last bit, and I didn't blame her.

"Keep it tender, Bebe," I said, "and quiet as we can. Short version is Havoc and Han are both hunting us now. Sven expanded the spell to be in this realm too."

"Oh shit." She groaned. "Seriously?"

"Yeah. Seriously." I kept up my swimming pace, the sides of the river flashing by. I didn't tell her that Havoc and I had had a moment. I didn't tell her about Fenrir. None of that mattered, not to saving the world.

And that was what I was going to do. I'd find a way. Stop Ragnarök and find my way back to Havoc.

Bebe balanced on my back. "It looked like Havoc kind of wanted to kiss you back there."

I swallowed hard, thinking the same thing. In all our encounters, we'd never kissed. I mean, we both thought it had just been fucking. Passion. Chemistry. Saving the world and then ensuring we'd saved the world.

Now I knew that we'd both been scared of being hurt and both of us had reasons for that. That there had been something between us right from the start, we were both just too fucking stubborn to let it happen. Until now.

"What's the plan?" Bebe asked as I swam.

"Find the Norns. Get the answers we need on how to save the tree of life. Avoid dying. Try to find a path where we all live happily ever after."

"I like that one the best," Bebe said. "And can I just say, I'm fucking sick and tired of all the water? Like, could we not end up in a river?"

I huffed. "Only since I've become a golden have I spent this much time swimming."

"It's your fault then?"

"Apparently." To be fair, the golden part of me was fucking ecstatic every time we leapt into the water. Swimming along, my damn tail was wagging with nothing short of pure joy. If I let myself, I probably could have lain in a puddle and experienced the same joy.

The one good thing, the happy emotions flowing from my golden to me allowed me to push back some of the fear and shit that was my current situation.

I would look on the bright side, damn it.

We made our way down the river in relative silence after that. To the left of me was the rock wall, to the right was the forest that extended from our old campsite. Raven wing rock. I kept my eyes peeled for a rock shaped like a raven's wing. Time slid by. An hour, maybe a little more.

"It's so quiet," Bebe whispered. "Is it because there's a predator around?"

"Fuck me, Bebe, you keep saying shit like that! Why would you say that out loud?" I whispered back, my skin prickling with awareness like she'd woken something up.

Twenty feet down the river and I thought maybe it was just a funny reaction to Bebe's words.

Nope, wrong again.

We'd had nothing but the sound of the river for so long the tinkling of rocks to our left sounded like a fucking gunshot as they tumbled down the rock wall. I slowed my swimming and floated, so we faced the left side of the cavern.

A dark hole yawned out at us, easily fifteen feet around. Rocks and pebbles slipped out of the abyss and down to the river, plunking into the water.

"That's probably not good," Bebe whispered.

"Yeah, probably not," I whispered back.

"What do we do?"

I couldn't swim upstream, Havoc and Han waited there. I couldn't keep shifting back and forth from four to two legs and back again. Not without using up too many calories. Which left me floating like a giant fluff ball in the middle of the river as the creature stepped out of its cave.

Black wings spread wide, the lower limbs thick with a deep rusty red fur, ending in oversized lion's paws. The upper portion of the body was not bird, but lizard, or dragon maybe with sparkling black rainbow scales that overlapped all the way up to its snout. The eyes were brilliantly green as they flashed and locked on us.

When you come to the raven wing rock, that is your path, you must go on foot.

That fucker, Fen, could have just said that it was a Rok, no 'c' involved, and I might have been a little bit better prepared instead of thinking I was looking for a rock formation.

"Cin? Am I seeing things?"

Bebe's voice hitched.

The monstrous bird hybrid launched toward us, and I did the only thing I could.

I dove for the bottom of the river and prayed the stupid thing missed on the first pass.

Those huge paws though, they didn't miss as they grabbed us both and yanked us out of the river.

18

WHAT THE FUCK, BEBE?

As the paws of the beast cupped my body, I curled inward trying to keep myself from being poked to death by its ridiculously long claws that circled me and Bebe. My dive into the river hadn't done us any good and the Rok had us before I was even a foot under water.

The weight of the monster pushed us further down and slammed us into the riverbed before it climbed again, dragging us with it.

We were going to get eaten by a monster if I didn't think of something fast.

But it wasn't me who saved us.

As we broke through the water surface, Bebe let out an unholy screech, so loud that it sounded as though she were ten times the size of her tiny body.

Then she launched herself at the foreleg of the Rok, her tiny claws slashing through its flesh.

"No! You aren't going to hurt her!"

Like a demon possessed she flailed and screamed, blood flowing, splashing across all three of us.

The Rok wailed, its call as high-pitched as a young girl freaking out that her favorite doll had been grabbed by a cootie-ridden boy, its eyes wide as if it couldn't believe what was attacking it. Hell, I couldn't believe what was attacking it, and scaring it.

More importantly, the Rok dropped us. Like we weren't worth the hassle. I mean, who wanted to eat razor blades hidden in cotton balls.

I huffed as we fell, hit the water and went under again. This time I swam hard for the far shore.

Bebe was beside me and she climbed back up onto the pack. "Go, go!"

Only I couldn't *go go*. I was easily ninety-nine percent sure that we had to go through the lair of that fucking bird brain that wanted to play patty cakes with us. It flew in a large circle around the cavern, its eyes sweeping across us, as if considering another pass.

Maybe it realized that what had attacked it was all of six pounds.

I swam hard for shore as a howl lit the air behind me.

As if one monster trying to kill us right then wasn't enough.

"Fuck." I growled as my paws found the far shoreline and I scrambled across the loose, skittering rocks, clambering hard for the flat wall that the Rok had made its home in.

Bebe bobbled on my back. "Don't look behind us, no matter what."

I gritted my teeth and ran harder, my feet slipping in the loose stones as the ground itself seemed to pull me backward toward the river.

Two howls lit the air, one that reached into my body and slammed me like a tuning fork that left my legs jiggling and loose, my heart pounding for more reasons than the physical exertion. The other howl sent a live wire of fear through me, promising to hurt me, to tear me limb from limb, to see me down to my last gasp of air.

I was pretty sure I knew which was which.

A splash of bodies hitting the water as they entered the river on the far side only pushed me harder.

That was all I needed to launch myself up to the next pile of rocks. I looked up and knew that I had to shift back to two legs if I was going to make it. There was no way that I could climb the sheer wall with either of my canine bodies.

I made the decision and wobbled as I stumbled from four legs to two, naked except for the backpack.

"You're going to climb naked?" Bebe leapt to my side. I dared a look behind me then to see a black wolf and a solid white wolf in the middle of the river. The Rok had taken after them, swooping down and grabbing at them.

I stuffed my hand in my bag, grabbed a pair of pants and yanked them on, followed by a shirt. "No."

Was it modesty? Not really. Okay, maybe I didn't want either of those boys following me up the cliff, looking straight up into my ass crack. I slipped the bag back on and reached for the first handhold.

"Cin!"

Havoc's voice cut through the sound of the Rok and the howls of the other wolf who had to be Han.

No, I wouldn't turn around. He wasn't the good guy right now, and to believe he was anything but someone who would kill me was a stupid, stupid move. It didn't matter that it was a spell, cast by that wooden headed Sven.

"Cin, help!" He bellowed and then the gurgle that followed...

"Don't look back!" Bebe leapt up and grabbed hold of the backpack, her body blocking me as I turned my head to do just what she told me not to. "It's a trick, girlfriend. You know that. He told you to run, he told you to kill him if you were given the chance! And he never called you by your name before!"

She was right. He'd only ever called me Goldie. Still...

"What if it's not?" I made myself move, even as I

asked the question, made myself start the climb. "What if he's hurt?"

"If he loves you," Bebe whispered. "He would rather let himself be killed than to draw you into that fight. No man who truly loves his woman would give up her safety, for his."

"Shouldn't it go both ways?"

"Not when you know you can't trust him." She butted her head against the back of my neck. "Trust *me* on this, Cin. You can't trust him—not right now. Which means you can't trust anything that comes out of his mouth, even if it tugs at your heart. Even if it breaks you."

I didn't like the tension in my chest, the way it grabbed at my heart and tightened my throat, the way my eyes blurred. I'd chosen him, and now I had to leave him behind.

"I...don't want to give up on him."

"I know. Neither do I. But right now, he's got to do him, and you've got to do you. You've got to stay safe, at any cost. You walk your path, Cin, and you rock this world to its core. And if he's going to be with you, then it will happen. You gotta just go with the flow this time, girlfriend," Bebe said.

"You're right." Two words, and damn they hurt as Havoc bellowed my name, at the sound of the Rok thrashing the water as it fished for the two wolves. My fingers and toes found tiny purchases as I dragged us up the sheer face toward the Rok's cave, my back and arms burning as I struggled.

Shifting so many times, so close together and then adding a wicked work out immediately was not easy, even on me.

Holding yourself perfectly flat against a wall of rock, the weight of a backpack and cat dragging you backward...it was a workout I wouldn't repeat.

There was a sudden rending screech behind us, then a wolf gave a guttural howl of defiance, and Bebe gasped. "I can't believe what I'm seeing. They killed it."

Fuck, fuck, fuck. Not that the Rok was my ally, but it had been keeping Havoc and Han busy, giving me a chance to get ahead of them. Without that distraction, my lead time was over. I redoubled my efforts, pulling myself up, pushing off with my toes, reaching for impossible hand holds.

Leaping, taking chances that I never would have taken before.

"Almost there," Bebe encouraged. "Maybe another two or three feet to the top."

I paused and sucked wind, shaking from the crown of my head to the tips of my toes. I didn't even have extra air for speaking. It had been silent below us for almost ten minutes now. There was no way that the two of them weren't climbing after me. No way they weren't catching up.

"Here, I'll help!" Bebe leapt off my back, for the top

of the cliff. Only thing was, her launching herself upward, pushed back and down on me.

That little bit of pressure was all it took to upset the balance I was literally clinging to.

My fingers on my right hand let go, and my right foot slipped. I screamed as I clung by one hand and barely the big toe on my left foot. With only four fingers, I gripped with all I had. I swayed and cried as my left big toe lost its grip.

One hand, one hand was the difference between me living and falling to my death. Would the world go down with me? Would a fall actually end things, or would it take one of the boys chopping my head off with a magical axe?

"Cin, reach for me!" Bebe called.

Reach for her. To give her the sun. I had to give it to her before I fell.

I rolled my eyes up, fully expecting to see a tiny paw reach for me, not a hand with outstretched fingers.

I couldn't question what I was seeing, I just flung my right hand upward, grasping at the lifeline offered to me. Bebe had found someone; she'd found someone to pull me up and right then I didn't care who that someone was.

There was nothing left in me to help with the upward motion, I had to let them yank me up and over the lip of the cliff. Shaking from head to foot, I kept my head down as I sucked wind on my hands and knees.

"Thanks." I lifted my head and stared at the naked woman who stared back at me.

Chartreuse eyes. Light brown skin with freckles across her nose. Wild dark curls flowing over her shoulders, so long that they covered most of her generous chest. I just stared.

She grinned, though it was a little wobbly and I swore I could see tiny little dagger canines. "Hey, girlfriend."

I shook my head. I was seeing things, that was the only answer. But I knew that wasn't the case, I could see my friend in the naked woman's eyes. "What the fuck, Bebe?"

"Yeah, so maybe we should talk about this as we run? It's a new development. Like it just happened. Just now."

She was on her feet in a flash, and when I blinked, she was a cat again.

Her hair was puffed up, as if she were afraid. I stumbled to my feet. Wobbling as the adrenaline of almost dying—again—fled. I pulled a pair of socks and shoes out of the backpack and yanked them on.

Because despite my confusion, about how she just turned into a woman right in front of me, and then back into a cat, I knew she was right. "Okay, let's go. And you better start talking."

I broke into a jog, shaky, but running, letting myself settle into the familiar movement, picking up speed with each step, pushing myself to go as fast as I could, all things considered.

"Here's the thing. I was cursed, you know that?" Bebe ran beside me, her tail straight up in the air like a flagpole. "The curse was because I messed around with Loki, but he...he softened the curse, the same way he softened yours. He told me that when...when I'd finally found true love, I'd be able to be a woman again. I thought that meant...I thought that meant romantic love."

Did she mean Richard? That she'd fallen for my brother and that broke her spell?

"You're my best friend and back there, with the Rok...I knew that I might die. I didn't care. I just thought to myself, at least she'll be okay. My best friend will be okay, I have to save her. There was no choice, I just did it."

I bit my lower lip and cleared my throat before I spoke. "You've saved me before."

"Not like that. Not knowing that I'd die, I always kind of knew I'd get through it. But this time...this time I was okay with it. Because...that's what true love is."

"I love you too, Bebe," I whispered.

"I love you more, girlfriend," she said. "I think...I think maybe I can shift back and forth now? But...I also think I can do more like this, as a cat. I'm just me, after all, no magic here. So, enough mushy stuff, pay attention, where are we going next?"

She was right. I needed to pay attention even though my heart was bursting with the fact that Bebe's love for me had broken her curse. Or at least it had broken part of her curse.

The walls of the tunnel were made of a glowing white stone, etched with symbols that no doubt meant things. A few I recognized from my crash course study of Norse mythology and the pantheon.

"How long do you think we have before they reach the top of the cliff?" Bebe asked as we continued to race through the dimly lit cave.

"Not long enough. Look for a side path, an opening, anything," I said as I searched the walls of the tunnel. I'd been so sure this was where we needed to go.

We took a corner, and I slammed to a stop.

A dead end. I put my hands against the white stone, and it was like touching a block of dry ice. I hissed and yanked my hands back, my fingertips bright pink and smoking a little. I put my hands to my head.

"This...this can't be it. There must be something else." I did a turn, looking at the wall, the symbols... that was what I should have been doing. Loki's symbol was right in front of me—the snakes woven around one another in an 'S'. The mark on my neck thrummed, pulling at me to lift my hand to the symbol, and I knew somehow that if I touched it, a doorway would open. I reached out then paused. How many doorways *could* we open? There could be a limit. I yanked my hand back.

"Look for a symbol that looks like a web," I said. "That's...that's what we need. You take the left wall, and I'll take the right. The symbol should open a doorway." I hoped.

"What if this web symbol takes us to a giant spider?" Bebe whispered.

"That would be shitty. But it's all we've got to go on." I turned and headed back the way we'd come, going as fast as we could while still checking the walls.

The symbols were all over the place, most of them I didn't recognize and then there it was.

A web etched into the wall just at my ankle height. Eight points of the web were embedded with tiny dark crystals, flickering as if they were lit from within.

"Here!" I dropped to my knees.

Bebe crossed to me. "You're sure?"

"It's this or we go visit Loki," I said.

"I'll take door number one."

"I thought so." I carefully pressed my fingers to the eight points of the web, the icy cold of the stones sinking into me. I grit my teeth and kept on pushing, feeling the wall slowly give away even as my hands felt like they would freeze solid, then shatter.

Smoke curled up from my fingertips, but I didn't dare let go.

One chance, I knew with an instinct I didn't understand that this was our one chance to get to the Norns.

I couldn't help the whimper as the doorway finally slid open...though I'd barely call it a doorway.

The opening was about two feet round, and disappeared into darkness, a waft of sweet smelling fresh air flowed up toward us, curling through me. That had to be good, right?

Cradling my seared hands, I scooted forward on my butt. "On my lap, Bebe, let's do this."

She did as I asked and I took a last look behind us, just as Havoc rounded the corner. His sharp blue eyes locked on mine. He gave a huff, a warning.

Go.

I nodded and forced myself forward, and into the darkness as he lunged toward me.

19

WATERSLIDE OF DEATH

The wall closed behind Bebe and me, throwing us into semidarkness. The sound of claws at the wall behind us did nothing to soothe my fear that Havoc and Han would be able to get through and follow us to the Norns.

I scooted forward, and the ground below me disappeared. I grabbed at Bebe with my arms, my hands still stinging painfully from pressing against the white stone and black crystals.

She screamed as we fell, and I just kind of held my breath. Would we drop into water? It seemed a definite possibility with the way my life trajectory had been going lately.

Only we didn't hit water, we hit something slick and hard, like a giant slide. Water sprayed around us. Check that, waterslide.

We were flipped and I had to let go of Bebe or crush her as I landed on my belly. "Fuck!" I blew out as I was flipped up and over, spinning down what could only be a waterslide of death.

Surely it was trying to kill us. There was no way that we wouldn't die.

"What the fuck is this shit?" Bebe yelled and I caught a glimpse of her before I was flipped again, the space below me gone once more as gravity took over.

I did the only thing I could. I held my hands in tight to my chest and just let it happen—whatever this was.

I don't know how many times I was spun, flipped, dropped…I knew that I was getting bruised and bashed to hell, I knew that there was something slippery that made it impossible to slow myself.

I tried a few times, but it just tore at my already tender fingers. Even if I'd shifted, there was no way my claws would have slowed us.

Bebe seemed to come to the same conclusion as I did and we stopped fighting.

I mean…at some point we'd come to a stop, right?

I hit a corner at high speed and the momentum took me all the way around the tunnel in a perfect loop over loop, knocking the wind out of me when I hit face down on the bottom of the waterslide of death.

A groan slid out of me and once more the ground

gave way below me and I slid over an edge into a free fall.

Only this one wasn't short.

And I could no longer feel the edges of the tunnel to catch me or slow me down.

"You gotta be shitting me!" I bellowed as I reached for something, anything.

The weird semi-dark made it so that there was no sense of space, of anything that could give me a place to focus on.

As suddenly as I'd lost all sense, the tunnel was back at my back, curving in a slow twist that began to slow my fall, the angle far less steep than before. I blinked and the semi-light began to grow, and I wasn't being spun so hard that I couldn't see.

Forest sprouted up as I watched, the tops of trees appearing first, flocks of birds flying up as we disturbed them. I sat up and the fall slowed further even as it gave me a good view of this amazing expanse.

Mountains in the distance, forest and valleys, and a desert beyond that, like a whole world had just appeared in front of me. "What is this place?"

Bebe slid into me and wobbled onto my lap. "I don't see a spider, that has to be good, right?"

The curving, mocking waterslide dropped us below the treetops and the interior of the forest turned into a fairytale. Flowers and tiny lights were strung between the trees over and over, creating a canopy of light and color that drew the eyes. The song of birds was sweet and gentle, the wind was warm and brought us new scents.

"I smell food," Bebe said.

I sniffed the air. "Someone is cooking onions and garlic." My mouth instantly watered and I couldn't help but wonder what the onion and garlic were for.

As long as they weren't being prepped to aid in someone or something eating me and Bebe, I was good. My belly rumbled, and I was suddenly ravenous.

Part of that was the shifting back and forth. Part of that was just the fact that it smelled amazing.

The slide spit us out onto the top of a bright green mushroom that was as big as a queen size bed, and easily as soft.

I just sat there taking it in.

"You think the guys got through behind us?" Bebe asked.

"Not today they won't."

We both twisted and jumped off the mushroom cap.

Behind us stood a woman of ethereal beauty, her white hair flowing around her as if caught in an unseen wind. Huge, solid white eyes stared down at us, seeing us though it looked as if she should be blind. Her dress moved in the same manner, the material gossamer thin, and yet there was very little shown of her midnight skin.

All in all, she was a stunning beauty.

That wasn't what had my jaw dropping though. She stood over thirty feet tall and made our mushroom landing pad look like a freaking footstool.

"How do you know they won't?" I managed to get the question out. Part of me said I needed to run for my life—this was a giantess. And giants were known for eating the flesh of anything that walked through their lairs.

"Because those are the rules my sisters and I have set in place. Any who would brave the lair of the Norns would find themselves safe—for a time."

I blinked up at her. "You are one of the Norns?"

She dipped her head toward me. "I am Helestia. The oldest Norn. And you are Cinniúint, daughter of Tyr, daughter of destiny. I am pleased to meet you, young one."

Turning, she motioned for me to follow her. "Come. You look worn from your journey to find us."

Bebe sniffed. "That's an understatement. I feel like someone stuffed me in a washing machine with a bunch of rocks and set the spin cycle to high."

I took a step, stumbled and went to one knee. "A moment, Helestia, please."

The Norn paused and looked over her shoulder. "Take all the time you need, child. Follow the path when you are ready, and we shall be waiting for you at the end."

I blinked and she was gone. "Bebe?"

"Yeah?"

"Weirdest shit so far?"

"Oh, yeah, a thousand percent. Zero stars for that little ride back there, two stars for the landing."

I stayed there on one knee, knowing I had to get up and move. Because despite what Helestia had said about the guys not being able to follow…I just didn't trust that they wouldn't find a loophole.

I dug around in my pack and opened one of the Tupperware containers. This one was just straight chunks of beef, potatoes, carrots in a thick gravy. The label on it said "Not Sleepy".

Fucker. Loki was a damn fucker. I sniffed the food anyway and didn't pick up on any sedatives or herbs. I had to take the chance that it wouldn't knock me out. I needed fuel, and this was all I had.

"Bottoms up," I muttered.

I stuffed my mouth as quickly as I could, chewing very little, swallowing a lot of the food whole. I had to refuel while I had the chance.

Bebe snagged a chunk of meat, then another and another. We sat for five minutes, eating as fast as we could.

"That will hold us for a bit." I wiped my face with the back of my sleeve. Best we could do.

I pushed to my feet, wobbled and took a step, then another and another, the calories helping. Apparently, it wasn't laced with anything, so I was going to take the win.

The forest around us was littered with the huge, fluffy mushrooms like the one we'd landed on. The path was wide enough for the Norn giantess, and it wove through as if it had been placed after the mushrooms and trees had grown.

Fantastic smells floated from all around us, cooking food, sweet treats, fresh baked bread, cinnamon, vanilla, strawberry...I breathed it all in and my stomach growled despite having just eaten. Something in me said it wasn't good to eat anything here. Like Alice in Wonderland, we would be in a world of fucking hurt if we took a nibble of anything.

Bebe stuck close. "This place is too nice. It gives me the heebie fucking jeebees."

"Me too, don't touch anything you don't have to, and don't eat anything." I kept to the middle of the path and picked up my pace. "Let's get this over with."

Almost as I spoke the path widened, opening us up to a gazebo made of woven willow branches, the same tiny lights as before, and bird nests.

Three women sat under the gazebo, a fire in front of their huge feet. The flames were a rainbow of colors, not unlike the bridge we'd seen in Asgard.

Helestia sat to the far left. All three of the women had the same silvery white hair, and white eyes, though each of them had very different skin tones. Helestia's skin was midnight dark. The middle Norn was so pale I could see veins running under her skin as if she were translucent. The third had skin that was blue, like a winter sky.

The one in the middle tipped her head to the side. "I am Proferia. You have met Helestia. And this is our sister Kleteria."

Bebe huffed and I reached down and scooped her into my arms so I could clamp a hand over her mouth. "Not a word."

"I would never," Bebe whispered. "What do you think I'm going to do, compare her name to a female body part?"

I glared down at her. "Yes. That's exactly what you might do."

"Is there a problem?" Helestia asked.

I held Bebe a little tighter. "I am only reminding my friend that we are in the presence of three goddesses, who hold our lives in their hands, and to remember to be respectful. She is a bit…"

"Forward?" Proferia smiled. "We know. We see her life. We know exactly who she is."

She motioned above our heads to the canopy of the willow tree branches.

I looked up and immediately went to my knees, as

if I'd been smacked on the crown of my head. "Holy shit."

They weren't willow branches, not the way I'd thought. They were color and life, flickering images held inside each strand. They were lives, woven over and over, some touching, some running parallel. Some ending abruptly even as I watched. It was overwhelming to say the least.

Proferia stood and pointed. One life drew closer to us, the strands that made it up flaring brilliantly bright red, glowing, vibrating with energy. "This is Bebe, as we see her. She is fiery, isn't she?"

A spark of lightning seemed to flare in the strand, and I couldn't help but laugh.

Proferia released Bebe's strand and it slipped back into the mass of lives that were too many to take in.

"It looks like her," I said. "Beautiful and spicy."

Bebe butted me. "What are you two talking about? You're not speaking English."

I swallowed and looked to my friend, but found myself speaking to Proferia. "She can't understand?"

Helestia shook her head. "She cannot. Nor can she see these lives as you and we can. It would be too much for her. You are like us, woven with destiny and fate and so it is something you can understand."

I bent and whispered to Bebe. "Hang on, we're negotiating. All good."

That seemed to satisfy her.

I wobbled a little as I stood. "And I can see these lives because...because I'm my father's daughter?"

"That is a piece of it," Proferia said. "Do you see anyone else you recognize?"

I blinked and looked through the lives, my eyes drawn to four...I reached out and touched them, drawing them closer to me. "My brothers and my sister."

"Yes."

They didn't tell me to trace the lines. Didn't tell me to look further. I just stared at how dark Kieran's line was, how all the lives around it seemed to be cringing from him. At how his life would end soon.

Very soon.

Richard and Ship were not like that—though I could pinpoint the moment I'd dragged them out from my mother's spell. Their lines went from dark to a wavering light, only growing in brightness.

Meg's line...that was far away, and it was not meant to cross with me again. She was safe and away from all of this, and that was the best that could be. "Be safe, Meggie."

"You would let her go?"

"You think she'd be safe around me?" I laughed, and shook my head. "No, I wouldn't bring her into this mess again if I didn't have to."

"But your brothers, you'd take the risk on them?" Helestia asked.

How did I explain that I'd tried to send them away? That they'd chosen to stand with me against whatever I faced. Their fates had been ones they had chosen. It wasn't the same as what had happened with them and Juniper.

Like the difference between choosing Havoc, or being forced to be with Han.

"That's different," I said. "But none of that is why I'm here."

Proferia nodded. "You come to find out what you must do next, how do you stop Ragnarök, how do you change the world?"

I grimaced. "I don't want to change the world. I just don't want it to end. And I'd prefer not to die."

I took note that Kleteria was saying nothing through all this, her eyes half closed as we all spoke. "Does your sister have anything to add to this?"

"She rarely speaks," Helestia said. "Be glad of that. She's a bit of a bitch."

Proferia nodded and motioned for me to look at all the lives woven again. "Before you ask your question... look for your own life."

I blinked. "My own life? You want me to see how my life will go?" Maybe that would help me understand how to stop Ragnarök?

I walked around the space under the woven willow branches that were in fact lives, three times before I shook my head. "I am not in here."

"No. You're not. Neither you, nor Havoc nor Han have lives with set past, present or future," Helestia said, her voice solemn.

"What does that mean?"

Kleteria stood, and we all looked to her. "It means that because of who and more importantly—what—you are, there is not a set path for any of you. And we cannot help you."

20

NOPE, NOPE, NOPE

"What do you mean?" I took a step back, "Your sisters just said you're the bitch of the three of you, no offense, but how do I know you're not just trying to get rid of me?"

Kleteria shrugged. "None taken. They are not wrong. I will say what must be said which often makes me the least favorite of our visitors."

"I only want to know how to stop what's happening. Are you telling me there isn't a way?"

"There is and there isn't. That's up to you and what you do next." Kleteria stayed standing and her sisters sat, heads bowing toward her. Those milky white eyes of hers were wide as saucers. "You finish the curse."

I frowned, not sure that felt like the right answer. "Okay. What curse?" Did she mean the curse I had as a golden retriever?

"And you can go to Hel," Proferia said, very clearly in English.

"Fuck you," Bebe snapped.

Kleteria glared at her sister, but Proferia acted as though she didn't notice. "Hel is where you must go. That is where the three deaths will occur. That is where the curse must be broken."

"Okay, but what about the tree of life? Suvenia is dying, rotting away, and I swore I would help save her." I couldn't do that if I was dead.

All three Norns looked to me and spoke in the same kind of freaky unison. *"The tree will fall, there has been too much damage, there is no way to save it. The realms are destined to fall with it. Unless destiny is changed."*

Shaking my head I took a step back. "No, that would...that would destroy everything. It won't matter if I break a curse, or if three wolves die" —fuck this was sounding worse and worse— "if the tree of life falls! Don't you think?"

That seemed to slow their rolls.

The three sisters put their heads toward one another, their lips unmoving, their eyes staring straight at me while they silently conferred.

After a few unnerving minutes, Kleteria spoke slowly. "You present a conundrum, child of destiny. Because your life is outside of our jurisdiction, we will not guide you in this further. Your fate is yours, and yours alone to discover. The survival of all rests on you, and you alone."

My eyes about bugged out of my head. "What?"

Kleteria's face and voice hardened and suddenly I understood why it would have been best for her not to speak. Not because she gave bad news, but because she clearly did not want to be a part of the solution.

I wanted to pull my hair out. None of this made sense. I read history for shits and giggles, read mythology of all sorts, dug into the legends of so many cultures but this bullshit...made zero sense.

Let the tree of life die? Just hope the chips fell in a half decent pattern?

The three Norns settled back, eyes closing, speaking in full unison. *"You must leave now."*

Except...Proferia opened one eye. "Go to Hel." Then she pointed to her right, my left.

That was the second time she'd said that. Go to Hell, or go to Hel? Hel was, as I recalled, daughter of Loki, sister to Jor and Fenrir.

Daughter of Chaos. Overseer of the dead. Damn it, I wished I still had the journal with me.

Or maybe it was best that I didn't know which path I was on. The journal hadn't exactly been leaving me feeling like there was any good ending for my story.

But Proferia...she seemed to want to help. Helestia opened her eyes and tipped her head in the same direction, mouthing the words.

"Go to Hel."

Two out of three wasn't bad in terms of getting a direction, I supposed.

I turned to the left and a path opened, leading me away from the Norns if I put my foot onto it. Why would Kleteria not want to give any advice? They were the weavers of destiny, the ones who should have helped me. Their lives were at stake too—if all the realms and the tree of life fell, we were all done for.

The Norns were still, their eyes closed, breathing quietly.

All three of them were huge, and getting a closer look at them would be difficult.

"What are you doing?" Bebe whispered.

"I'm missing something here." What had Fenrir said? To be myself?

I took in a deep breath, scenting the air. Something was there, a scent that was faded and yet familiar. I followed it over to the Norns and looked at them as best I could from the ground. I barely came to the bend in their knees. Could just look up into their laps. The smell was there, just at the edge of the three of them.

Proferia and Helestia were still, but Kleteria fidgeted like a child being asked to sit through a three-hour sermon. Could she be hiding something? A clue to all this?

"Bebe," I motioned for her to come close, then

scooped her up and tossed her into Kleteria's lap before I could think better of what I was doing. "What do you see?"

"Gods, why would you do...oh...oh shit. Yeah, I got it!"

Bebe shot forward and grabbed something from the Norn's lap.

She leapt off as the giantess rumbled. "That is mine."

"Bebe!"

"Yeah, we gotta go!" She mumbled around the thing in her mouth. I turned and sprinted to the left, down the path that would lead us to Hel. Or Hell, depending on the day I supposed.

The rumble and groan of the Norn behind us had me moving as fast as I could go, dodging the tree sized mushrooms. I didn't know just how pissed off a giant could get, and really I didn't want to. Bebe was at my heels and together we raced through the oversized fungi farm, the slope of the land taking us down and down.

The temperature dipped, and my breath came out in puffs of condensation.

A quick glance over my shoulder gave me a moment's relief. "She gave up."

Bebe spun and looked back, then spat out the item she'd snagged from Kleteria. "Why did she give up?"

"No idea. Let's keep moving though."

I bent and scooped up the thing Bebe had spat out, as I continued down the path. A thin string, like a piece of fishing line, or maybe of spider web, had been wrapped around a long-pointed item, over and over. A hundred times or more.

"What is it?" Bebe stood on her back legs, trying to get a look. "It smelled funky."

"I'm sure this is what I smelled too. It's familiar. But I can't nail it down." I ran my hand over the wrapped item. Like a mummy wrapped in layers of thin cloth. I tugged at the edges with my fingernails, trying to find the starting point.

Whatever was inside was indeed *funky*, as Bebe had said. I lifted it to my nose and breathed in, trying to identify it. Harder in this form, I was sure I could have figured it out as a wolf or golden.

"Is this why she wasn't helpful you think?" Bebe was in front of me now, leading the way. "You think she...shit, you think she was bribed? Or spelled?"

That gave me pause. I found the edge of the string and began to unspool it, fast as I could.

It didn't take long, and the item encrusted inside the strands of white material flipped out, through the air, and landed point down into the path in front of us.

A piece of dark wood, shaped like a small dagger. I grabbed the handle and pulled it out carefully. The tip looked as if it had been dipped in blood. The smell was stronger now, and I recognized him.

"Sven. This was a piece of that bastard." He'd used a piece of himself to what...influence the Norn?

"Well shit, that's going to put a bug in the margarita, isn't it?" Bebe said. "What do we do now? Is this even the right path? They could be working for him, screwing us over."

I rolled the wooden dagger over in my hand. "Yes. Proferia and Helestia told me to go this way. Even if their younger sister tried to be difficult, spelled or not by Sven. I think she was the only one affected." I hoped.

I brought the backpack around and tucked the dagger in. Maybe we'd need it. Maybe we wouldn't. But if it was used for controlling one of the Norns, I needed to take it away.

Bebe bobbed along ahead of me again. "You know, I love the idea of strippers and ice cream, but I don't think we're going to get that."

I laughed. "No, I don't think we are."

"That's okay, I don't think I need the strippers anymore." She paused. "I think I might be falling for your brother." Bebe shot me a look, her eyes uncertain. "But he's been lovely to me, and doesn't treat me like I'm stuck like this—which I'm not now. He's...he's special. And I see how he treats you. How protective he is."

I played dumb. "You mean Richard? He is handsome. But he can be overbearing, are you sure you want to take a swing at that?" I grinned, happy that my best friend had seen what I saw in Richard. Strength. Loyalty. Kindness. "Although, he does like his women curvy as fuck, so you've got that down pat."

"Hell yeah." She swished her tail. "I wish…I wish I wasn't a cat shifter now. But I suppose my curvaceous booty will make up for my diminutive size."

"Are you going to ask me for permission to pursue my brother, is that what's happening here?"

She sniffed. "You wouldn't say no, would you?"

"Then we'd be family for real," I said softly. The air around my face was a solid fog, I could barely see her at my feet.

Bebe froze and her head drooped. "Girlfriend, don't you know? We already are family. We don't need me banging your brother to seal the deal."

I laughed and held up my hands. "I don't want to think about you banging my brother. Thanks. But go for it. Have at Richard."

"You're the best, girlfriend." Bebe sighed.

We walked in silence and if not for the fact that we were headed toward the land of the dead, I might have enjoyed it. The air was sharp and cold, and the forest around us was slowly devolving from giant mushrooms to bare trees that reached for the sky, covered in thick frost.

"Bebe...does that tree look like something to you?" I motioned at a tree that was on our right, the two main arms of the branches were a little more straight out, less upward than the others.

"Like a cross maybe?" Bebe shook her head. "Why...oh, it's got eyes?"

I picked up my pace. "Yeah, that's what I was seeing too." And hoping that I was wrong.

The ice crackled around us, the trees lifting their roots and stepping toward us. "Bebe, up."

She leapt up to my arms and I set her on the backpack. "You watch behind. I'll watch the front."

"Good plan." She shivered as she hunched down in the space between my back and the top of the bag. "Maybe Loki gave you a blow torch in here?"

I picked up the pace but didn't run. Not yet. I was going to ascribe to a notion I'd read when I was a little girl, in a book I could no longer recall the title of. Don't run from the supernatural. You'll draw its attention.

I kept my pace steady even as the frost covered trees came to life around us. They groaned and swung their arms (branches?) but didn't seem to be coming at us. "What are they doing?" Bebe whispered.

"No idea," I whispered back, keeping my eyes peeled as the path sloped downward. I had to jump to the next level of land. That sharp movement was all it took. That, and I landed on a small sapling that was running around, arms flailing like a toddler.

It cracked under my left boot. Let out a pitiful cry and went still.

Fuck. "Sorry!"

The trees bellowed, spitting splinters and bark toward us.

I didn't wait around. I sprinted down the path, staying tight to it but weaving and dodging the creatures that were—rightfully so—pissed that I'd stepped on one of their young ones.

"Faster!" Bebe said. "They're coming in hot!"

I was moving as fast as I could. The thump of huge feet, the crackling of ice as they broke free of the weather filled my ears.

"Jump!" Bebe yelled. I didn't question her, I just leapt straight up as high as I could. A tree slid under me, the boom of it hitting the ground shaking the air around us. I landed lightly on the trunk as it slid down the path, arms flailing, branches still reaching for me. But it had no mobility to reach behind.

I balanced sideways, as if I were surfing.

On the path below I could see a...well it looked like a hole in the middle of the world. Nothing around it, nothing above it, just darkness within.

"Bebe, we're headed for that!"

"Nope!" She dug her claws into my shirt, skimming my skin. "Nope, that's a terrible idea!"

I caught movement out to one side and ducked as

another tree took a swipe at us. "We don't have a choice!"

Besides, I had no doubt that was where we were headed. A whole lot of nope, right into Hel's waiting arms.

21

HEL-RACIOUS

Using the tree for a surfboard really was the way to make an entrance. The creature bellowed and screamed as we got closer to the big round portal that sat smack in the middle of the path. I couldn't see into it, there was nothing but darkness.

It expanded as we got close, allowing for the extra size of the tree.

I crouched. "Hang on, Bebe."

"I ain't fucking letting go now!" She buried her face against my neck. "Tell me when it's over."

Funny, with all we'd faced, I hadn't expected her to freak out here. It wasn't like we could even see what we were going into.

I drew a breath right before we slid through the portal.

Because maybe we'd land in water again.

Maybe we'd land in a place that had no air. Who fucking knew?

The tree skidded away as the portal enveloped us.

I couldn't see a thing and I stumbled a few steps before the place opened up and gave me a view.

We stood on the top of a rock shelf that was hundreds of feet in the air. The tip of my boot hung over the edge. Rock formations were everywhere, as if I were standing at the edge of an underground Grand Canyon.

The screams of the frozen tree as it fell drew my eyes straight down. Below my feet, off the cliff edge was a classic boiling pit of lava—very hell like. Only it wasn't red, it was frothing and blue, as if it were a giant Kool-Aid slushy.

"Not a bad way to go I guess," I muttered. Bebe peered over my shoulder.

"How are you standing here not freaking the fuck out?"

"Good sense of balance."

I turned and a figure stepped out of the darkness.

Han launched himself at me, his hands going for my throat.

Bebe hissed and slashed at him as I stepped back, the heel of my boot now hanging over the edge. The only thing keeping me on the cliff really was Han and his hand around my throat.

His fingers tightened, cutting off the blood to my brain. "Time to die."

"Stick," I whispered.

"Stick?" He cocked his head to the side, and he might have loosened the pressure on my trachea just a bit. Enough for me to breathe.

"Why stick?" Han was hesitating, for whatever reason. And I would take it.

Bebe gasped, understanding, and dug into the backpack. I reached up behind my back as far as I could, and she dropped the piece of Sven toward my hand. One shot, we had one shot.

The splinter dagger belonging to Sven hit my palm. I closed my fingers and jerked the weapon forward, driving it into Han's side.

He bellowed and jerked away from me, so we both stumbled from the cliff edge. I wish I could say I had a clean get away.

But his brother was not to be left out of this.

Han hit the back wall of the cliff, and I sprinted toward a path that wove down the edge of the cliff.

Havoc howled and my body reacted, but I fought it back. I had to. I kept a hand on the wall and ran as fast as I could, even though I could *feel* him drawing close behind me, practically nipping at my heels.

"Bebe, how close?"

"Ten feet," she said. Same as I could feel Havoc, I could sense Bebe prepping to launch herself at him.

"Stay with me, Bebe," I yelled.

She stilled. "Ok."

I made it to the bottom of the cliff path and the ground was flat, hard rock. I raced on a path that seemed to keep pulling me forward.

The ground gave out below me. I leapt forward and caught myself on the edge of a chasm that hadn't been there a moment before.

Havoc dove across, his body a blur of dark fur. When he landed, he shifted to two legs. He snapped his fingers and clothing flowed over him. Leather armor, thick metal belt, his axe hanging from said belt.

He didn't say anything as I clung there. He just stared down at me.

Bebe jumped straight up and forward, and she shifted to two legs. Her right hook caught him off guard and it sent him to the ground.

Bebe spun and reached for me, helping me haul myself up. But we were too slow.

Havoc grabbed her by the back of her head and threw her away from me.

"Havoc. Don't." I scrambled backward until I was against a wall. I couldn't get away.

"You have to die." He shook his head, and his throat bobbed. Sweat dripped down his face. He was fighting the spell.

Bebe cried out. "No! Not Cin!"

His hand went to the axe, and he pulled it from the

loop. Everything slowed down. I stared up into his eyes and…he wasn't there. Not the Havoc I…loved.

I blew out a breath. "I love you, Havoc. I'm sorry I couldn't save us all."

His movement stilled. Or maybe I just thought it stilled.

A body slammed into him, so one minute he was standing there, and the next he was just gone.

"Run, Cin!" Han yelled.

Han was saving me? The world had to have turned upside down.

I got to my feet and Bebe ran to me, back in her cat form. She leapt up to my arms and maybe we would have made a run for it.

But I couldn't move.

My feet were sucked down into the ground, like quicksand that went to my knees.

"Bebe, get out of here!" I tried to let her go, but my arms were locked around her.

"I can't move!" She yelped and maybe she struggled but I couldn't feel her moving.

"Fuck," Han snarled. "I can't move either."

"Fuck you," Havoc snarled right back at his brother, apparently also stuck.

Like flies on a glue strip.

The soft feminine laugh that followed was not from either of the brothers. I was able to turn my head, so I saw her walking toward us.

A long black dress trailed around her, as if she were going to a goth wedding—the bodice was sheer and showed off an open ribcage held together with her corset. Her face was split between beauty and death. Her long dark hair on one side of her head was done in a hundred braids. The side of her head that was death had long straggling white hair that was matted and thin.

The chill in the air as she approached dropped to an arctic level. "Hello, nephews. Whatever are you two boys doing here?"

"Hunting," Havoc growled. "And you interrupted."

"Well now, this is my land. Did you ask permission and fill out the proper application forms?"

My eyes widened. Was Hel going to help me?

Their lack of answer was answer enough. She laughed again and turned to me. One eye socket was empty in the rotting side of her face. The other eye was a stunning aquamarine that was framed with long dark lashes. Her smile twisted her face. "And you are the prey, I assume?"

"I was coming to speak with you, actually," I said. "I'm trying to—"

"Save the world, blah, blah, blah. Loki has been trying to convince all his children to help. You know that, right? But we know he's up to no good. Most likely he's put you on the path that will destroy us all. That's always been my father's endgame." She shrugged her intact shoulder, the delicate bone structure so at odds with the grotesqueness of the other side of her.

"The Norns sent me to you," I said.

Hel paused and turned back to me. "Which one?"

"Not clitoris," Bebe mumbled.

Hel's good eyebrow shot up and she laughed softly. "I don't much like her. Tell me then, Proferia or Helestia, which one sent you to me?"

"Both."

Her reaction was unexpected. Her eyes widened. "Interesting." She snapped her fingers, and the world blacked out.

When I came to, I was in what could only be called a cell. A dungeon. The bars all around me gave me about a ten foot by ten-foot space.

Hel stood outside my cell. "You four will stay here until I know what is going on. I will go and speak with the Norns to see if you are telling the truth."

"Wait, there isn't a lot of time!" I reached through the bars. "The tree of life is dying!"

"I am aware," she snapped, giving me the ugly side of her face. "You killed the bitch who tied her life to Suvenia. We thought it was on purpose. But since Suvenia is still alive, it wasn't a complete bond."

"That's good…isn't it?" I tried.

Hel ignored me and spun, her skirts swirling out around her as she strode from the dungeon. The clang of more metal shutting behind her had me sliding down the inside of my cell. "Bebe?"

"I'm here." Her voice came from my right. She was in a much smaller cage, the bars too tight for her to squeak through.

"For what it's worth, I am here too," Han grumbled. "And you're welcome for saving your ass."

I turned to see him on my left, with Havoc in a single cage. Han sat slumped, his hand over the wound I'd given him.

"Thank you, for this." He motioned with one hand at the wound.

I raised my eyebrows. "You're welcome?"

His smile was brief and seemed to tangle up with a grimace. "It broke the spell. I don't know how, but it did."

Havoc grunted. "And then he tried stabbing me with it."

"Did it work?

I took a step toward their side of our joined cages and Havoc's hand shot through toward me, his fingers just able to snatch at my chin. "I'll take that as a no." I stepped back, what little hope I had that something would go right, sliding away from me.

I went to the far side where I was closest to Bebe. I laid down and reached across for her. She reached through her bars and her paw just touched the tip of my finger.

"Ice cream would be really good right now," she said.

I smiled and laid my head on the cold floor. "Yeah. Ice cream would be amazing."

The drip of water had my attention, and I let the steady dripping hypnotize me.

"Are you giving up?" Han asked.

"No. Maybe? I don't know how to move forward." I sat up and leaned against the bars so I could look across at him and Havoc.

Han was sitting, like me, against the far side of his cage. Havoc stood in the corner, watching me. Unmoving.

I'd been lying here, thinking about what everyone had kept saying about me. That I was a daughter of destiny. That my abilities—whatever they were—would have come on when I started carrying the sun. But I'd not felt any magic, not felt any different than I'd ever felt before.

What did it mean to control your own destiny?

Fen's words came back to me. Something about the meeting I needed to know. I wracked my brain. Odin had done most of the talking...what the hell had he said?

She is changing everyone's destiny!

Was that it? Was that...what I could do? I frowned. I'd survived when everyone thought I would die.

Because...because I chose not to.

I was bonded to Havoc because...because I chose him.

Was it that simple?

"Do you think we were ever actually mates?" Han's question was unexpected.

I looked over at him. "Do you?"

He shrugged. "I've never had a mate, or a mate bond before. I've never experienced anything like it. The desire to protect, to keep you safe...it consumed me. It's why..."

"Why you let me almost die on multiple occasions?" I frowned at him.

He shrugged. "I knew what you were the moment I saw you in the shelter. But I didn't want it, you are right about that. Still, I took you with me when I knew what you were."

Bebe snorted. "As if that makes you a hero?"

"She didn't die in there, did she?"

I stared across at Han.

If I was right about my ability, then maybe I'd made him take me. I'd all but begged him in my mind to take me.

But I didn't share those thoughts out loud. "Maybe we were never really meant to be mates. Maybe that's why you could turn it off so easily."

He huffed a dry laugh. "I couldn't turn it off any more than you could. That's just it. I blocked it, the same way you did. But all those efforts came tumbling down when we came through the gateway to the Norns. To be fair, they'd started to come down once Sven removed the spell."

Havoc let out a low growl. "She was never meant to be yours."

"Loki thought so." Han grinned up at his brother. But the smile slid and he closed his eyes. "You know, I think I might actually be dying? It's a very strange sensation."

I didn't dare get any closer to their side of the cages, but my thoughts were tumbling out of my mouth which brought us closer in a different way. "Destiny brought us together, Han, and you did save me. But maybe we were just meant to be pack, and not mates."

His eyes were shuttered with pain. "Pack." He said the word like it was foreign to him.

"Something you've never had, or maybe not for a long time. I'm just guessing."

Why, why did it matter now? It had to do with the choice, I was sure of it.

But something in me said that I was closer to the truth than I'd ever been. Han was a dick…he'd tried to kill me. But so had Richard and Ship.

Havoc stepped between us. "Do not try to convince him to save you again. Your life is over when Hel returns."

I closed my eyes and leaned my head against the bars, thinking. The drip of water was steadier yet, the puddle splashing the only sound outside of Han's ragged breathing and the occasional snarl from Havoc.

I wasn't done. I wasn't giving up. I would find a way out of here. That was my choice.

A blow of air and water turned me around. A single eye peered up at me from the puddle. Jor blinked once, then rolled so the corner of his mouth escaped the puddle. "It's too small."

I grabbed the bars. "Jor!"

"Heard you were talking to my brother. Now he wants in on the coffee dates!" Jor blew the words out with a blast of water.

"Stop wrecking the puddle!" Bebe motioned at Jor, then looked over at me. "You think you can make more water? The pipe runs over your head."

I was up and climbing my cage before she even finished speaking. "Hang on, I'll get it."

Havoc let out a rumbling growl that made my whole body clench but said nothing to me.

He and Han spoke in low tones.

"What will you do?" Han asked. "You care for her, as apparently, I do too. Or I just feel obligated perhaps."

"I will finish what was started all those years ago. Ragnarök will be stopped if she dies now, and all will not be lost." Havoc spoke the words, but there was no conviction in them. No belief.

"Wrong!" Jor blew the word out. "That's no longer

true! Her life changed the rules! Which is why this is such a shit show!"

I hung from the top of my cage and reached through. The water pipe was a bit big to get my whole hand around it. I needed to reach through with both hands.

Awkward much. I scrabbled at the pipe with one hand, then jerked myself upward and shot my second hand through the bars to the pipe.

The move slammed my face against the bars, but I managed to get my hands around the pipe. Linking fingers, and holding the pipe as tightly as I could, I lifted my feet so they were set against the bars.

"Here we go." I pushed off the bars, bending the pipe.

I caught my breath, readjusted myself and pushed again, straining with everything I had. The pipe creaked and the straps holding it up loosened.

"Keep going! You got this, you're a bad bitch!" Bebe yelled. "We aren't done yet!"

I tipped my head back and pushed, baring my teeth. She was right. We weren't done yet.

I was a bad bitch. The strain on my muscles increased, my hands bit into the metal, and a scream bubbled up as I fought with the steel. The scream burst from my lips, and it turned into a howl that ripped from me. The sound seemed to shake the entire room, as if the cage was made of a giant tuning fork.

The pipe let go, and I fell, catching myself on the top of my cage as the water poured in around me, soaking me.

Jor burst up out of the now massive puddle outside my cell door. "Coffee dates forever!"

I dropped to the floor. "Can you get me the key?"

Jor grinned, flashing his teeth. "What about the boys?"

What about them indeed? Well. There was only one option I could see.

"We take them with us. But we have to tie Havoc up."

Jor laughed. "Kinky, I like it!"

The key turned out to be Jor's mouth. He bit down on the steel and ripped one of the bars clean out of the cage. Bebe's cage was not made of steel, and I was able to pull the wooden slats free on my own.

Then we turned to Havoc and Han.

"I will kill you if you open this cage," Havoc said. Warning or promise?

I chose to believe that it was a warning.

"Right. I need you not to do that or you'll never get to touch me again." I turned away as I searched the dungeon. Surely there was a set of cuffs, or something for binding a person. What self-respecting dungeon master didn't have manacles?

"Here!" Bebe called from a corner. "There's something here that might help."

What she'd found was not manacles.

Two axes, one double headed, one single headed, rested against the wall. "What do you want me to do with those?"

"You could threaten him with it," Bebe said.

"Yeah, but he'd just take it from you." Jor looked over my shoulder. "I mean, no offense, but he's pretty strong."

Han groaned. "You are an alpha, are you not?"

"Yes."

"Then command him to obey you."

I looked at Han. "Do you believe that would work?"

He shrugged and grinned. "Maybe? You're an alpha, and essentially a Norse demi-god. Give it a try."

I did as Han suggested, but I could tell it wasn't working. I didn't need to have a connection with Havoc to see he was faking it as he tried to smile at me.

The smile kept turning into a snarl.

"You're a terrible actor."

He grunted and shook his head.

Jor's coiled body let out a deep shudder that rippled his length. "Let me talk to my sister, she might be able to help."

He left, diving back into the water that still puddled on the floor. I wasn't sure Hel was the answer, despite what Proferia and Helestia had said.

"I don't even know what I'm supposed to do here." I looked at Bebe. "Come on, let's see what we can find."

"You're just going to leave me here?" Han groaned.

"For now, yes." I turned my back and Havoc growled, the sound going right through me. I clutched at the doorway and forced my legs to keep going. If he howled I was going to use one of those axes and...and what? Not kill him.

Because I could still feel his breath across my skin as he'd told me to get away. To kill him if I was given the chance. If our roles were reversed, I didn't think he'd be able to kill me any more than I could kill him.

Not now, not with the memories we'd shared. Not with the choice I'd made. He was it for me, end of story, I just had to figure out how we were going to make it work.

Bebe and I jogged up a set of stairs that led out into a large open space that was tiled in black marble. Or maybe it was just carved into black marble? The air was cool still, and the blue frothing lava poured along through a channel that bisected the black marble room.

A throne sat at one end.

The other was an open doorway, a light glimmering and beckoning on the other side. I started toward that—it seemed a better beacon than the big black throne of death.

I sighed. "What a fucking mess."

The voice that answered me was not Bebe's.

"You have no idea."

22

ROTTEN TO THE CORE

I spun to see Sven sitting on the black throne. Next to him stood a wolf I knew all too well.

Kieran.

"Kill her." Sven waved his hand in my direction and Kieran took no time in racing toward me.

I shifted, pulling on both my golden and my wolf without thinking, and they merged with ease. I needed them both and they combined as I landed on all fours. Kieran slammed into me, and I spun, diverting his larger weight so that we danced around one another.

"You should have died years ago," he snapped. The darkness in his eyes, the demon, or spell, or whatever it was that had a hold of him had enveloped the brother I'd once known.

I didn't answer him. I didn't need to. He would die here.

The strand that had been his life in the Norn's tree had shown me his death and it was now.

Teeth and claws, we tackled and bit one another. I kept my chin tight to my chest, protecting my neck where I could.

Bebe tried darting in, but I snapped at her to stay out of the way. Not because she wasn't amazing, but I couldn't be distracted. And if she got hurt, I wasn't sure I could focus on what I had to do.

This was the moment that had been coming for so many years.

He'd hurt me.

A hundred times he'd hurt me, beating me until I was unconscious.

He had been Juniper's weapon. The sword she'd held at my neck for so fucking long.

And I'd cowered under his rage.

The golden retriever and the wolf in me were in agreement.

I lowered myself to the black marble and whimpered. Cowering before him. I was a far better actor than Havoc.

Never again. But he didn't know that—he didn't know that I wasn't that woman anymore. That wolf. That I wouldn't run from him.

That I wouldn't let him beat me.

He stalked toward me, panting for air. "Bitch. You

know you can't win. You've never been strong enough. Didn't you learn that when I stuck you with that spear? When we threw you in the river? When I beat you bloody?"

His words struck a hard chord. Pain from the past reared its head, demanding that I see the darkest of my moments—all of them at his hands.

"You should have protected me," I whispered.

"You were never one of us," he growled. "You were *never* going to be one of us."

"I loved you as my brother, you betrayed that trust." I was speaking not to slow him down, but because this was our reckoning. There would be nothing after this.

Because one of us would be dead. And it would not be me.

I kept my eyes lowered, watched his feet step closer. I rolled to my side.

"I never loved you," he growled.

"I would have saved you too," I whispered. And I would have. I would have forgiven him if he'd turned from the darkness.

Forgive me, Mars. I am going to kill your son.

"Don't let her fool you!" Sven snapped.

"You don't know her like I do! She's weak!" Kieran turned his head as he stood over me, exposing his neck. Because he thought I was done. He thought I was weak, just like he said.

How very wrong was he.

There was no moment that would be handed to me like this again.

I leapt up, and latched my jaws onto him like I was one of the scaley-dilly's from the swamp. My teeth cut and crunched through cartilage, crushing his windpipe.

He thrashed, the tips of his claws reaching hard for my belly, but the angle was off. I stood to the side as he fought for his life. I could have killed him, but I held off, something in me telling me to wait. Not a mercy, no...a necessity?

It was as if there were a voice in my head, telling me to wait. It sounded suspiciously like Proferia.

I threw Kieran to the side and stared up at Sven as my brother's body tumbled to a stop.

Sven sighed and stood up, his gangly legs and arms reminding me of the trees I'd run from through the forest of the Norns. At his side a pouch hung, deep green and it...moved. He tracked my eyes.

"Ah, you like it? It's the last bit of my mother."

He opened the pouch and pulled out a shard of a tree. The tree of life. Suvenia. "No."

"The last piece," Sven rolled it in his hands. "I will be the center of all the realms now. I will recreate them in my image. Make them better."

I could do nothing but stare at him. "No, you can't

do this! So many people will die. Sven. You showed me kindness, you can't be this evil. You put cream and sugar in my coffee."

Even as I spoke, I slid from golden wolf back to two legs, crouched on the black marble. The air around me was cold and I had no clothes but as I stood, a long golden gown slid over my body, the material like silk. A belt slid around my waist, a warm band holding me tight.

"I did that because I had no idea who or what you would become." He sighed. "Everything was going as planned. We had Soleil in our sights. I had to get her the night of the dead moon, and I almost did. But then you showed up and stuck your nose in my business."

The marble erupted around me, shards flying every direction.

Bebe cried out and I spun. My legs were caught in my skirts. No, not the skirts, roots.

Roots had ripped through the marble and were wrapping around me, binding my arms and legs together, pinning me in place.

Sven strolled toward me. His face wasn't tight with anger, more resignation. "You see, the realms were always my mother's children. Far more than I was."

Bebe scoffed. "Wait, stop, this is all because you have mommy issues? You're shitting me."

Sven didn't stop walking toward me. He held up the

splinter of the tree that had belonged to the tree of life. "But I think you, Cinniúint, daughter of destiny, have perhaps offered me an even better option. You see if Ragnarök had come to pass, then I would have had to still contend with the same players. But with the tree of life gone...there is nothing to be reborn. So I have a true clean slate from which to build a world as I see fit, in my image. I will be the greatest of all the gods. I will raise up those I see fit, and cast down those who cause harm."

He was right in front of me now. "And you...you are the final piece. Juniper foolishly tied her life to my mother...of course, I gave her the key of how to do it."

His words sunk into me, and I could only stare at him.

Sven smiled. "I had no idea she'd actually done it, when she carried you in her belly no less! Juniper's death assured my own mother's. And I knew you would do it. You had the makings of a great alpha shifter." He lifted a gnarled hand and cupped one side of my face. "And then to carry the sun too? Ah, two blows in one. You killed Juniper, setting us on this path. And now I will kill you, extinguishing the last light of the last sun. Perfection."

I stared up at him, my thoughts racing. "You don't know that the world will end with my death."

"No. But you've caused me grief. And that is enough to end you at this point. A bonus to take out the last of the powers that once were. The clean slate that I wish for."

The pain was sudden and sharp beyond anything I'd ever felt before. I hadn't even seen him move until he stepped back from me.

I looked down at my chest. Blood bloomed over my left side, spilling down the gown as if it wouldn't sink into the material.

"No!" Bebe screamed. "NO, take me instead! Please! Don't...don't let her die!"

I blinked, my vision going fuzzy, rapidly. "Don't stop fighting, Bebe," I whispered, reaching for her. If I could give her the sun, we might still have a chance. But she was bound as tightly as me and we couldn't touch. "I'll...see you on the other side, my friend."

Her scream was guttural, as if torn from her very chest, and I knew from the depth and volume of it she'd shifted back to two legs. The roots slid from around my body, and I went to the ground. Or I would have if not for Bebe.

She caught me first. Someone else had their hands on my body, helping to lower me down.

"Take it," I whispered.

"Then she will die too," Sven laughed. "It is over."

I stared up into Bebe's eyes that streamed with tears. "Please don't leave me," she whispered.

But I couldn't see her anymore. My vision was dark

and though I knew she was shaking me, it was no good.

I slipped into the darkness of the beyond. I floated there, no pain, no thoughts, just nothing.

"So, my son thought stabbing you with the last cutting off my tree was smart? What a fool."

23

REDEMPTION OF THE DEAD

I stared at the spirit of the tree of life. Suvenia stood with me in a space of nothing, with light shimmering around the spirit of the tree of life, and that was all I could truly see. There was no tree, no threads reaching out to the nine realms.

Nothing.

"We've got to quit meeting like this."

Suvenia laughed softly, the wooden bark of her face crinkling. "Your loved ones are still waiting for you, back there, you aren't dead yet. We shouldn't leave them waiting long. But I need to give you this, and my son foolishly gave me a way to do so when he stabbed you with the last of my body."

She held out her hand and pressed something round and hard into my palm. I looked down on the seed. It was a deep brown, but tiny flecks of silver sparkled through it as I rolled my palm. "It's beautiful."

"It is my last seed. Plant it close to your heart, where love flows, and wind caresses, where peace finds you, and the sun gives its...*all*. It will be safe there for three years."

I clutched at the seed, holding it tight to me. "This...this will save the realms?"

She shrugged. "Given time and given a proper caretaker. The realms will be unstable for those three years, but that is not terribly new. Three years after planting it, you will need to re-plant it."

"I kill green things," I whispered, horror filling me. This was almost worse than if I'd been asked to go on an epic quest to save the world. That was possible, that was something I could at least attempt.

Me keeping a green *anything* alive was not.

Her smile was gentle. "You must *find* the proper caretaker, I do not think it will be you. You will know the person. This seed needs love. And care. And sacrifice. To help it grow and take hold, a gift of life freely given before it is planted. Then, when the first blooms come upon it, it will be strong enough to go on a final journey to be replanted at the center of the realms."

Her words were a little bit overwhelming, but through it all I heard only one thing. There was a chance to save the worlds, to save the tree of life itself.

To set things right that I'd put into motion when I'd killed Juniper.

I held tight to the seed. Avoiding the question I really wanted to ask.

"Why would my mother bind herself to you? It didn't save her."

Her sigh was heavy. "She thought it would give her power. But she—and my son—do not understand everything. The fact that he stabbed you with what was left of me proves it."

"Once he understood what she'd done, he knew I would kill her one day." I frowned. "And in killing her, it would shatter your life force."

"I believe so, though it was only recently he learned what she did. He gave her knowledge of how to make and steal mate bonds, many years ago, for a price of course, but even he didn't know what she'd done until he went back to Grayling with Han." She dipped her head in my direction. "What he did not take into account was that you were a child of destiny—that every choice you make creates a ripple in the world. You threw a curve ball, as they say."

Her words solidified what I'd been thinking. "That's a shit power."

"I don't think so." Her smile was gentler than when I'd first met her. "We all make choices, yours just…hold more oomph to them. They interact with destiny because of the way your life is tied to the world. It's an unusual ability. But not shit."

I knew I had time here, but even with the time, I was anxious to get back to the others.

"And Ragnarök?"

"I do believe that you have changed too many things...new prophecies will be laid out by the Norns, a new oracle will be born. New heroes will rise. New monsters will challenge them."

I grimaced. "You mean it's not really over yet?"

She shook her head. "The story is never truly over. But your story...your story is nearing the end."

That took me to the question I didn't want to ask.

"And the sacrifice you mentioned, needed to start the seed growing?"

Sad, she looked so sad, and I knew what she was going to say before it ever came out of her mouth. "The life of one taken, the life of one given, and the heart of a warrior."

I swallowed hard. "The three wolves, like the journal."

She dipped her head. "Three souls, yes. Go to the center of Hel's home, to the vortex. Cast the sacrifices there. The energy will disperse to the seed, you only have to make that choice."

I didn't want to leave her, not because I was happy here, but because I knew what waited for me out *there*.

In Hel's realm I would have to say my hardest goodbyes yet.

She leaned in and pressed her forehead to mine. "Trust, young one. Trust in your heart and your instincts."

I drew a deep breath, the scent of wood and woodlands sinking into me. The pain of being stabbed returned to me full force as I left the spirit of the tree of life and found myself cradled carefully in Bebe's arms. I glanced down. The splinter was gone, transformed into the seed that was now inside of me.

"Not by a long shot," Hel said.

Everything was fast, so very fast. Like the world had sped up.

I knew what I had to do, but sending Bebe away… that would be the first step. My mouth felt full, as I lay there, and I rolled the seed around in my mouth. Carefully I pulled it free, and Bebe gasped.

"Cin! Cin! Talk to me! The wooden stake is gone! You're alive! Hel showed up, and she took care of Sven. But you were still dead!"

She clutched me to her, and I returned the hug. Over her shoulder I could see that Sven was still there, trapped in a box of ice. And boy did he look pissed.

I closed my eyes and held my friend for a moment.

"I need you to take this, Bebe." My voice was cut with pain as the wound pulled and stretched. I lifted the seed to my mouth and released the sun into it. The seed began to glow, warm with the power of the sun. "Please, everyone's life depends on it."

Bebe took the seed and stared at it. "You aren't coming?"

I shook my head. "I need you to go plant it, right now. Near the pond. And then...ask Bob and George to look out for it."

Bebe was shaking her head. "No, I can't leave you! Wait, who's Bob?"

"Bob is a good friend of mine. He's got a green thumb. And you have to do this. I can't."

"I left you once already, I won't do it again!" She leaned into me. "Don't ask me..."

"You are my second in command, Bebe. I am telling you as your alpha to go and plant this seed. You can't help with the rest of this journey." I pressed it into her hands.

With everything I had, I pulled away from her and stood, barely able to keep my feet under me. I locked my knees, my one hand still tangled with hers.

Bebe stayed on the floor where she was. "I can't...I promised."

"I know. But you need to do this now."

I looked at Hel. "Would you mind taking her?"

Hel sighed. "I suppose. You don't want Jor to take her?"

I shook my head. "She needs to go now."

Hel dipped her head. "Seeing as you've just come

back from near death, and Ragnarök is no longer on the table because of you, I will do this."

The death goddess reached over to Bebe and took her by the hand. Bebe stared at me. "Cin, you're my best—"

They disappeared. I swallowed hard. One down.

"Jor," I said, "can you help me get to the vortex at the center of Hel?"

Jor's body quivered. "That's a place we don't go unless..."

"Unless we're going to sacrifice something," Han said.

Havoc stepped toward me, and I stepped back. "I am going to die. That's what you want, isn't it? That's the spell that Sven wove into you?" That gave me pause as I glanced at the ass who'd spelled Havoc. "What if we killed him?"

Jor chuckled. "See, this is why I like you. You seem kind, and then you're like...let's kill that prick!"

Havoc's jaw tensed and his hands twitched as if it were taking everything in him to not strangle me right there. "It would remove it."

Sven was locked in a block of ice, and I could feel my life leaking out of me. There was no time to thaw him out, and light him on fire. I didn't have that kind of magic.

I sighed. "Awesome. Jor, can you take me?"

He slid toward me and lowered himself so I could

more easily swing a leg over his thick body. "I don't like this. You mean to die then? Really?"

"I don't want to, but it's the sacrifice the tree of life demands to live on." I steadied myself on his back and turned to look at Han and Havoc.

One life taken. "We can toss Sven in; he can be the life taken seeing as he caused all this. That should kill him."

And Havoc would be free for a few moments.

Jor's tail flicked out and he wrapped it around the block of frozen tree man that was Sven.

I swallowed hard. "I need one of you to...sacrifice yourself with me."

Han's chin dropped to his chest. "Fuck. I should have known. We are...the three of us are tied so tightly together..."

Havoc didn't look away from me. "One of us dies. Not just you."

I nodded slowly. "Yes."

"Good."

That was...not quite the answer I'd been expecting.

He moved toward Jor and leapt up behind me, his hands went around my waist, his warmth and proximity too much. It was dangerous, but I leaned back into him, peace flowing over my skin as I just allowed myself to *be* in that moment with him. "Just don't kill me before we get there."

Han shook his head. "This is fucked up. Can't we just offer a pint of blood or something?"

"I agree," Jor grumbled. "This is stupid. I lose my coffee friend, and we've only really had one coffee together!"

I patted Jor's scales. "I am sorry, my friend. Take Bebe out for coffee, she will need someone who understands what we've been through. And Richard. Take Richard too."

Jor snorted. "Might as well bring Fen along then. Make it a party."

That thought and resulting image actually made me smile. "I think he would like that."

Han took a step back. "I won't do it."

Of course not. "I can't make you, no one can." Because the point of it was the sacrifice. That's what the tree had said. One life taken. One life sacrificed. A warrior's heart.

My wolf grumbled under my skin, fury lighting her up. My golden seemed to wrap around her, calming her. Whispering that it wasn't the time for rage.

It was time for goodbyes.

Jor started moving across the black marble floor. I let my hands rest on top of Havoc's.

Han watched us, I could feel his eyes on me still. The mate bond was ridiculously still intact for him.

"Goodbye, Princess."

"Goodbye, Han." That at least was an easy goodbye.

I closed my eyes and just leaned against Havoc. His hands twitched. "Is it very hard to control the urge to kill me?"

"Less now that I know what's coming."

Now that he knew I was going to die in a few moments.

He lowered his head to the crook of my neck and pressed his mouth there, the softest of rumbles sliding up from his throat and into me.

There was no orgasmic thrill, no clenching of my body, no screaming of names.

Communion of a different kind, an afterglow without the passion, the knowledge that I'd fought away a fate that would have tied me to the wrong man, to be here in this moment.

That I'd made the choice to love him.

And he'd made the choice to love me.

"Funny," I whispered, my fingers wrapping around his. "Isn't it?"

"What's funny?" Havoc tugged me closer to his body, simply holding me as Jor took us deeper into hell.

"That I had to come all this way, to find out that where I belonged was never a place."

The air whooshed out of him and Jor shivered. "You're going to make me cry."

"I didn't want any of this," Havoc lowered his voice.

"Neither did I."

He pressed his mouth to my neck. "I would choose this path again. I would choose the *pain* again. You were mine from the beginning, Goldie, I knew it and tried so hard to fight it."

Tears slipped out of my control, down my cheeks, falling off my chin and landing on our joined hands. He reached up and brushed his thumb across my face, wiping them away.

"Gods!" Jor snapped. "This is awful! Fucking stupid!" He shivered and his skin kept rippling.

Jor was not happy.

But for just those few minutes, the world was where it needed to be. Or at least my world was. Havoc wasn't trying to kill me. Sven had been stopped. My family was safe.

"You aren't afraid," Havoc said. Of course, his nose was pressed close to my skin, and he would have been able to smell my fear.

"No. I never thought I'd have a long life. Not growing up in Grayling with Juniper for a mother." I turned my head to look him in the eyes. "You aren't afraid either."

"I am with you."

He swallowed hard and his dark eyes flickered, the blue of his wolf there for just a moment. "*I am with you.*"

"We're here. Gods, I hate that we're here," Jor cried and threw himself flat on the ground. Sobbing.

The Midgard serpent, destroyer of worlds had his head flat on the ground and was sobbing as if his heart had been torn free. "I hate this!"

I slid off his back and gave him a gentle pat. "It will be okay, Jor. I promise."

"No, don't make me promises you can't keep!" Jor snapped, his head coming around. His big eyes were bloodshot, and tears dropped to the ground, sizzling. "You won't be here. Do you know how long it's been since I've had a friend? My family hates me. You understand that. Of all the people..." He tipped his head back and bellowed.

I stepped back from him to see this vortex where my life would end. The ground was a thick green grass that came up to my knees, and all around us were trees that rose hundreds of feet in the air. The forest circled an open hole. Sparks and bits of light trickled up, as if a fire lay in the bottom. I crept closer to the edge.

I'd fully expected the vortex to be fire and darkness, fear and screaming souls.

You know what it fucking well looked like?

A frothing, foaming river, the water was blue and white as it spun and slammed into the side walls of the hole.

"You gotta be shitting me," I whispered. Why was it always a river?

A low growl turned me around. Havoc was hunched. "I can't...I can't fight him."

He held out his hand and his ax appeared, his fingers wrapped around the shaft and he lifted his eyes to mine.

Only it wasn't his eyes looking back at me. They were neither black or blue.

They were dark brown and sparkled with malice.

I looked past Havoc to where Sven stood at the tail end of Jor. Dethawed.

Grinning.

Because he had us all now.

24

WOOD DOESN'T ALWAYS FLOAT

Sure, I knew I was going to have to jump into a vortex of water, my last dive into a river so that I could give whatever energy up to the seed. But I had a feeling that letting Havoc kill me via Sven would not be quite the same thing.

"Havoc. Listen to me." I held my hands to my side. "You can fight him. You love me. I know you do."

"He can't." Sven laughed. "That is the beauty of my spell, it taps into his *purpose*. His reason for existing was to kill the one who carried the sun. You are the last, Cinniúint. You are the one he is destined to kill."

Destined.

I stared up at Havoc. "No, I was always his destiny, but not to kill me."

He lifted the axe and I stepped toward him, caught his face in my hand and kissed him.

Our first and last kiss.

Sven was laughing. Jor was swearing. But they faded away as I breathed in my choice.

Havoc was my choice. He was the destiny I chose.

And no one could take that from me.

The clatter of the axe hitting the ground, then his arms went around me, and he leaned into the kiss, his tongue and lips claiming mine for his own.

Mine. Mine. Mine.

"Cin." He growled my name and held me to his chest. "You...you broke the spell."

"That's impossible!" Sven bellowed.

We turned together to face the woodland king. "People keep saying that to me." I smiled. "But I don't think that word means what you think it means."

Jor snickered.

I looked up at Havoc. "I wish..."

"I know."

"I'll kill you both then."

We turned as Sven rushed us. His body exploded with roots and branches shooting toward us, flying daggers of sharpened wood, too many to avoid.

Havoc spun, putting his back to the certain death.

"NO!" Jor bellowed and threw himself between us and Sven.

"Jor!" I screamed his name as the hundreds of wooden spears still attached to Sven ripped through the big serpent.

He writhed and rolled, humping his body so he didn't crush us as he flung himself, and Sven toward the edge of the vortex.

Jor's eyes found mine as his big body slipped over the edge. He clung there a moment. "I'll see you, coffee date."

I reached for him. "I'll see you wherever the other side is, my friend."

He let out one last bellow. "It was worth it. I will feed the tree of life. I give my life freely." And then he let go of the edge and disappeared.

"I do not!" Sven screeched and screamed and then they were gone, silence slid over the space.

Trembling, I stood there in Havoc's arms.

Havoc tightened his hold on me. "You don't have to—"

I looked up at him. "I think I do. The tree of life… it's about sacrifice. What are we willing to give up, to see all the realms survive?"

His one hand whispered up, slid over my throat and cupped my face. "Then we go together. Wherever this leads, I am with you."

I stepped into his arms again, and whatever fear had started to curl through me slid away. Okay, maybe not all away. But I could do this.

For Bebe. Richard. Shipley. Mars. For those I loved, as few as they might be, this was a small cost to save them all.

Havoc stepped back and held out his hand to me. I wove my fingers tight with his. "Together. I choose you, Havoc. In this life, and whatever comes next. I choose you."

His smile curled up one side of his face. "Through fire and pain, I chose you, Cin. You are the crucible of destiny that I would cast myself into a thousand times."

A deep breath slid from me as I took the first step toward the edge. Perhaps a tiny part of me thought maybe…maybe someone would come and stop us. Maybe Hel would show up, and she would tell us that Jor and Sven had been enough.

Maybe my father, Tyr, would arrive at the last second.

Fuck, I'd even take a Loki intervention.

But there was no one coming this time, and I knew that.

Our toes were at the edge of the vortex. "Like going for another swim," I whispered.

"Only this time, you aren't alone. And neither am I."

I turned my head to look at him. "I'm ready. I give everything I am to the tree of life, to nourish it."

He nodded. "I give everything I am to the tree of life. A willing sacrifice."

The words echoed and the vortex seemed to flash brighter, I thought maybe I saw Bebe on her knees, burying the seed. But maybe I was just seeing what I wanted to.

I squeezed his hand. "I love you, Havoc. See you on the other side."

He growled, "I love you, Goldie."

Together, we took that last step, and fell into the frothing, ice cold of the vortex.

25

LOKI'S PLAN

"You think that heroes are dead, and the love is not real, after this little display?" Loki spread his hands wide at the large screen tv on the wall. Only Odin would want a TV screen that encompassed an entire wall instead of getting a projector.

The entire Norse pantheon had watched Cinniúint and Havoc step off into the vortex. More than a few of the women were openly sobbing.

Tyr stood with his fists on the table, shaking, tears streaking his cheeks.

Loki motioned at the screen. "Two of my grandsons defied me. And one gave his life..." he bit back the quaver in his voice. "Jor saved them...that is the effect she has had on those around her. Showing them pathways that have never existed before. The Midgard serpent...has become a hero. She chose a new destiny for us all."

A few gasps went up around the room. Thor grumbled about stupid serpents.

"She has done what none of us could do," Freya said. "She stopped Ragnarök."

Tyr did not wipe his face. "My daughter saved us all. By throwing every prophecy, every legend into the air and reforming them to follow her heart, the destiny of all changed."

Loki nodded. "She has. And the tree of life has already been replanted. Nourished by the life of those sacrificed. And carrying the power of the sun itself for warmth and strength."

"Bah, poppycock," Odin said.

Every Norse deity turned to him. He purpled a little under his beard.

Petunia crossed her arms. "Have they not proven that even the oldest, and most stubborn of souls can find their way back to the light? Back to a path of destiny that serves us all better than running headlong into an end of the world scenario?"

More grumbling around the room.

"What are you proposing, Loki?"

"Well—"

The doors to the meeting room were flung open and a woman stalked in, her hair wild and her chartreuse eyes flashing. There was no magic to her, and yet she was here.

Doing what she should not have been able to do. All for love.

Loki was impressed and he dipped his head in her direction. He saw Hel peek around the corner. So that was how Bebe got here.

"You will bring my friend back *now!* And Havoc!" Bebe went straight to Tyr. "You're her father, make them bring her back!"

The last word cracked and quivered. Tyr nodded. "We are discussing that."

"No, no discussions! This world would be nothing if she hadn't fought for all of us!" She slapped her hands on the table and leaned forward. "Most of you sat on your lazy asses and watched, did nothing! The few that helped, like Jor—"

"He's dead," Loki said. "He died trying to protect her."

Bebe's hands went to her mouth. "No."

The fact that she grieved his son...gods, she was a woman now, far more so than when he'd met her all those years ago. He tipped his head toward her. "Thank you for that. For grieving him." He almost regretted letting her go, and letting Petunia turn her into a cat.

"If we bring them back, the sacrifice will mean nothing," Freya said. "Then all would be for naught."

Loki held up a finger. "Actually...the demand was for a life taken, a life sacrificed and the heart of a warrior. There is nothing saying that couldn't be less than three lives...and she just needs a gentle push in the right direction."

26

SPLIT PERSONALITY

My feet were on solid ground. The water we'd stepped out and into was frothing around us. As if we stood on a platform and the watery vortex wasn't quite ready to take us in.

All around us, I could see Jor, his body undulating through the watery tornado.

"I'm a hero!" He grinned, flashing his teeth. "My brother is going to freak out!"

I laughed, I couldn't help it. "Jor, you were always my hero!"

He rolled and flashed his belly, then dove deeper into the vortex. I looked to my right. Havoc stood next to me, but his eyes were closed, his face slack as if he were asleep.

"Havoc?" Fear caught at me. How was he out cold, and I was here, like this?

"He's on the cusp of death."

I held on tighter to him as Hel stepped out of the frothing water. The mishappen side of her face was turned toward me. "You both didn't have to get in here, you know. One more sacrifice was all it would take."

"If you think I could have made him stay behind, you're welcome to send him out."

Hel huffed. "My nephew is a stubborn one."

A smile flicked over my mouth. "Yes. But you didn't come here to tell me something I already knew. Did you?"

She shook her head. "No. I came to offer you my father's plan."

The mark on my neck burned, flaring to life so hot that I slapped at my neck, yanking my hand from Havoc's. "What's happening?"

"A choice, a different kind of sacrifice," Hel said and shoved me into the swirling water.

My eyes closed and I saw them immediately.

My golden retriever and my wolf. They sat at my feet staring up at me. The golden's tongue lolled out as she smiled up at me. My wolf's black fur was sleek and her face calm as she took me in.

Hello, sister.

I blinked and crouched, holding my arms out to them. "Hello ladies."

The golden's joy was instant and she launched

herself at me, licking and climbing in my lap, fighting to get as close to me as she could.

My wolf was more reserved. But as she stepped forward, she rested her chin on my shoulder. I swung my arms around her neck and held her tight, breathing her in. She was the side of me that I'd leaned on my whole life. The reason I was alive.

Sister. You have a choice to make.

The golden's voice was soft and gentle, almost a hum under my skin.

"What choice? That's what Hel said."

My wolf sat down again but put her paw on my leg. *The choice is simple. One sacrifice taken. That was the woodland king. One sacrifice freely given. That was the Midgard Serpent. The sacrifice of a warrior's heart. The sacrifice does not have to be a death.*

I stared at her. "What...what are you saying?"

The other gods think that you can sacrifice one of us. Give up your connection to a piece of you...that it will be enough. The golden sat next to my wolf, her big brown eyes sad as she spoke. *I will be sad to leave you. But...it will be best. I know I was an accident.*

I shook my head. "I...you mean I would go back. I would be alive? What about Havoc?"

He will be given a choice as well. He will have to give up something if he wishes to survive. But we do not know what that might be. My wolf let out a heavy sigh, her eyes flicking to the golden.

As if she were saying goodbye. "But I...I need you both," I whispered. "You both bring strength to me."

My wolf, my beautiful wolf let out a long, mournful howl that echoed in my bones, a goodbye that I did not want to have. *But only one of us understood that you needed to find your heart. That you needed to find joy. My time with you is done, sister. I protected you when you needed that. I fought for you when you needed that. But now...you are safe.*

The golden sat up. *No. You agreed. I have only been with her a short time! I am grateful for the time I had with you both.*

My wolf huffed and butted her head against the golden. *I know her better than you. It is you she needs now.*

I stared at my two sides, the light and the dark. I reached for my wolf and she stepped back. *Let me go, sister. Let me go to protect the tree of life. To be the guardian I was born to be. It is the last sacrifice that you will be asked to make for a long, long time. And it is a worthy calling for me.*

I could do nothing but bow my head and sob. Not because I didn't love the golden, but because my wolf... she had been my only friend, my only family for so many years. How was I to live without her?

I am still here. The golden tucked her head under my chin and all but crawled into my lap. *I am with you.*

I clung to her, my tears dropping into her thick fur,

unable to find the words. Finally, I managed to whisper what I needed to say, choking the words out. "I sacrifice my wolf to the tree of life."

A howl ripped through the still air, reverberating through me, to my bones and back again, tearing free of me. As loud as it was, the howl cut off, and my wolf was gone.

I'd let her go.

27

THE END. MAYBE

I was staring up at the underside of a tree whose branches spread wide across my vision. Lines of color and varying thickness sparkled and danced like those I'd seen at the foot of the Norns.

Lifelines flared and I saw my brothers, I saw Bebe, I even saw Han.

They were alive and well.

I blinked and the vision was gone, and the cold of the ground made itself known to me. I groaned and rolled to my side, breathing in the smells all around me. Living things, dirt, stagnant water.

I pushed to my feet slowly, taking in the fact that I was naked, and smelled as ripe as the things around me. "Where the fuck am I?"

I think we're back in Alaska. My golden said, her voice gentle.

That was new. "You...you can talk to me now?"

Until you don't need me in that way. We thought it best.

How the hell did you hug a piece of yourself? I started to walk, picking the easiest path through the trees. The scenery looked familiar. "Thank you."

I got you. The golden huffed and I could feel her joy at being with me. Her absolute fucking joy oh...look. A pond. The pond behind the bookstore.

My feet were moving before I could stop myself. I dove into the water and came up squealing. "That's... not what I wanted to do!"

Sorry not sorry! This is an amazing pond, can we come and swim here often?

I laughed. "Sure."

Wading out of the pond, I headed toward the back of the bookstore. I was alive.

The world was saved.

"Cin!"

The screech spun me around. Bebe was running in cat form straight for me. I held my arms out and she leapt into them, her panic and relief bubbling out of her. "Oh my gods, you did it! You're back! I was so fucking worried don't you ever do that to me again, girlfriend!"

I held her tight and lifted her to my shoulder. "I need to get some clothes."

"And ice cream. We can at least have that, right?" She clung to me, her claws digging at me mercilessly.

Up the back stairs I went while Bebe chattered on and on, telling me how she'd gone to Asgard and demanded that they send me back to her. How Hel had dropped her off and then disappeared, and it had been Tyr who'd delivered her back to earth.

"You went to bat for me, Bebe." I set her down on the back of the couch. "You're the best friend I have ever had. You know that, right?"

"Best. Bitches. Ever." She grinned.

I showered—damn it, my hair was a mixture of blonde and black like I'd just kind of gone crazy with the highlights. The mark of Loki was still there but faded. Like a pale scar. I had a new mark around my wrist that looked like a light green tattoo. The scales wrapped around my wrist, and Jor's eyes stared up at me from the underside of my wrist. "Hello, friend," I whispered, running my fingers over the mark.

"Anything you want to tell me?" I said once I was in clean sweatpants and a sweatshirt and curled up on the couch with a hot tea.

"What do you mean?" Bebe sat next to me, making biscuits against my hip, as if she'd massage my fatigue away all by herself.

I frowned at her. "Are you something more than you've told me? Like what Han and Havoc said about you being more than you have admitted to?"

She didn't shift into two legs. She curled up next to me. "No. I'm not magic like that. I'm...hell...I'm human,

Cin. Or I was. But I've been trapped as a cat with Petunia's magic a long fucking time. Longer than I let on. And I think...I feel like it's changed me. Shouldn't I have aged? Cause I haven't."

"How long has it been?"

She grimaced. "It makes me look bad. Like how long it took me to break the curse, to love someone truly."

"How long, Bebe?"

"About thirty years." She flattened her ears to her head. "So I'm close to your age then."

"Maybe you'll find out you have more magic than you thought," I said. "Who knows?"

She began to purr. "I hate to admit it, but I'm almost more comfortable being a cat than a woman now. I mean there are times being a woman rocks of course but in between the hot and heavy this is pretty good."

I hadn't dared to see if my connection to Havoc was alive. I was afraid of what I would find. Or worse, what I wouldn't. I needed a distraction.

"I had to give up my wolf," I blurted the words out.

She gasped. "That...that was what they made you give up?"

"I had a choice, and my wolf made it for me. She knew that I needed my golden more. That I needed to know joy and love, compassion. That my time with my wolf was done; she'd taught me all she could."

Yup, broke down crying right there. Bebe shifted to two legs, grabbed some clothes and held me while I sobbed. So much grief, and like Bebe, so much gratitude. I had my golden. I had Bebe. But there was someone missing.

"I don't even know if Havoc made it. He said he'd follow me into death; what if they didn't tell him that I didn't actually die? He wouldn't have..."

She stroked my hair and held me close. "You'll find him, Cin. I know you will."

I wanted to believe her. I wanted to believe I would find him.

I just didn't know how. Because when I finally looked at the bonds I had tied to me, he wasn't there.

THREE WEEKS later I was in the bookstore, helping sort out a new order. Denna was back, having made a long trip across the country, and pissed that we left her out of everything. But I also saw the relief in her that she hadn't had to face anything else terrifying.

She was a good friend.

Bebe lounged across the coffee table in front of Richard. As far as I knew, my brother didn't realize that she could shift to two legs. I didn't ask what Bebe was waiting for.

Ship had gone back to Grayling, to try and pull the pack together. He wasn't as strong an alpha as me or

Richard, but I understood that he wanted to try and make his way in the world, without Juniper.

No one had seen or heard from Mars. Richard said he could sense him, but there was a feeling of distance. Like Mars didn't want to be found.

That cut deep, but I couldn't make Mars want to be here. He had his own life to live. Maybe he was trying to figure out how to undo his curse too.

Havoc's pack was gone. Berek and Claire had gone the second I'd taken Jor up on his ride across the world via my back pond. Not that I blamed them. I'd have kicked Claire's ass for helping Havoc at that point.

Han was...no longer my mate. There was no mate bond of any sort attached to me. So wherever he was, he was on his own. And strangely, I found myself wishing him luck.

Maybe now that he was free of Sven's spell, he could find a path that was truly his own.

"This little seed is ah-mazing!" Bob held up the small pot. He'd dug the tree of life out of the spot Bebe had buried it, found a beautiful golden pot and replanted it. "Look at how much this beauty has grown already!"

He wasn't wrong. The tree had sprouted up several inches in the first week. The wood was still quite green, which meant there was no way to see what the final bark color would be. Mahogany. Oak. Fir. Cedar. But always, there was a glow around it, the sun peeking through the bits of bark and tiny green shoots.

I stroked a finger over the budding leaves, feeling a deep connection to the plant. "She is a beauty."

The softest tones, like a distant howl rippled through me from the tree. My golden huffed in recognition. I put a hand to my chest. My wolf was still with me, as long as the sapling was here.

"Oh, did I tell you, Cin, about the new guy in town?" Bob set the tree of life down (no, he had no idea what it truly was). "He's de-lic-ious. You should see if he would take you out on a date. As long as it isn't another brother of yours come to town." He made a gesture to Richard. "They are handsome, your brothers."

The door tinkled behind us and Bob gasped. "From my lips to god's ears. Tell me he isn't related to you."

I turned and time slowed and the only thing I could see was Havoc. He hadn't lost the scar over his eyes…eyes that were now darkness ringed in blue as if his wolf had merged more fully with him. He never looked away from me as I walked toward him, and slid my arms around his neck.

I wondered what he'd given up to be here. To be with me.

The rest of the world fell away as his arms wrapped around me. "I chose you," I whispered.

He smiled down at me. "Good thing. Because I'm

not going anywhere, Goldie. Though I'm mortal now, so let's not do any more near-death trips."

"Deal." I smiled up at him.

My golden about turned inside out, her joy flooding me, pushing back the grief and sadness, the fear and uncertainty. I leaned into her emotions as he pressed his mouth to mine, the joy flooding us both.

Giving us the happily ever after we both deserved.

For now.

ACKNOWLEDGMENTS

Cin's story was meant to be longer, and it was strange for me to have her tell me that she was done with her story in just three books. But...I realized that it was because she'd grown so much in the time her story took place. Going from a place of fear and loneliness where she let her wolf lead and fight with everything she had, to finding a place of peace and letting her golden show her that love was still possible, and that joy could be found, even after the darkest hours of her life.

Sometimes we must find our wolf to survive what the world throws at us, to bare our teeth and howl into the oncoming storm that we will not be broken, that we are the warriors our ancestors need us to be, to break the cycles we have been born into.

And then when the time comes, we must be brave enough to gently lay our wolf down, and embrace a softer side when the battles are done. We need to recognize when it is time to breathe deeply and start fresh, where we don't have to fight so fucking hard to be safe, loved, and cherished.

I hope...that for everyone who has read this, for everyone who has resonated deeply with Cin and understood that you must survive at all costs, that you find your golden...you find your peace, you see the joy in this world again, and that above all else, you find your heart and the safe place to rest it.

CONNECT WITH ME

Email me at Shannon@shannonmayer.com or find me on social media.

FACEBOOK READER GROUP:
Mayer's Magnificent Readers

Join my newsletter for updates on upcoming books, behind the scenes info, and exclusive content.

instagram.com/hijinksink
tiktok.com/@hijinksink

CAGED BY FATE

(FREE PREVIEW)

DIANA

Sixty years ago...

The forest was blooming with color and scent, the sound of small animals scurrying ahead of me, the feel of a late spring breeze tangling through my hair. I breathed it in, letting the earth center me when all I wanted to do was rage.

I slowed my feet and closed my eyes, fighting the urges threatening to take over. Still, the blood in me ran hot, vampire and werewolf combined, and after all these years, I struggled with keeping myself in check.

My mind dipped back to the argument with my father earlier today, which only spiked my heart rate again.

"You need to find a mate. That is our way, Diana." Lycan didn't move from his spot behind the big wooden table. His breakfast was spread in front of him, and he barely lifted his head as he spoke.

"No. I don't," I bit back. "There is none that so much as flicker my interest."

"Not even Lochlin?"

I snorted. "He's a brother to me. A cousin. Not a lover."

Lycan tipped his head to the side. "Our pack is not just you and me. I am king, Diana. And one day when I am gone, you will reign as queen and you will need an heir."

I barked a laugh, though my ire rose with each of his words. "Perhaps I will make myself an heir, as you did."

His face closed off. "Do not mock—"

"I'm not. I am the last of your children, but I was not born here. Why can I not—"

His fist hit the table, making every plate on it jump, and the legs below groan. "Because of what you are. That will never be forgotten no matter how many years pass. Even now, there are whispers that I should not trust you."

My heart felt as though an icy fist reached through my chest and took hold. "And do you trust me?"

"Of course I do!" he bellowed. "Even if any of your siblings had survived, I still would have named you my heir. And I would not have named you heir had you not been the best choice! But there are some who will never trust you. Some who only see you for what you once were."

My wolf inside of me, she fought to break free, to unleash on those others.

In part because they were not entirely wrong. I was a werewolf, but I had not always been. Born as a half-human, half-vampire, biologically the daughter to the vampire king, my blood was stained in the eyes of my pack. Even though I'd undergone the most brutal of changes to become a werewolf in truth, burning the vampire blood out of my body... it was not enough, even now.

"I have defended the pack against our enemies, and that includes the vampires." My voice deepened, as I fought to keep my wolf in check. "I have been obedient to my king, and done everything in my power to serve our people!"

Lycan grunted and went back to eating, but I knew him. Knew that this conversation was not done.

Soon enough, he spoke again. This time, with a note of finality in his voice that made my stomach turn.

"Find a mate, Diana. This is not your father speaking, but your king. It is a must. I don't care if you love him. I don't care if he means nothing to you and is just a trophy. But do it. Before the year is out."

I knew a dismissal when I heard one.

Spinning on my heel, I'd left at a good clip, heading for the deep forest bordering us on the north.

And so here I was, feeling sorry for myself.

"A mate I do not love."

I opened my eyes and kept walking, finding myself in the graveyard, beyond the black willows that wept with us when our dead were buried. Past the north creek, and deeper still until I stood on the border between us and the angels. Angelic in nature in only their own minds.

What had drawn me here?

My mate?

I laughed at myself. "You're a romantic fool."

The crack of a twig spun me around and I dropped to a crouch, my hand going to the knife at my belt. Shifting would take too long. But a blade would protect me just fine.

Movement across the border stilled me further, and I lowered myself until I was almost flat to the ground.

Stumbling, a man tripped over a log and fell, sprawled out on his belly. He should have sprung up, but he didn't move. A low groan slid out of him, a sound that cut into me. Whoever he was, he was clearly injured and in pain.

Did I dare try to help him? He was still technically on the other side of the border...

I pushed myself back into a low crouch and peered over the brilliant, orange poppies that hid him from view.

Face up, he'd rolled onto his back as he'd fallen.

I just stared at him, not sure why I couldn't look away. His hair was long, a deep brown, and in a few places around his face it was braided, beads set into the ends. His face was covered in a bit of scruff that hid the fact that he was a bit baby-faced still—as if anyone couldn't see that from the smooth skin of his cheeks.

His shirt was peeled open and large gashes ran in patterns over his chest.

Demon sign. He'd have had to cross at least two borders to get here.

"Fuck," I whispered. I crept forward. Demons did not mark their own like that. They marked captives. I was on the edge of the border when the sound of wings snapped my head up, the animals around us going silent.

Decision time, Diana. Help him, or leave him?

I had my hands under his arms and was dragging him across the border before I even had a chance to change my mind. Bending at the knees, I scooped him up over my shoulders and ran back the way I'd come.

A screech in the air behind us set the hair on the back of my neck on end.

Why was I risking my life for this human? Because human he was, I could smell it all over him.

A second screech ripped through the air, and I had no choice. I set down the human and wheeled around to face the incoming demon. Demons running through the territory held by their high and mighty cousins? What was going on?

"You cross our border, and you will start a war!" I yelled as the demon ducked in and out of the trees, weaving through darkness.

"Ah, but you took something of mine, little wolf! He did not make it to your lands."

I grinned, baring my teeth. "Finders keepers."

"Then prepare to weep," the demon laughed and shot toward me, wings and body coming into view as the shadows around his—no, her—body gave way. She flung a five-pointed star at me and I knocked it from the air with my blade. The clink of metal on metal rippled through the air.

She did not slow, and I met her head-on, weaving and ducking to one side so I could grab a hold of one, black wing. Digging my fingers in, I gripped the leathered skin and yanked hard, dragging her off course and away from the human.

"He's mine!" she shrieked.

The wolf in me howled, and I snarled back. "No. He's *mine*."

We went down in a tangle of limbs and claws. I wasn't just fighting for my life, I was fighting for his —even if I didn't understand this need to protect him.

Her fingers raked across my neck, grappling for a hold on me. She slid through a shadow, her body turning into smoke, only to solidify behind me. Her one hand was around my neck, the other my head.

I knew I was about to have my neck snapped like a pencil. Father would have to select another heir. Maybe he'd choose one who could find a mate. Despite my maudlin thoughts, there was no regret. If I had to do it again, I'd have done the same. Something about saving this human felt like...my destiny.

Behind me the demon stiffened, and a gargled shriek slid out of her. Her hands loosened on my neck and she fell to the ground twitching.

Behind her stood the human male, a glowing blade in his hands. His eyes slowly lifted to mine. One blue, one green.

"Are you...all right?" He swayed where he stood, asking if I was okay.

I looked down at the demon. "Y-you saved my life."

"You saved mine first." He shrugged. "It was nothing."

Only it was more than that, it was very much something. "Stay here."

He popped off a jaunty salute with the hand that still held the glowing knife, and then slumped to his knees.

"Don't mind if I do. I...don't feel particularly well."

His chest was still oozing blood, but it was the rivulets running down the side of his face from his hairline that had me worried.

Shit.

"I have to move the demon's body. I'll be right back. Don't move."

I wanted to ask him his name, ask him what he was doing here, ask him how he came in possession of a blade that could kill a demon with such ease...all the things. But I had to get rid of this corpse first. If it was found on our lands, war would break out, and it would be all my fault. That wouldn't do at all.

Scooping up the body, I took it to the river. The waters ran into the angel's lands and from there to their demon cousins. The current would carry her home as well as wash away some of mine and the human's scent. Perhaps the combination of distance and time in the water would be enough. The fact that she was killed by a blade that I had no knowledge of would help.

I hoped.

Once she'd floated well out of sight, I made my way back to where the human knelt. I found him motionless, his chin dropped to his chest.

For just a moment my heart seemed to stutter. Had he died while I'd been gone? I hurried to where he was and dropped to my own knees beside him.

"Hey! Wake up. Please wake up!"

He startled and the blade came up so fast, I didn't have time to move. For the second time in the space of only a few minutes, I was sure I was going to die.

He had the blade pressed to my throat, the steel of it glowing a bright bluish-white. But he didn't cut me as his wild eyes tried to focus. "Who are you?"

"Diana," I said, my throat moving against the blade. "And I just saved your life, remember?"

His jaw and throat worked and his eyes fluttered closed. I yanked the blade out of his hand and tucked it into my belt as he slumped forward, his head landing on my shoulder. "Maverick. My name is Maverick."

"Well, Maverick, seems like you've found yourself in a bit of trouble."

"Thought you said your name was Diana," he mumbled.

A laugh huffed out of me as I stood and helped him to his feet.

The moon was high in the sky by the time we made it to one of the old and rarely-used hunting lodges that dotted the Territory. I had brushed the cobwebs off the bed and tucked him in with a coarse blanket before heading over to the keep. It didn't take long for me to dig through the laundry sent down the chutes and recover a pair of pants and a shirt that smelled like Hamish, one of the guards. Hopefully, between the remote location and Hamish's clothes making his scent, that would be enough to keep anyone from finding him.

A tiny part of me wondered why I was hiding him,

but I already knew. He was…different. And if only for a little while, I wanted to keep him to myself.

Crazy. This was sheer insanity. Or the influence of my father's discussion with me over breakfast about finding a mate. I surely had not found it in this scruffy, demon-slaying human.

Once I returned, I helped him wash and change into the new clothes, doing my best to be careful of the wounds on his chest. I asked him no questions until I had tossed his clothes in the fireplace, burning them into a pile of ash. There could be no evidence of the female demon's death.

"What happened to you?" I sat on the edge of the bed, tending his wounds. The ones on his chest and back were deep, but not so deep that he needed stitches. And, although the knock on his head had stopped bleeding, it had lumped up nicely. I'd need to watch him carefully. He probably had a concussion.

"I was a prisoner of the demons. I…I overheard them talking about a blade they had confiscated from another prisoner. One that could kill them. A week ago, while they were sleeping, I was able to escape my bonds and search our camp. That's when I found it. I snatched it and made a run for the hills, as they say. Almost made it, too…" He winced as I wiped alcohol across his chest. "Why are you helping me?"

I shrugged and shook my head. "I've been asking myself that same question, Maverick."

"Are you human?"

I lifted my eyes. "You think I could have taken on a full-grown Fallen female—a demon—as a human?" I wasn't offended so much as surprised. He had to be new to the Territories. There was no way he couldn't understand how incredibly dangerous it was to fight one of the Fallen. The fact that both of us had survived was still something that made me wonder just how we had pulled it off. His stolen magical weapon had definitely helped.

"Where's the blade?" He suddenly sat up and I pushed him gently back down.

"I've hidden it. If the demons come around asking questions, we need to make sure there is no evidence."

He frowned. "Why would they come here?"

"If they figure out that she died on Werewolf Territory, then they will come. They have been looking for a reason to start a fight with us for a very, very long time." I sat back and dropped the cloth into a bowl. "That is the best I can do for now. You need to rest, and heal."

"And then what?" His eyes searched mine, and despite the injuries done to him, I could see him working over the choices for his future. A quick and agile mind lay behind that pretty face.

"Then we see what you're made of." My smile was stupid, and sudden...and stupid. Something about him drew me in. He was different. I was different. And in that, I felt a connection to him. For whatever reason, I got the sense that I could trust him. So I let my guard down. We spoke for hours in our little lodge in the forest, and I felt my heart slipping into his hands. Felt myself sharing more of who I was with him than I had with anyone else in my life ever.

Two weeks passed, and they were the most amazing two weeks of my life. My father, in a bid to give me more time to find a mate, had relieved me of some of my duties, and I used it all on Maverick. To my surprise, nothing ever came from the demons. If they hadn't come by now, I knew they would not, and my worries faded.

"You look happy, Diana," Lycan's voice called to me across the dining table the morning of the fifteenth day.

I smiled. "That's because I am happy."

He lifted an eyebrow. "And?"

"And what?"

"You're going to make me ask, are you? Fine then. Who is he, and when do I get to meet him?"

Panic settled in my chest.

"What do you mean?"

"Well, clearly you've got your sights set on a mate now. You've hardly been home, and you're practically walking on air. When do I get to meet my new future son in law?"

My heartbeat slowed some and I managed a weak smile.

"I promise, if it gets to that point, you'll be the first to know."

It was going to have to happen, and sooner than later. But it would be a fight, I knew. And I wasn't ready to share yet. I just wanted to keep Maverick to myself, hidden away for a little while longer.

Back at the lodge a short while later, I flung the window open to let in some fresh air. "Are you feeling well enough to sightsee tomorrow, maybe? The merchant ships will be here, and we can walk the harbor. Maybe we can even take you to meet my father soon. We will just have to come up with a story of how we met. A story that doesn't involve border-crossing and murder..."

Maverick leaned against the headboard, his shirt flaring open to reveal his wounds mostly scabbed over, some even smooth already. "You think the wolves are ready for me?"

I laughed softly and shook my head. "Never. But my father is suspicious. He knows I am hiding something."

Or someone.

I made my way over to the chair beside the bed. We'd been careful not to touch too much. I could feel the tension in him, could smell the desire rolling off him. He wanted me. But he never so much as leaned too close. Never tried to take advantage of me, though he watched me when he thought I wasn't looking.

I MADE my way over to the chair beside the bed. We'd been careful not to touch too much. I could feel the tension in him, could smell the desire rolling off him. He wanted me. But he never so much as leaned too close. Never tried to take advantage of me, though he watched me when he thought I wasn't looking.

"I brought you something," I said, grinning as I reached into my pocket. His eyes widened as I produced the four leaf clover I'd found on my walk back to the cabin. "I've heard they're supposed to be lucky in your world."

"I've never found one before," he said, eyes shining as he accepted it. "Though I've been so lucky lately that it almost seems like I had. And I've been meaning to give you a gift as well."

I cocked my head, wondering what it could be as he reached for the bedside table. He hadn't had much of anything when he'd arrived, and had spent all of his time in my room, so what could he possibly have to give me?

"It's an anklet," he said, gesturing for my leg. The green thread was strung with shells of all kinds, with lots of deep purples and bony whites.

"It's beautiful," I said, eyeing it closely. "Where'd you get all these shells?"

"Here, try it on," he said, smiling softly at me, ignoring my question.

I raised my leg instinctively, and my ankle tingled as he gripped it lightly in his hands and tied the beautiful anklet in place. "Thank you," I said. "The colors are beautiful."

His hands lingered for a moment, caressing my leg before letting go to gesture to the room around us. "I tried to find lots of purple ones, since you seem to love it so much."

My heart stopped for a beat.

"*Find?* From here?"

He looked away. "I wanted to do something for you, some kind of gesture for taking care of me for all this time. I snuck out to the beach a few times earlier this week, while you were off at the keep."

I rolled my eyes, but the warmth inside me only grew, even as I chastised him. Hot, daring, *and* thoughtful. "That was reckless, Mav. You could've been killed."

"And it wasn't reckless when you ran headfirst into that demon to save me? We both have a bit of a reckless streak. Besides, if there's one thing I'm good at, it's being slick," he said, waving off my concern. "All that matters is that you like it."

"I love it," I said, warmth rolling through my body in waves. I paused for a long moment, just staring at the anklet and enjoying the moment. Just a few weeks earlier I'd been so certain that I didn't want a mate, and now I was here, giddy and starting to fall in love.

I ran my fingers over the back of his hand. "Mav. If…there was a way…would you stay here? With…me?"

He turned his hand over, lacing his fingers with mine. "A way? What do you mean?"

We'd talked at length already about him not wanting to be a prisoner, and I felt him tense. I held onto him a little tighter.

"A way to become…like me. A werewolf. A way to stay here in truth, a part of this world."

His hand tightened on mine. "You told me there was a way your kind could hide their true nature when you went to the mainland. I thought maybe you could come back with me—"

My stomach flipped. Leave my pack? My family?

"No. The Crimson stones are kept in my father's chambers. There is no way he'd give us one. And even if he did, I need to stay here for my people." I shook my head. "But you could…" Gods of the forest, this was hard. To be vulnerable…tell him how much I wanted him to remain here with me. "If I could find a way to keep you safe, would you stay?"

His hand slid up to my cheek, his mouth finding mine. Tentative and careful. Sweet. Kind. He was so very kind. "It would be my honor."

It would be his honor…

But that, like so many of the things he'd told me, was a lie. Instead, he had betrayed me and left me heartbroken and alone.

~

Present Day

A knock at the door snapped me out of the memories that burned in my gut. I stood in front of my window holding two items in my hands.

"Enter."

"Your Majesty, the meeting is set to start in under five minutes. Are you prepared?"

"Yes, I'll be there in a few moments. Just gathering my thoughts."

The item in my left hand was the second of two crimson stones. The other had been stolen by Maverick that same night he'd kissed me and then escaped to the mainland, hidden in one of our ships.

In my right hand lay the hilt of the dagger that Maverick had used to save me. A blade that still glowed bluish-white.

A knock at the door snapped me out of the memories that burned in my gut. I stood

I balanced them as I stared out the window of my room. The skies should have been brilliant with a noonday sun, but instead were black as night. The window flung open, clattering and slamming the panes against the wall, and the storm ripped into my room, flinging objects around, and scaring my attendant right out the door. The wind howled like a bitch on the hunt for blood. I bared my teeth as I gripped both the dagger and the stone, the storm matching my mood.

I'd managed to put him out of my head eventually, but it had taken decades. And now, here we were, full circle once again. If we had any hope of saving the world, I would first have to face the man who had broken my trust and then stomped on my heart. Only this time, I was a lot older and a hell of a lot smarter.

Maverick was going to wish that I'd let that demon have him by the time I was done with him.

DIAN

Give me the strength, father, one last time, to see this through despite my grief...

I sucked in a deep breath and let it out, pausing to study the faces around the table of my war room.

It had been a scant five weeks since he'd been killed and the grief had not eased one bit.

Lochlin, seated in the chair beside me, where my father used to sit. My packmate, long-time confidant and friend. Now, my right hand and advisor. Usually quick to smile despite the scar that bisected his face from one brow to the corner of his mouth, the auburn-haired, bear of a man was stoic today. I had no doubt he wouldn't like my plans, but that was alright. We'd locked horns plenty over the decades, and while I appreciated his counsel, I was Queen.

We'd do it my way.

Beside him sat Will, the youngest of my three brothers. Now that we'd defeated and killed our oldest, Edmund the Vile, Will was King, and he deserved the title. A good man. A fair man...despite being a bloodsucker and all. His brand new wife Bethany was seated to his right, holding his hand in a quiet show of support. That was good. He'd need it. Despite enjoying the backing of most in their Territory, there was still a fringe faction of his kind who would never accept his marriage to a natural-born human, even if she was a vampire now...

I turned my head and locked gazes with my other brother, Dominic. Dark, dangerous, and General of the Vampire Army. He'd been crucial to the success of our mission to take Edmund down. But just as crucial, his wife and beloved, Sienna. I still marveled at that one. A human—or so we'd thought—with powers beyond anything I'd ever seen. Stories of her healing magic had spread across the Territories far and wide. And now that she could ride the bloody Hunters as if they were her own private ponies, she'd reached an almost god-like status. And still, she stayed humble and kind...and stubborn and foolhardy at times.

All part of why I liked her, honestly.

Next to them sat Nicholas of Southwind. A vampire aristocrat raised in a family of diplomats with an interesting skill set I'd yet to witness personally. And Raven, another vampire whose presence I still questioned. He was far too handsome, and charming in a way that raised my hackles. If it wouldn't please him so much to get under my skin, I'd have already demanded to know why he'd even come to this meeting.

Finally, I shifted my gaze to the woman directly across from me, Evangeline. My savior. The woman who had protected me from Edmund as a child, and spirited me away to Werewolf Territory. Defying the king himself and risking her life to save mine. A Duchess with a heart of gold and a spine of steel.

Although you wouldn't know it now. She looked like a husk of her former self. Those snapping brown eyes, always lit with determination and wit, were now downcast as she stared at the intricate pattern on the mahogany table. Losing Lycan had been tough on us all. It was as if a live grenade had been tossed in our midst, tearing through us all. The pack was still reeling, friends and clan members from far and wide had been in mourning for weeks now. And me? As much as I tried to play it off...show the strength and fortitude so necessary in a Queen, some days it was hard to even put one foot in front of the other and get through the day.

And still, Evangeline was suffering more. She'd barely left her quarters and seemed so deep in a fog, I was starting to wonder if she'd lost her grip on reality. Or maybe she'd just been lost in memories of the past.

I'd spent a fair amount of time doing the same lately, so I could hardly judge. Still, I hated having to leave her like this. Especially without knowing when—or if—I'd be coming back.

I spared one last glance out the window and pursed my lips. There was a fair chance it didn't matter what I or any other creature on this planet did now. The end was near. Ever since the Veil had fallen fifteen years before, we'd been on a downward slide.

It had been slow at first. So slow, we didn't even notice. But then the winters grew colder. Longer. The summers sweltering. The winds and tides unpredictable. And lately, especially these past few weeks, the weather was off the rails. Storms even while the sun shined. Snow and sleet mixed with hail and thunder. If we got caught at sea in something like that, we'd all be at the bottom of the ocean. Wolves were stronger and hardier than humans to be sure, but Mother Nature was the great equalizer.

Shoving aside the big-picture problems, I focused on the ones I had a shot of actually solving.

"I think that's everyone," I said, forcing a smile to my lips as I rose to stand. "Let's begin. I'm sure you've all seen how—"

The door flew open, banging off the stone wall with such a crash that I instinctively laid a hand on the hilt of my sword.

"Sorry I'm late!" rasped the tiny, misshapen woman

who hobbled into the room. Her face wasn't visible due to the towering plate of food she held balanced in front of her, but I didn't need to see it.

"Myrr?" I demanded, immediately irritated. "What are you doing here?"

She plopped into a side chair closest to the door and shot me a mostly-toothless grin. "I'm the Oracle, ain't I? I need to be kept apprised of all the haps, don't I? I swear, I won't interrupt. I'm just going to sit here and eat my breakfast while you all do your plotting and scheming and such, hmm?"

I let out a sigh. I wanted to remind her that, as the Oracle, technically, shouldn't she already be apprised of "the haps"? But I wasn't about to call her on it. Dominic, a non-believer who was only just starting to come around to the idea of someone truly seeing the future—barely—had no such reservations.

"Aren't you supposed to be all-knowing?" he demanded. "All-seeing?"

"Not all, no." Myrr hefted what looked like an entire haunch of venison in her gnarled hands and glared at him through one, milky eye. "But I knew you lot were meeting here without me so I guess I know *some* things, eh, big boy?"

Sienna laid a hand on Dom's arm as he seemed ready to fire back, and he settled against his chair with a sigh.

"Fine, do as you please. You will anyway," he muttered.

It wasn't that Myrr wasn't helpful...exactly. It was just that it took some time—a lot of it, in some cases—to see how she was helping. Since I'd found the note my father had left for me in the event of his death, I'd met with her to talk over breakfast—at her request—a half dozen times to get some guidance. All I wound up with was a headache from grinding my teeth in irritation after listening to her chew for an hour straight. Now, with my journey imminent, she was just as likely to harm as she was to help. Many of her visions were cryptic and erratic, muddying the waters more than they offered clarity. Others were so ominous and full of impending doom that it made it hard to stay the course and keep morale high. If the weight of the world was on my shoulders, I needed morale at its highest, and the water to be crystal clear.

The time for prophecies and the doubts they could bring had passed. Now was the time for action.

I turned to her and lifted a brow in stern warning. "Just observing, yes? If you have something to add, we can meet afterward."

Or not.

The Oracle set down her venison to mimic the locking of lips before throwing away the key.

I dipped my head and then turned to face the others at the table.

"The reason I've asked you here is because I..." I glanced at Raven and Nicholas of Southwind and let out a sigh, "Or my brothers trust you implicitly. As you all know, Sienna has an enemy out there working behind the scenes to wreak havoc on both her and on the Territories as a whole. This enemy, she has considerable power, and she is using that power to prevent the rebuilding of the Veil, a process that apparently involves Sienna and four other keys." I turned to Sienna. "Care to step in and share your experiences with this entity?"

Sienna sucked in a breath, her expression darkening as she spoke. "She was feeding me false prophecies and dreams for some time. She was also the one responsible for the werewolf Elka's possession, and subsequent attack on me. She has the ability to intrude on my dreams somehow, and even cause injury from within them. It's jarring because you don't know what she'll do next. She even spoke to me through Will's bloodworm at one point. Her powers are chillingly strong, and largely unknowable at this point."

I nodded. "So be wary of strange dreams or other such intrusions. Beware of voices giving false directives, no matter how alluring they may seem. We theorize that Elka was targeted because of her dark emotional state at the loss of her brother, Jordan. We believe that the entity is most likely to make her move at times of strong emotion, or weakness."

"In hindsight, I'm fairly certain that my second in command, Scarlett, was possessed by her too," Dom cut in, and Sienna nodded at his side. "Perhaps for quite a long time. Unlike Elka, Scarlett didn't seem like a woman possessed. It was almost as if this entity prayed on her jealousies and insecurities, and wore her down over a long period. It's also very likely that she has a way of keeping track of us, given the nature of her powers. She clearly doesn't need to be directly present to invade someone's."

I turned to Myrr as I continued, "But it's not all bad news. There does seem to be another force out there that is trying to aid us. Elhimna, the enemy called him. He has spoken through Myrr on several occasions, and seems familiar with our enemy and her tricks. He has counseled us to gather the remaining keys and keep them safe at all costs."

Myrr nodded, setting down her venison for a moment to add, "There's something about his words that rings true. I'd stake my name as Oracle on his words being reliable."

"We have scholars studying the history books for any record of his name or of a dark force with powers like the entity we're facing, but have found nothing. For now, keep your guard up at all times. This will be most important when it comes to this next bit." I reached for the stack of papers before me and handed them to Loch. "Can you take one and pass the rest down?"

I didn't need to keep one for myself.

"I found this note shortly after my father's death. I've spent over a week trying to decide how to handle this, and now that my path is clear, I wanted to share it with you all."

I cleared my throat and began to recite from memory.

"'If you've found this, Diana, that means I am gone. Likely too old and too slow to keep up with the pups in battle. Such is life. What you need to know most of all is that you were my greatest joy. I cannot imagine how empty my life would've been without you in it, and if that was all my Evangeline ever gave to me, it would've been enough. I am so proud of you, and all you've accomplished. You are already a better leader than I ever was. Enough of that, though. Now, for the hard bit. I hate to burden you further, my daughter, but I'm afraid it can't be helped. I've been in search of something that might help us fix what has been broken. Something The Oracle told me in secret could save you all. Decades ago, when I was still king and you were more trusting, a man came to our keep. Charming, silver-tongued, and handsome. That man left our territory with a jewel he had no right to take. I believe he is still in possession of that jewel, and we need to get it back, daughter. Only then can we find the other keys... Only then can we restore the Veil.'"

The rest of the room was silent, except for the Duchess's' now-labored breathing.

She met my gaze through the thin, black lace of her widow's veil as she pushed back her chair and stood.

"I'm sorry, Diana, but I can't be here. I hope you'll forgive me."

I swallowed past the lump in my throat to reply. "Of course."

She swept from the room, closing the door behind her. I knew it had been a gamble to request her presence, but I didn't want her to feel excluded.

It was probably for the best that she wasn't here. Emotions were sure to run high and we needed to think with our minds, not with our hearts, now more than ever.

I glanced around the table as I continued. "I know who this man is. I know the gem my father spoke of. In fact, I am the reason it was so easily taken. But that's a story for another day. What's important is that I own its mate, so I know exactly what we're looking for. And, thanks to our amazing tech team, I know that it's located in the human realm. What I need now is a few volunteers to come and help me find it."

Sienna's arm instantly shot high. "I'm in."

Dom grabbed her hand and yanked it down. "*I'm* in."

Bethany shot Sienna a glance. "If she's in, I'm in too."

Will nodded. "In."

"Me too," Loch said.

I pinched my eyes closed and let out a sigh. *Gods give me strength.*

"As much as I appreciate your loyalty and passion here guys, none of that's going to happen. Loch, I need you here in my stead. And William and Bethany are the brand new King and Queen of the Vampire Territory. They need to be here for their people to waylay any concerns and ensure that the last of Edmund loyalists have all been rooted out. Dominic cannot be separated from Will. It's his literal job to ensure his safety. And obviously, Sienna, being the one key we *do* have, needs to be protected at all costs."

I crossed my arms over my chest.

"I brought you all here because I need some recommendations. Dominic," I said, turning his way. "I need one of your men to come with me and offer some cover. Someone strong who can handle himself if things go sideways, but also smart and well-connected, with deep knowledge of the human world, whose presence won't be questioned. Someone who can call in some favors if our quarry proves to be hard to find."

Raven cleared his throat and hunkered down in his chair, silent as he eyed Dominic through heavy lids.

"That's Raven," Dom said with a clipped nod. "He's

been my right hand since...since Scarlett's passing, and spent more time in the human realm than any other warrior I know."

I instantly balked.

"Raven? What's he going to do, seduce Maverick into giving him the stone?"

The man in question met my gaze, a grin stealing over his firm mouth. "Your Majesty, make no mistake. While there's no doubt I could do it that way, I'd be much more inclined to fight the man than fuck him. I like my lovers...softer, if you will."

Heat stole over my cheeks for no good reason, which pissed me off. What was I, some blushing maiden? Hell no. I was a werewolf queen, damn it.

"Be that as it may," I said with a tight smile, "I was thinking Nicholas of Southwinds."

Anyone but Raven.

"Nicholas should go as well," Dom agreed. "His talent for...reading people could be useful. But you have your pack and this whole Territory relying on you, Diana. You need protection as much as anyone else in this room. If I could convince you not to go, I would."

I opened my mouth to speak but he held up a hand.

"*But* since I know I can't change your mind, it has to be Raven. There's no man I would want beside me on the field of battle more than him. If I have to put your life in someone's hands, it will be his."

"I'm honored to go," Nicholas said, his tone solemn.

Dominic turned to look at Raven, who slumped back in his seat and let out a groan, his eyes rolling hard enough that I wondered how they stayed in his head.

"I mean, yeah. Alright, then. I did swear fealty to King William, and now report to Dominic. If he says I go, then I go."

"Your enthusiasm for the task gives me the utmost confidence," I said through my teeth.

His smile never faltered. "I'd be a lot more willing about the whole thing if you didn't act like such a high-handed bitch all the time."

Something inside me snapped, and an instant later I was across the table, my short blade pressed against his neck.

"You dare call a queen such a slur in her own home?" I whispered, adrenaline pounding through my veins, making me feel more alive than I'd felt since before Lycan's death. I held Raven's mocking gaze, getting angrier by the moment as I called over my shoulder. "Brother...you say this is the strongest fighter you know? He couldn't even stop me from getting the drop on him."

Raven had the balls to wink at me. "Alas my Queen, if I chose violence today, you'd already be dead."

"Raven!" Will snapped. "Enough!"

Raven's voice dropped to a whisper, low enough for only me to hear.

"I get it. It's not your fault. Most women have a hard time letting me go."

As much as I wanted to take all the pent-up anger and grief of the past weeks out on this bastard, I couldn't. With all eyes on the two of us, it was best to let this little pissing contest die a quick death or risk creating a rift. Our pack had a strong ally in the vampires for the first time ever. I needed to keep it that way. No matter how satisfying it would've been to wipe the smirk off his face.

I lowered my knife and stepped back, smoothing the braid down my back as I forced a smile.

"You see I'm right, though. He's difficult, Dominic. There is zero chance he'll obey me. The last thing I need is to be dealing with a wild card bloodsucker who can't do as he's told. And while I understand that the you and Will trust him, I do not. For all I know, he'll try to eat me while I sleep."

His mouth quirked. "If I decide to eat you, Your Majesty, you wouldn't be asleep for long."

"Godsdamnit, Raven!" Dominic growled, thumping the table with his fist. "You're not making this any easier."

"Just pick someone else. Anyone," I managed,

suddenly flustered and trying not to think of this irritating man bent before me, mouth pressed to my–

"Wordplay aside, our brother is right, Diana," Will said, clearly not thrilled by the thought, but resigned. "I know he can be vexing, but in this time of political upheaval, there is no one else I would trust with your life, either."

Will pursed his lips and shot a glance at Dominic, who leveled his friend with a cold stare.

"Raven. Apologize. Now."

With a sigh, the bastard rose from his chair to stare down at me just long enough to let me clock his sheer size and presence that far overwhelmed my own before dropping to one knee.

"Forgive me, Your Majesty. It was never my intention to offend. I apologize for my insolence and offer my fealty." He bent his head low to the ground until it touched the tip of my boots and I was staring down at his gleaming, dark hair. Then he looked up. "From this day forward, I am yours to command."

He looked so solemn, his voice suddenly ringing with such sincerity that I actually believed him. Raven mocking me and acting a fool was one thing. This Raven was far more unsettling. I could hear the pulse in my neck pounding and, judging by the way he was staring at it with barely repressed hunger, so could he.

He had just ceded control to me, but somehow I felt more out of control than ever...

Nope. Not happening.

I was about to put this nonsense to bed once and for all when Myrr dropped the iced bun she'd been holding and spoke, her tone the low drone of prophecy.

"Yes. Our Queen Diana, Nicholas of Southwind, and Raven of the mainland. This is the trio that will save the Empire."

Oh, sure. *Now* her visions were clear as glass?

I knew I should've kicked her out when I had the chance.

RAVEN

The waves on the rocks outside my window mimicked the waves in my dreams, the ones that crashed against the shoreline and threatened someone I couldn't protect. Panic and fear raced through me as I struggled to get through the surf, my hands outstretched as I screamed for her. Fought to get to her.

Too late, I was too late.

Sweat soaked through my sheets even though I'd gone to bed naked.

Jerking to a sitting position, I swung my legs to the side and bent at the waist, sheets pooling around my middle.

"Fuck." I growled the word, hating that I could still be denied a good sleep from something that had happened too damn long ago. Then again, I wondered if the dreams were even real now, because no one else remembered the things I did.

My skin was tight and hot, and my guts ached.

Curling my tongue over my fangs, I was reminded I had to feed today. Before we left on this so-called quest. Or Diana was right, she might just wake up with me eating her.

A flash of her on her knees in front of me instead of how it had actually happened was a pleasant enough thought that I considered relieving myself right then to the image but...no. I was not about to let her get to me.

Something about the woman dug at me in a way that made my skin itch, made me want to poke at her. Made me want to force her to deal with me. Which was only more reason for me to not go with them back to the mainland.

Yet I could not deny my King, or my friend.

"She's not even my type," I muttered under my breath as if saying it out loud would help me.

To be fair, the women who found their way to my bed were typically soft, with generous curves, and hair like silk that I could bury my face in while I fucked them ragged, making them beg for more before I brought them screaming to completion. Mind you, they rarely lasted more than a night or two—didn't want them getting attached, after all. But there was always another waiting in the wings. A maid who'd heard someone's panting through the walls.

Caged By Fate

My lips turned upward and then immediately slid into a frown.

Diana...she was everything that I would expect from a wolf queen, right down to her leather pants and the weapons she was never without. Her body was lean and strong, her muscles tight, and the way she held herself, with more confidence than I'd seen in any other leader.

I wanted pliable. Sweet. Not a sharp-tongued, battle-hardened she-wolf.

Grumbling to myself, the last remnants of my nightmare banished at the thought of the queen staring down at me when I'd apologized. I'd known exactly what I was doing, looking up at her, the same way I would have had I been feasting on her pussy.

Sure, she hated me, but I could see the blood rise to her cheeks as that knowledge had hit her, and the darker thoughts ripple through those frosted blue eyes. Her wolf had stared out at me with curiosity even while the woman was pissed as fuck to even consider the thought.

And now I had to spend goddess knew how many weeks with her.

"Stake me now and be done with it," I muttered as I slid into a dark shirt and pants. I ran my hands through my hair, not caring if it was tousled. It would give the impression I'd just fallen out of a lady's arms after pleasuring her all night. An image I had to uphold if I was to continue as the rogue.

I grimaced, anger snapping through me. There had been no woman to take my attention away from this stupid political game—the only two that had caught my eye were married to my two closest friends.

Strike one and two. And worse, I now considered them family, and would fight to protect them.

I made my way to the side table and opened the refrigerator hidden behind the panel in the wall. I stared at the stock of cold blood with mild distaste. Nothing like taking it straight from a warm, willing woman, but Dominic had reminded me that I had to drink and drink deeply before I got on the damn boat...A deadline that was rapidly approaching.

Familiar footsteps sounded outside my door.

"Bossy bastard." I smiled as I reached for the first of four bottles.

"Talking about me again?" Dominic opened the door as I spun the lid off the bottle and tipped it back.

Even cold, the flavor wasn't unpleasant. This vintage was from a human, female, early thirties and she tasted of chocolate and fruit. Not bad.

I put the empty bottle down and reached for a second. "No, of course not. How many bossy bastards are in my life? Wait....I suppose that it's just you."

Dominic raised a brow and leaned on the edge of the door frame. "Still mad?"

"You're sending me on a quest of some sort, with a woman who despises me, and a whelp who has barely been tested in battle, on a boat that likely was made when the Territories came into existence." I looked over my shoulder. "Sounds like the start to a bad joke, don't you think? Why would I be mad?"

I spun off the cap on the second bottle and snapped it back. Female, human again, and tasted strongly of whiskey and…peanut butter? It was an odd combination, but smooth and it slipped down my throat with an ease that had me sighing. I set the second bottle down and picked up a third, but didn't open it just yet. Instead I turned to my friend.

"Choose another to go. Your sister doesn't want me there, and conveniently, I don't want to be there either. I came back to the Territories for a reason and this surely was not it." I pointed the bottle at him. "You have many, many men and even some women—who would be more than capable of doing this job, and you fucking well know it. So why me?"

"Diana is strong enough to take care of herself," Dom said. "But you know the mainland better than anyone else. You have the connections she might need to find this thief. And despite how you behave, you're skilled in areas outside the bedroom. Your swords are deadly, Raven."

I smiled at him over the third bottle and gave him a

wink. "You would know it. You still bear the scars of our first fight, do you not?"

Dominic's nostrils flared. "You cheated."

"I won. Have you not yet learned? All's fair in a fight to the death." I tipped the bottle at him and then poured it into my mouth. This one caught me off guard. Werewolf, female, tasting of a wild spring storm and driving itself into my veins in a way I hadn't felt in so very, very long, making me want to run and howl at the moon, to find a partner and fuck her until I couldn't breathe any longer, then lay in her arms as the stars burned above. Eyes closed, I put the bottle down and leaned on the wall. "Gods, I forgot how hard other Territory blood hits. That was a doozy."

Dominic grunted. "I do not forget."

I lifted my eyes to him, my veins still humming with the unknown female's blood. "Sienna?"

He gave me a sharp nod. "When it tastes of magic, I believe you might have found your mate."

I grabbed the fourth bottle, almost hating that I had to drink it down and wash away the previous one. "There is no magic in blood that comes from another Territory. Power and strength, yes. But mates are for those who believe in fairy tales and happily ever afters." I paused and put the drink back. "I lost faith in those many, many years ago."

Dom motioned for me to follow him. "So did I.

Then I met Sienna. Things change, Raven. Let them. And...drink your last bottle before you leave."

I saluted him. "Yes, you bossy bastard. Where are we going now?"

"You need a tune-up. I want to make sure you can protect my sister."

I laughed, blowing a kiss to a maid as she scurried past. Her eyes widened and her mouth dropped into a perfect O that would fit right over my—

"I want to see if you can still spar. I've no doubt you'll be in a few fights before you find the thief."

I stared after the maid who had slowed and was looking over her shoulder at me. Yes, that one would be lovely to hold and yet...I winked at her and turned back to Dominic.

"Sparring, sure. I do keep up, you know." I tapped a hand on my chest. "Ladies don't like a man who lets himself get soft."

Dominic looked over at me, his eyes thoughtful as I kept my smile pinned in place. Let the fool I was thought to be stay on the surface.

"I see you, Raven," he said finally. "I know who you are. You will protect her with your life if you need to, as would I. Which is why I am sending you. Because I trust you to do what you must to make sure you get the job done and both come back alive."

His words cut into me, his faith in me still shaking me from time to time. I was just the palace maid's boy, before we were cast to the mainland. I did not come from blood, or fancy titles.

Dominic had never cared.

"You have my word," I said, all the light teasing tones gone. "I will protect her as if she is family."

He nodded and that was that—an understanding from one to the other.

We made our way to the covered courtyard, set up for the vampires who'd stayed behind in the Werewolf Territory. Will would need to leave soon, he'd gone back and forth for the last five weeks, dealing with both his own court and supporting Diana. Now he would finish his official takeover of the Vampire Territory as our new king.

The courtyard was empty. The day was only just beginning. We'd leave for the mainland this afternoon —just the three of us, if you didn't count a bare bones crew to help man the boat.

Diana, Nicholas and myself. That was enough to draw irritation through me again, and I scooped up not one, but two swords.

Dominic lifted his eyebrows. "In a mood then, are we?"

"You said to spar. So let us spar." I lifted both swords and settled into a waiting stance.

Dominic scooped up a sword and a shield. A more traditional set of tools for this fight. "Come at me then. Bird boy."

An old insult and one that only made me roll my eyes. "You can do better than that, you bastard."

He grinned. "Bird brain?"

"Perhaps that's what I will call you from now on."

Diana's voice made my hands flex of their own accord around the hilts of both swords. Though she wasn't my type, even I couldn't deny that she was striking as she came into view. Stalked into view was more like it.

Her long dark hair and frosty blue eyes like a winter morning could make you feel like kneeling at her feet.

Again.

I bowed at the waist. "Ah, the queen of all arrives. Come to watch the peasants fight for your honor?"

Dominic sighed so heavily, it fairly rattled the air. "Must you, Raven?"

"Oh, I must." I smiled and dipped my head. "I cannot feed on this trip. I cannot bed any women, and I must be subject to the ice queen's whims. Fairly played, but let me have a little fun."

Diana's eyes narrowed on me. "I barely saw you on the battlefield against Edmund, and have yet to ascertain with my own eyes if you have any skill, or if all you do is talk your way out of having to fight."

I shrugged. "A win, is a win, is a win. I don't care how I survive, *Your Majesty*, only that I do." And, now, that she did too.

Diana moved into the sparring square that had been marked out, her eyes locked on me as she circled around. Hunter and prey, I could see it in the way her body shifted ever so slightly.

Another woman I might have laughed at, seeing her set herself up to attack me. With her, I was going to have to be careful. She'd just as soon tear my throat out.

"How are you going to track this thief?" Dominic asked, cutting through the growing tension. "He's been gone for years, correct?"

I was not so stupid as to take my eyes off the stalking wolf. She paused and turned to her brother, and I realized that had been his goal. To draw her ire away from me. I stabbed the tip of one sword into the ground and leaned on the handle.

"Yes, I'd be curious about that as well. Unless you're hoping I'll do all the work for you?"

Dominic shot me a look and I just grinned at him. I couldn't help it. She was fun to irritate, and I liked the way her eyes flashed at me a little too much.

"My tech team has been studying the crimson stone here, and have found a way to mimic the resonance within. They then sent out a similar sound and got back four pings."

My eyebrows shot up. That was...actually pretty clever. "Four pings, better than the whole world at least."

Diana tucked her hands behind her back. "Of the four locations, there is only one that Maverick would willingly go."

"Indulge me," I drawled. "I'm curious as to the other places we might end up."

"Antarctica, Madagascar, Moscow," she said and I winced as she went on. "But from what I know of him, he'll be in the fourth place. Isla Naranja..."

"How can you be sure?" I asked. "Being wrong will truly fuck us over."

I thought the question would piss her off, but she laughed and the sound caught me off guard, wrapping itself around me.

"Because that's where the party is. Casinos, brothels, pubs. And he is, at heart, a scoundrel and a gambler. And he sure as shit isn't gambling with penguins." Her eyes sparked and she turned to her brother.

"Hand me your weapons. I want to see if he's any good."

"He survived the battle unscathed," Dominic said. "And I've seen him fight. He's that good."

Good enough to beat the General himself more than once. But while I might brag about my skills in the bedroom, my skills on the battlefield...I chose to keep that to myself as much as possible. The more someone thought you were good at fighting, the more challenges came your way.

"You want to spar with me, Frostbite, far be it for me to stop you. Although I can't help but wonder if this is just a ploy to get close to me." I flashed her a wide smile as I tugged the blade from the ground and swung my two swords up into a ready stance.

"I'll get close enough to run you through the heart, just for giving me that stupid nickname." She smiled so very sweetly up at me, that I knew I was in trouble.

We circled one another, and Dominic watched from the sidelines. "He's weak to the right."

"Fucker," I growled at my supposed friend. "You'd help her cheat?"

"Giving her advice, it's a rather brotherly thing to do." Dominic laughed as Diana came at me, fast and low, springing up with her sword and shoving me backward.

I could have beaten her right then, her belly exposed to my right-handed blade, but I fell back, let her push me around the ring.

Always keeping just out of reach.

Letting her direct the flow of this dance. Watching her body work, and admiring it none too little.

Keeping pace with her and noting when I could strike. Because I didn't want to hurt her—despite how she was getting under my skin.

On two legs, I outmatched her in speed, and reflexes, so I kept myself reined in. If she got seriously pissed, and shifted to four legs....well, that would be a whole other ball of wax. Werewolves were far more deadly when they had claws and teeth that could tear your head from your shoulders.

Not that I'd ever admit that.

The fight rolled into ten minutes of parrying and thrusting, and her softly golden skin had a sheen of sweat coating it, beads sliding across her collarbone and down her neck. Her lips were parted as her breath came in harder, and faster with each passing minute, the sound drawing me closer, wanting stupidly to feel her breath against my ear.

The top of her shirt slid just a fraction of an inch, exposing the very top swell of her breast and my eyes locked onto a bead of sweat as it ran down her skin there as I wondered how she'd feel under me, sweating and writhing, panting for air.

A bit of material that was not her shirt caught my eye. Binding? She bound her breasts to keep them out of the way?

The shield snapped into my face and sent me backward, flat onto my back, the world spinning. The tip of her sword followed, settling into the hollow of my throat. "If you can't keep your eyes on the prize, then you will die, Raven."

I laughed and smiled up at her, letting her see my fangs as I ran my tongue over them. "Who said I didn't have my eye on the prize, Frostbite?"

The flush of her cheeks could have been from the

exertion of the fight, but I didn't think so. With a snarl she tossed her shield and sword away and strode from the covered courtyard.

I pushed to my feet and dusted myself off as Dominic picked up the weapons and set them in the racks. "You just can't help yourself, can you?"

I shrugged. "I find I enjoy getting under her skin. If I must go, at least give me this."

Dominic sighed and shook his head. "Just try not to get yourself killed."

I hope you LOVED reading this preview of Caged By Fate as much as I loved writing it.

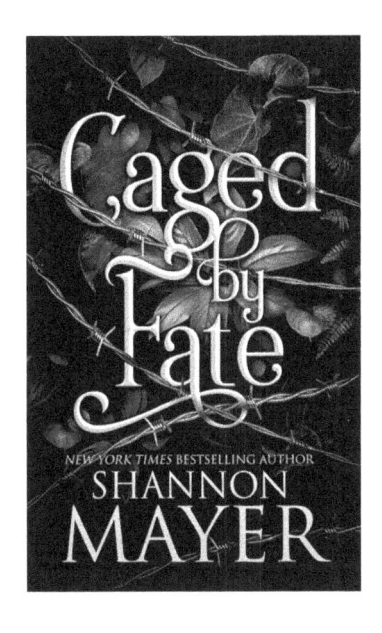

You can continue reading by purchasing or borrowing a copy through the links below:
PAPERBACK
HARDCOVER
EBook

Milton Keynes UK
Ingram Content Group UK Ltd.
UKHW041509081124
2701UKWH00039B/160